"Just say boo and Vicki'll be wrapped around you in no time flat," Mom said. "She's nuts about you. And then you'll end up living at her house, like your brother is at Juliet's all the time. What do I need a nine-room house for? I have no kids left!"

Oh, boy. She was really off. "Mom, come on. . . . I'm just dating her. It's not like Ty and Juliet."

"It will be."

"It won't be. Relax," I said. How ironical can you get? I feel delighted if I can get Vicki to take her bra off, and my mother has us living together!

Mom sighed. . . .

ANGEL FACE
NORMA KLEIN

FAWCETT JUNIPER • NEW YORK

RLI: $\dfrac{\text{VL: 5 \& up}}{\text{IL: 9 \& up}}$

A Fawcett Juniper Book
Published by Ballantine Books

Library of Congress Catalog Card Number: 83-21657

ISBN 0-449-70282-0

This edition published by arrangement with The Viking Press

Printed in Canada

First Ballantine Books Edition: May 1985
Ninth Printing: August 1990

TO ROBERT CORMIER

ONE

IIII

"WHO IS SHE? WHO IS SHE?"

My father had his suitcase on the bed—he was trying to pack—but every time he'd fold something up and put it in, my mother, who used to be on the fencing team at Vassar, would pick up a shirt or a pair of pajamas on the end of her foil and wave it triumphantly over her head. At that rate, it was going to take my father all day to pack. But it was Sunday—maybe he figured he had all day.

"Her name is Randall Wormwood Hamilton," Dad said.

Mom turned to me. "What kind of a name is that? What *is* she—a man? Randall? You're leaving me for another man?"

"It's a family name. . . . She's known as, that is, she goes under, Randy."

"Randy . . . Wormwood . . . Hamilton." Mom repeated each name with great precision. She turned to me again. "Jase, have you ever heard of anyone named Randy?"

Actually, I've known two kids named Randy. Last year in English class there was this guy they used to call Randy Andy because all he did was read *Penthouse* and *Playboy*

1

during study period. He used to cut out photos of some of the female teachers, especially the ones over forty, and paste them over the faces of the Playmates of the Month. But I decided not to mention him. "There was Miranda Brice," I said. I thought Mom would remember her because she used to play tennis with her mother.

"Oh, right," Mom said. She was wearing shorts and a T-shirt and had her hair wrapped in a towel because she'd just had a shower. "Miranda's a *real* name . . . but Randy? What is she—an Episcopalian or something?"

When my mother was a teenager, before her father went bankrupt, she used to go to this really fancy school with a lot of very rich kids. Not just ordinary rich, but rich like they had mansions and their fathers owned department stores and stuff like that. My mother's family were Presbyterians, but there was compulsory chapel attendance and she used to pretend to be Episcopalian because everyone else was.

"She's not Episcopalian," Dad said, tossing in some socks. Usually my dad's a very neat packer, but I think by this point he figured he might as well just toss in whatever he could.

"She's got to be," Mom insisted. "All the girls at Newcomb with those fancy-shmancy names were Episcopalian."

"She's a Quaker," Dad said.

"A Quaker?" Mom looked horrified, like he'd said ax murderer. "You mean, the ones that sit around and don't say anything? The ones that make funny little painted signs and don't believe in listening to the radio? *That* kind of Quaker?"

"Those aren't Quakers, Mom," I put in. "Those are Amish people." I knew because we studied them last year

2

at school. I'm lousy at school and they almost made me repeat ninth grade, but a lot of unnecessary information sticks in my brain.

"So, which ones are Quakers?" Mom said, frowning. The towel came unwrapped and her half wet hair tumbled down her back. "I'm getting all mixed up. Listen, I *know* they sit around and don't say anything. Unless the spirit moves them or something. I had this friend once and—oh, no, that's right, she was a Friend. Aren't Friends and Quakers the same thing?"

You'd have to know my mother better than you do so far to realize that having this kind of discussion when someone you've been married to for twenty-seven years is about to leave you for another woman is not at all unusual. It's usual, in fact. My mother has a mania for irrelevancies.

"The similarity," Dad said, going into the the bathroom to get his shaver, "is that both groups are often politically active. They both tend to—"

Mom smote her brow. "Of course! Okay, okay, now I get it. Say no more. She's this little Quaker type in a gray dress with a white collar and, like, she's really into the nuclear freeze thing. She probably marches on Washington every three seconds for some cause. You met her on some thing, some intense we're-going-to-change-the-world-type thing, and she's very earnest and has a great figure and perfect teeth and a ponytail or something and—"

It is very, and I repeat *very* hard to stop my mother once she gets going, especially when she's excited about something. But I ought to mention that one major difference between my parents—and they're basically about as different in every possible way as anyone you'll ever meet—is that my father is very active politically. In fact, that's his profession. He used to be a speechwriter, but everyone he

3

wrote speeches for lost—not because his speeches were bad necessarily, but because he was always for the underdog. Now he's editor of a magazine called *Human Rights*, which is about anything bad that's happening to any special group anywhere in the world. He doesn't so much write the stuff, though he does sometimes. Mostly he goes over what other people write and fixes it up so it sounds good. I think he basically likes it, but sometimes he says it's a thankless job and he should have run off and joined the circus when he was my age, the way he wanted to then.

If anyone should have joined the circus, it's my mother. She can juggle four tennis balls, she can ride horses bareback and not fall off, and like I already said, she can fence just like Errol Flynn in those old movies. She says she's a compendium of useless skills. Compendium is a word I memorized last year because Mom was on this kick about improving my vocabulary. See, the problem now is that my oldest sister, Andy, who's twenty-three, is in law school, and my other sister, Erin, who's sixteen, is in boarding school, and my brother, who's two and a half years older than me and a senior in high school, is madly in love with this girl, Juliet Moscowitz, so he spends most of his time at her house. He even sleeps over there a lot, not just weekends. Which leaves just me for my mother to scream at and force to improve my vocabulary. Now that my father's pulling up stakes, it could get even worse. I'm not going to even start worrying about that.

"Fay, I don't want to discuss this now," Dad said, picking up a shirt my mother had heaved on the floor.

"When *do* you want to discuss it?" Mom said, advancing on him, sword held forward.

She was just joking with the sword, but my father backed away uneasily. "When you've calmed down," he said.

"I'm not *going* to calm down!" she yelled. "Why should I calm down? You're walking out with this little Quakerette that you've been screwing around with, and I'm supposed to sit there like I'm in some kind of goddamn Noel Coward comedy making witty remarks? No, sir. You picked the wrong lady, bud."

"I'm aware of that," Dad said dryly.

That was dumb of him, but I guess he was getting kind of riled up. "So now you've picked right, huh?" Mom said. "Now suddenly at forty-nine the perfect little wifey has crawled into view, on all fours with a rose between her teeth. Pitch out the old, on with the new!"

"I don't want to talk about it in front of Jason," Dad said, glancing over at me with a worried expression.

"Why not?" Mom countered. "He's not supposed to know? I'm supposed to lie? 'Daddy's gone on a little vacation. Maybe he'll be back someday soon. . . .'"

"It's okay, Dad," I said.

"He's only fifteen," Dad said, as though I wasn't there.

"Really? Gosh, you could've fooled me. A mere fifteen . . . And I guess until this moment he's been under the impression that his parents were madly and insanely in love."

"Listen, I can go inside," I said nervously. "I can just—"

"Did you think we were madly and insanely in love?" Mom questioned me.

"No," I replied. Which is true. I never did. I more wondered how come they got married in the first place.

"Did anyone in this family? Did Andy? Did Erin? Did Ty?"

Just as I was shaking my head, Dad said, "It's not a matter of that. I just don't see the need to expose a child—"

"He's *not* a child," Mom screamed.

"Yeah, I'm not a kid, Dad," I said.

It's true, though. My parents have gotten along badly ever since I can remember. Andy says she can remember a time when she was around six or seven when it wasn't quite as bad, but she's the only one of us that can. About five years ago they both decided to stop wearing their wedding rings. My father just took his off; my mother buried hers in the front yard in what she called an unwedding ceremony. It's probably still there unless some dog dug it up by mistake. And this isn't the first girlfriend my father has had either. Three years ago he moved out for six months because he was "seeing someone," but then he moved back in again. And five years ago my mother took me and Erin, and we all spent the summer at this ranch in Montana with a guy she called her boyfriend whom she met at a group called Parents Without Partners. He was around my mother's age and, like her, he loved horses, and I have to admit they seemed to get on pretty well, a lot better than she and my father ever did. But at the end of the summer he drove us back and waved and Mom said, "There goes a terrific half of a man. . . . If anyone ever finds the other half, wow." Like many of my mother's remarks, you could spend a lot of time trying to figure out what the hell it meant, or just forget it.

My father had managed to pack. He snapped his suitcase shut, then took a deep breath. My father is not too tall, about five foot nine, and a little paunchy. He has all his hair, but it's pretty gray. "This is different," he said.

"Different from what?" said Mom.

"Randall and I . . . I want to, we're getting married."

Mom made a little dance around the room like she was square dancing without a partner. "Oh, goody, a wedding, I

6

love weddings! Are we invited? Will it be all in white? Do I have to dye my shoes?"

"I've gotten in touch with Burt Ciampa," Dad went on tensely, "and of course you can use him too. I realize he's a friend of both of ours. . . . But I think you should get *someone*."

"Are you kidding? Of course I'll get someone! Don't lose a wink of sleep over that, sweetie. I'll get the best someone there is. You and Quakerette will be living in a one-room walkup over McDonald's. . . . Were you worried I was going to play the martyr and say: Take everything! Take my house, my money, my kids. Don't *worry*. I'm dumb and a tad self-destructive, but there are limits."

"Good," Dad said, with just a trace of a grim smile. Then he turned to me. "Jase, look, I'm going to give you a number where you can reach me. It's Randall's apartment. Let's—we'll have lunch sometime and—"

He looked so pleading and strange, as though I was going to refuse to have lunch with him, that I said, "Sure, Dad, that's fine."

"Everything's going to be fine," Dad said, talking just to me. "Lots of people have, many people go through things like this, but—"

"Don't worry about it," I said, real cool.

"We are going to be just *fine*," Mom said. "We're going to be right as trivets, aren't we, Jase? Listen, you know what we're going to do for dinner? We're going to open a bottle of champagne! Jase, go look inside and see if we have any champagne. And if we do, chuck it in the freezer, okay?"

I went into the dining room where my parents have a wine rack under the buffet. There was a bottle of champagne that said, "Great Western." I put it in the freezer. Then I went back. My parents were in the front hall.

"Did it say, 'Brut'?" Mom asked me.

"I don't know," I said.

"Brut's the good stuff," Mom said. "And we deserve nothing but the best. We're going to celebrate. To a new life! Right?"

She was looking at me, so I said, "Sure."

Dad sighed. He looked like there were various things he might have said, but decided not to. He reached over and hugged me hard. There were tears in his eyes. "Take care, okay, son?"

I just made some kind of gesture. My father never calls me "son." No more than I ever call him "father." He sounded weirdly formal, like a father in a movie. I felt really sorry for him, he looked so rotten. Not that my mother looked great. But Mom always looks that way. Her hair was almost dry now—it's blondish gray and it was all crinkly and wild because she hadn't brushed it yet. My mother's tall and skinny with bright blue eyes like me. She's a restless person, always smoking or talking or jiggling her leg back and forth.

We both watched my father pick up his suitcase and leave.

TWO

||||

AFTER MY FATHER CLOSED THE DOOR BEHIND HIM, WE BOTH stood there in silence. Finally Mom said, "There were tears in his eyes." But she said it in that flat, ironical way she has. "You know what they were for, Jase?"

"'Cause you're getting divorced?"

She shook her head. "They were for him. . . . Because life was supposed to be perfect. Because Mama said be a good little Jewish boy and work hard and get good grades and marry and have kids and all that shit, and he did it and it didn't work out. . . . Of course Mama *didn't* say fuck around on the side with little Quakerettes or little Catholic secretaries. I mean, listen, we have something to be thankful for, right? What if he'd married the little Catholic kid? She'd have had ten more kids before they got home from the church. This—I have to admit it—it sounds like a perfect match. Doesn't it to you?"

"I never met her," I said.

"Neither did I, but I can tell. It's perfect . . . Randall Wormwood Hamilton. I bet, let's see, she's what? Thirty-six? I bet she jogs—want to bet? I bet she doesn't smoke. She's probably calm and neat and—oh, shit." Suddenly

9

Mom started to cry. She cried in big, choking sobs, putting her arms around me.

I held her. My mother is five seven, exactly my height, and I'm skinny too, but, holding her, she felt fragile, like she was about to come apart at the seams. Boy, I felt lousy. Somehow all through the confrontation with my parents, it had been almost like a show I was watching, maybe because at times they seemed to almost forget I was there, and also because they'd had so many fights before. But then my father hugging me and looking like he was going to cry, which he never does, and now Mom breaking down completely. Did I wish Andy was there! I'll tell you about Andy later, but she's the only one in the family who could've handled this.

"It'll be okay, Mom," I said softly. "I'm still here . . . I've got three more years of high school." More like five unless I buckle down and work a little, but I didn't add that.

"Oh, honey," Mom sobbed. "Why was I *like* that? Why can't I be composed and dignified?"

"You were," I said. I would've said anything just to cheer her up.

"Was I?" She looked so pleased I felt even worse.

"Sure, you were great."

"I didn't seem sarcastic and crazed and off the wall?"

"Not at all." Partly, though I can't stand my brother, I was using a technique that he said worked when his girlfriend, Juliet, got really mad at him once. He said, forget the truth. Figure out what they want to hear and tell them that.

Suddenly Mom looked almost cheerful, though her eyes were still red. "So listen, why *don't* we have the champagne, okay? I mean, why not?"

"What should we have it with?"

"Oh, find something in the freezer and toss it in the oven, would you, hon? I'm just going to collapse on the couch. Call me when it's ready."

For the last couple of years meals around our house have been basically frozen stuff. I looked in the freezer. We had a lot of Lean Cuisine things Andy bought last time she was home. Like Dad, she's a little chunky and is always trying to lose weight. Some of it tastes like mush, but some of it isn't too bad. I put in two glazed chickens.

When it was done, Mom said to bring it and the champagne into the living room. She said she was too tired to move. She was lying on the couch, but when I brought in the champagne, she sat up. "One thing I'm terrific at," she said, "is opening champagne bottles. That's one advantage of having had a father who was a souse. See, the trick is not to let it foam all over the place. Watch me."

I watched. At the rate I'm going, I doubt I'll be rich enough to order a lot of champagne, but who knows? Maybe I'll have to someday. It did foam over a little, but Mom poured it quickly into these paper cups I'd brought out. We clinked cups.

"What I like about champagne," Mom said, "is you don't get mean drunk or out of control. It just makes everything seem kind of soft and fuzzy, like it half wasn't happening. Do you know what I mean?"

I do know what she means because that's the way pot makes me feel—which is why I smoke it Monday, Wednesday, and Friday, plus either weekend day of my choice. I won't go into the whole thing, but last year I was really into drugs. I mean, I doubt I went to school unstoned more than a couple of days all year. Those were usually half days, like

11

the day before Christmas vacation. I just couldn't hack it otherwise. Eventually Mom and Dad caught on and I was grounded, got a big lecture, and had to promise under pain of no allowance and a lot of other stuff, to give it up. I was pretty good over the summer, but since school started a couple of weeks ago, I've gone back. But like I said, I have this schedule, and I figure if I can get through two complete school days without anything, I deserve the other three days. If you went to my school you'd know what I mean. I'm not saying most of the kids smoke as much as me, but it is acknowledged by everybody, including my parents, to be a pretty lousy school.

See, the thing is my parents just don't have a lot of dough. That's for a couple of reasons. First, Mom has never really worked at a steady job, partly because we moved around so much. And Dad, though he's always been an editor, kept changing jobs. It wasn't like he was bad at them and was fired. It was more he'd do them for five years or so, then decide he wasn't happy at them. First he was an editor for a chess magazine, because he used to be a chess whiz in high school. Then he did that speechwriting thing I mentioned. Then he was with a university press that was trying to publish fiction for the educated reader, but Dad claimed they discovered there were only about ten of those in the country and most of them used the library. He really likes what he does now because people in positions of real power, senators and guys like that, read his magazine and even write him letters. But he still isn't pulling in a whole lot of cash. Also, *he* went to a lousy public school in Brooklyn when he was growing up, and he feels private schools coddle you and if you're bright, you'll find your way. Mom, who went to private schools till her dad cashed in his chips, disagrees, which is why she made Dad send Erin, who has dyslexia and is spacey in various ways, to this "special" school in Pennsylvania for kids who need extra attention. But the rest of us have all had to hack it through Elmwood High. It's in Rockland County, about forty-five minutes from New York. Our house, which is a pretty standard four-bedroom split level, is close enough to school so I can walk.

Mom and I each drank about two or three glasses of champagne. It was good stuff. The only other time I had champagne was when Ty was bar mitzvahed a couple of years ago. It wasn't exactly your typical bar mitzvah, since it was held in a Unitarian church and we all went to a Chinese restaurant afterward with about a hundred of Ty's and Mom and Dad's friends and relations. At the restaurant a waiter went around asking us what we wanted to drink, and since all of us "kids" were at one table we ordered whatever we wanted. It wasn't as good as this, though.

Mom was half falling asleep. But every once in a while her eyes would open and she'd look over at me with a tender, woozy expression. "We'll make it though, Jase, won't we? Don't you think?"

"Sure," I said. I was feeling a little sleepy myself. I yawned and blinked and shook my head, trying to stay awake.

"I mean, look, I'm forty-six, I'm not Ms. America, but who knows . . . ? Somewhere out there there's probably some terrific wealthy, virile guy who's been looking all his life for a woman who can juggle four tennis balls and make a mean chili and do a super impersonation of Groucho Marx. There's got to be, right?"

I smiled at her. "Right, Mom."

She smiled back at me. "Jase, you're such a sweetheart," she said. "I don't want to make you gay or hopelessly screwed up about women, but I really love you a whole lot."

I hesitated, just because you hate to go through all that mushy stuff when you're over six years old. "I love you too, Mom," I said finally. I don't know if she heard me. She was out cold by the time I got the words out.

I don't think Mom has to worry about my being gay. Maybe about my flunking school or being a pothead. Not that I'm all that experienced with girls, but if you could tape the average sex fantasies that go through my head at school, they'd supply material for about a million X-rated movies. I look at Ty and I figure, hell, if he got Juliet Moscowitz, someday I'll get someone too. Not that I'm crazy about Juliet, but she has a really fantastic figure. Small, but curvy. I got so bugged last year because she complained to Ty that I was staring at her "in a funny way" whenever she came over here. Well, first she never wears a bra, and then, whenever Mom and Dad were out, she and Ty would go at it like crazy in his bedroom, which is right next to mine. What was I supposed to do? Try and concentrate on my work? Forget it. This year, like I said, he's practically living at her house, or mansion (they have four cars and six color TVs, just to give you an idea), so that problem has been more or less eliminated.

I want to tell you about my family. I just feel you ought to know the basics. Well, about Mom and Dad you get the idea. It's always been like that, more or less. According to Mom, they spent their whole honeymoon arguing. According to Dad, he knew the day before the wedding he was making a horrible mistake. Mom said she was nineteen and what did she know and she would've married anything in pants that didn't smell of garlic or read *Time* magazine. Dad says he was on the rebound from someone named Cerelia Blade, whom he went with in college but who ditched him for someone else. Anyhow, they supposedly have been talking about getting divorced for the last twenty-seven years, but in between Mom had us and I guess they had other stuff to worry about. Don't ask me to explain it because I've never been married and I doubt I ever will be. I'm just telling you what they say.

One thing I guess I ought to mention before I get on with Andy, Erin, and Ty is that for some reason I'm both my parents' favorite kid. Figure that one out, and if you do, come back and tell me. I've probably given them more trouble than any of the other three, but they both favor me. It's strange, and I misuse it, I admit it. It's gotten me out of a lot of trouble, and it's one reason Ty hates my guts. Not that Ty likes anyone much (other than Juliet), but I'm like, real low down on his list of favorites. *He's* pretty low down on mine, too, but mainly because of the way he acts with me.

But what I want to do is describe everyone in the order that I like them, which means Andy comes first. Andy (that's short for Andrea) looks basically like Dad. She's short and chunky and has dark frizzy hair and glasses. She's not a knockout physically, and she didn't have a great social life in high school. But in college she had a really nice boyfriend with whom she broke up in senior year. They're still friends, though. I personally think she'd be great as a girlfriend or a wife or anything. She's definitely the smartest person in the family, but she's not the kind who rubs it in your face all the time. Despite going through the same rotten schools the rest of us have, she always got all As, and got into Princeton on a full scholarship. She has a scholarship to Harvard Law School too. The thing with Andy is, she can just look at a page and one second later she has imprinted in her brain *forever* everything that's on it. She says it isn't something she ever *tried* to do. It just happens. So she's always been able to do a minimum of work and be right up there at the top of her class. I could give you a million reasons I like Andy so much, but I'll just tell you the main one. She's the only one in our whole family—this includes Mom and Dad—who will listen to anything you say and give you a totally straight answer. She never says what she thinks you want to hear, but she doesn't lecture you, either. Like, take the drug thing. She knows I do it and she thinks it's dumb, but she doesn't come up to me and pull out the old soap box. She says a day will come when I won't need it anymore, and then I'll stop. She's great. Take my word for it.

My sixteen-year-old sister, Erin, is the one I have the least to say about. She looks like Mom, I guess, but Mom has a kind of wild, zany energy, whereas Erin is pale and thin and quiet. Like, we'll all be having dinner and all of a sudden someone'll say, "Where's Erin?" and it'll turn out she left the room an hour ago. She reads a lot of poetry and she has about a million stuffed animals. The other thing about her is she was almost anorexic a few years ago. You know, that kind of girls' disease where they get thinner and thinner and even sometimes die from being so thin? She never died or even was put in the hospital, but she was thin in an ugly, sick kind of way so her veins stuck out and she got winded if she even walked down the block! Every time she comes home from this school she's in now, Mom and Dad say how much better she looks. It's true she's gained

16

some weight, but she still doesn't say all that much. Basically, I don't either like her or not like her. If I met her someplace and she wasn't my sister, I might try talking to her for about five minutes and then probably give up. Maybe some other guy will have more determination or something. I hope so.

I'm going to try really hard to be objective in describing my brother, Tyler. Okay, let's see. Well, first, he isn't bad looking. His coloring is in between me and Erin, who're blond, and Andy, who's dark. He has blondish-brown hair and brown eyes, pretty good features. His big problem, in *his* opinion, is that he's short. He's seventeen years old and he's only five feet four. Dad used to tell him *he* was short all through high school and then suddenly shot up, so Ty's been waiting for that to happen for the past few years. If you ask me, it's not going to. He measures himself every morning, and maybe he grew an inch or half an inch over the summer, but that's it. I really think that, apart from hating me because Mom and Dad like me better, he hates me because I'm fifteen and three inches taller than him. If I grow any more, he'll probably kill me. But Juliet, whom he's been going with since last spring, is only five feet one and a half, so I guess he doesn't have to worry so much.

What Ty did—I mention this in case anyone who's reading this is short and a guy and not too great at sports—was, he took up ice skating. Not ice hockey, where you have to be some kind of maniac and risk getting all your teeth knocked out. Figure skating. He became kind of an expert. He can jump over hoops and do triple figure eights. That kind of stuff. And the reason that paid off is that almost everyone else taking lessons was a girl. That's how he met Juliet, in fact. So all these girls (and some of them were not bad) were so bug-eyed that he was a boy, they didn't care *how* tall he was. They just wanted someone to lug them around the ice and do the "Skater's Waltz." It improved his social life about a thousand percent. I mean, true, it had nowhere to go but up, but ever since he started, when he was about fourteen, he's done okay.

I'm trying to think of other reasons Ty hates me, and I have to say, though this may sound both conceited and unfounded in reality, that it's partly because I'm smarter than him. Ty works really hard and he gets As and Bs, but his SAT scores were low, *way* down there. Even after Mom and Dad hired some kind of tutor to help him raise them, they're still too low for him to get into any top college like Andy did, *or* to get a scholarship. He'll probably go someplace out in Minnesota or Canada where there's a lot of ice. I'm not saying I'm smart the way Andy is. Why would I be doing so badly in so many subjects if I was? But I do think I *could* be smart in some things if I could somehow get motivated. Teachers talk about that all the time, and I think about it too. I guess deep down I don't give enough of a damn. That's the truth. I'm aware it's a serious problem; I'm not trying to get off the hook. But I still think I'm smarter than Ty.

In relation to Mom and Dad, this is how it goes. Andy admires Dad. Maybe because, like him, she has a really logical mind and she's sort of an idealist—she wants to be the kind of lawyer who does good stuff. She says she "pities" Mom but that she doesn't see why Mom doesn't get her act together and get a job or go back to school, the way lots of women her age do. I don't know *what* Erin thinks. I guess she has kind of a crush on Dad. She calls him "Daddy" and makes little pictures for his birthday. Ty sort of hates Dad; it's somewhat mutual. I mean, obviously no one *hates* their own kid, but Ty bugs Dad, a lot of times on purpose, somewhat the way he does with me but also in a different way. He talks in this very superior, sarcastic way. Like Dad will be right in the middle of explaining something, and Ty will get up and say, "Dad, I'm afraid I have to interrupt this talk to defecate. I'll be back in a minute." Not that Ty is real close to Mom, but they basically get along.

Okay, so there you have it. Your typical American family. We're not in jail, we're not in debt, we'll probably all go to college, but still it kind of makes you wonder, if you're the wondering type.

THREE

IIII

*M*OM WAS SLEEPING SO SOUNDLY ON THE COUCH THAT *I* didn't want to wake her up. I just covered her with a blanket and went into my room and fell asleep with my clothes on. When I woke up the next morning at six-thirty, I all of a sudden remembered. Shit. Today was the day everyone in our class was supposed to come to school dressed as either Rhett Butler (if you were a boy) or Scarlett O'Hara (if you were a girl). The seniors do this every year. They pick a theme—this year it's Sex Symbols Through the Ages—give each class a costume, and at the end of the day the teachers pick who they think is the best.

Rhett Butler is a guy in this book *Gone With the Wind*. Some girls in my class read the book and a bunch of others saw the movie. I never did either one. I gather it's sort of like the Three Musketeers, only set in the South around the Civil War. I meant to ask Mom and Dad over the weekend, but I totally forgot. Not that I would've done a big number the way some kids do, but to show up without *any* kind of costume would be pretty pathetic. Then I had this great idea. I decided to borrow one of Mom's swords. She has this old-fashioned one with a leather belt that I know fits me because I tried it on once. Luckily she was still sleeping so I snuck into her bedroom and got the sword. Then I found this hat Andy left behind when she went to college. It's green felt with a feather. And I have this old leather jacket that's a little tight on me, but which I can still get into. I drew on a kind of moustache with a black flair pen and went to the full-length mirror in the hall to look at myself.

I thought I looked fantastic. I'm not bad-looking, though for some reason girls haven't discovered how terrific I am yet. I think that's partly the way I act around them, which is pretty dumb. Andy says I have gorgeous eyes (they're blue) and if I stood up straight, I'd look great. Of course she's my sister and not totally objective, but still it gives me some hope for the future. I'm not all that muscular. It's my fault. The only exercise I ever do is running, and I don't do it very often. Still, with the hat and sword, I looked cool. You know who I looked like, actually, a little? I looked kind of like the Pirate King in *The Pirates of Penzance*. We all saw that last year. I have to admit I felt pretty good, having put together a costume on such short notice.

On the way to school I met my best friend, Otis, at this place we usually meet. Otis is black, and he's about two inches taller than me. Otherwise we're quite a lot alike, except like Andy, he can goof off in school but still remember things the teacher is saying. He says it's a matter of mind control and he's tried to teach me tricks about it, but it doesn't work.

When he saw me, he started to laugh.

"Hey, what's wrong?" I said.

"Who're you supposed to be, man? Robin Hood?"

I shrugged. "I thought it was some kind of historical novel."

"Some kind . . . yeah, but why the sword? It takes place during the Civil War. Nobody had swords then."

"They didn't? I thought they were always having duels and stuff like that."

"Jase, it was 1860! What'd you think, they were all out there in the battlefield yanking out their swords like the Three Musketeers or something?"

That's exactly what I did think. All of a sudden I knew why I had thought that. One class we had, they talked about guys using muskets to fight with, and I thought that was why they called them the Three Musketeers. I thought muskets were a kind of sword.

Otis was still shaking his head. "At least you didn't bring a bow and arrow. . . . That's a pretty nice sword. Where'd you get it?"

I told him about Mom being captain of the fencing team. He was impressed.

Suddenly I realized Otis didn't have a costume on, or anyhow he was wearing a tan raincoat over it. He was carrying a big paper shopping bag. "So, come on, what's your costume?" I said, trying to pull open his coat.

He wouldn't let me. "No way . . . Wait till we get to school."

"Why? Is it so embarrassing?" I was sure his was even worse than mine.

"Relax, you'll see it when you get there."

"I wonder what the girls will look like."

Otis grinned. "Especially Marcella." He raised his eyebrows.

Marcella was Italian. She came from Italy last year with her family. She has quite a heavy accent and long thick black hair, down to her butt almost. She's what my father would call "generously endowed." Once Ty and me went to

an R-rated movie with Dad that had this almost unbeliev-
ably sexy girl in it. All Dad would say when we got out
was, "Yes, she was certainly very generously endowed."
That's the way he talks a lot of the time.

When we got to school, Otis said, "Okay, turn around a
sec."

"You're really making this into a production, aren't
you?" I said.

"Turn around, Jase. Or close your eyes."

I turned around and stayed there till he said, "Okay. You
can look now."

Wow. Talk about doing it up right. He had this black suit
with velvet lapels, a little white carnation in one buttonhole,
a ruffled light-blue shirt, a funny kind of top hat and a *real*
moustache stuck on his upper lip. I just stared at him in
amazement.

"What do you think?" he said nervously.

"Was he supposed to be gay?" I said, meaning the ruffled
shirt.

"No! . . . Why don't you see the movie, you jerk?
He's this great lover. He carries women up flights of stairs."

"And then what? Rolls them down again?"

It's not that I take this kind of thing seriously, but if that's
the way Rhett Butler really looked, then I was going to look
kind of absurd. I didn't have to worry, though. By the time
everyone filed into our class, there were so many weird
getups, it looked like Halloween. The most far-out was this
guy Russ Pharr. He's on the football team and has a great
physique. Over six feet tall and really muscle-bound. He
showed up wearing nothing on top, just bare to the waist (I
guess so all the girls could admire his gorgeous body),
really tight jeans, boots, and—ready for this?—a bow and

arrow! So evidently I wasn't the only one who hadn't read the book *or* seen the movie.

Most of the girls looked pretty, but in the same kind of way. They mostly had flowered dresses on. A few had big hats. The pretty ones looked pretty and the others looked uncomfortable. We didn't get a really good look at Marcella till the beginning of Social Studies. Our teacher, Mr. Boyle, asked Marcella to hand back our tests from last week. She was wearing this extremely low-cut dress, and when she bent down you could see this little black spot, a mole I think, on one of her breasts. I was so interested in the mole I forgot to look at my score, which was 70, not so bad for me. Boyle had written in red on the side, "We covered most of this in class!"

"Well," he said. "I know you'll all be pleased to learn that we're going to be studying the Civil War, and I think some of you will make some interesting discoveries about that period. . . . Does anyone here know when gunpowder was discovered? Just a ballpark guess?"

A couple of kids guessed, but it was way earlier than anyone thought.

"So, I think Mr. Pharr's bow and arrow and Mr. Lieberman's sword, though attractive, wouldn't have been too effective if they'd had to face someone of the period armed with an actual gun."

The second class of the day was one of the few I don't totally dread: Biology. I'm pretty good at it, and our teacher Ms. Korbel, has so far just been going over stuff we did last year. It's funny with teachers. There are some teachers who seem to hate me before I walk into the room, practically. Or, if they don't hate me, they act in this kind of sneering way, like they *expected* me to do terribly. Maybe it's because they've read my record or something. But then there are others—not as many, unfortunately—who like me for no special reason either. Ms. Korbel is one of those. She'll smile and say, "I bet Jason can explain this better than I have. Do you want to give it a try, Jason?"

I don't want you to think I'm obsessed with breasts, though I admit my thoughts do wander around topics concerned with the female body pretty frequently. But there's one thing about Ms. Korbel that's been on my mind ever since school started. Someone started the rumor that over the summer she had cancer and had to have a breast removed. Or maybe both. I think it was just one. I keep staring at them, wondering which is the real one or if either one is real. They both *look* real. I'm glad about that for her sake, because she's not married. It would be kind of strange if some guy tried to take her clothes off, pulled her sweater over her head, and her breasts came off too! I guess she must explain ahead of time, but even so it would be sort of a shock. She's not that old either, just in her twenties, I think.

Today she stood up and started asking how we'd made out with our assignments. She just stood there, talking in her usual way, but there she was, dressed like Olivia Newton-John in these tight black spandex pants and a red top with a V-neck. All the female teachers had to dress up like Olivia Newton-John and the male teachers like John Travolta. She's blond, but usually she has her hair in some plain, regular teacherish way. Today it was all fluffed up and tucked behind one ear. Somehow it was ten times more of a shock to see a teacher looking like that. Especially when her personality seemed just the same. Maybe she realized that's what we were feeling, because she smiled awkwardly and said, "Do I look the way Olivia is supposed to look? I've only seen her in a photo."

25

There were a few whistles and someone called out, "All right!"

Ms. Korbel blushed. Then she said crisply. "Well, let's try and pretend this is a day like any other." She smiled at Otis, who was in the front row, right next to me. "I love your shirt, Otis. Why can't men dress like that all the time?"

Otis looked pretty pleased with himself. He must have known he looked good. Otis has had somewhat more experience with girls than me, not quite everything, but a lot closer than I've ever come. I think it's partly that he's much calmer around girls than I am, even if they're gorgeous. He says he *feels* nervous, just like I do, but he doesn't start making idiot jokes and horsing around. My problem is that even when I can see by the girl's face that she's completely turned off by the way I'm acting, I can't stop. It's like a compulsion, almost.

Still, it was one of the better days in school. We were given homework and had regular classes, but everyone, even the teachers, was in a different mood than usual. I wish they'd do something like this every day.

In math class something kind of embarrassing happened, though not to me, luckily. Mr. Blake asked one of the kids to come up to the blackboard and simplify an equation. Vicki Katz raised her hand. She's a math whiz. I get the feeling she's with math like Andy is with reading—it just comes naturally. Anyhow, she walked up to the board in this really old-fashioned dress she was wearing. It wasn't low-cut—the opposite, in fact. It had a high neck with lots of lace in front, a very full skirt, and dozens of little buttons down the back. The trouble was, she's small, smaller even than Juliet, and she evidently couldn't reach all the buttons. Maybe she meant to ask her mother to do them up and then

26

forgot. But there were about six buttons that were undone, and you could see her bra clear as day. I had an unusually good view because I was in the front row.

She stood there doing the equation, which was pretty long, and gradually various guys in the class caught on and started to giggle or snort or make noises. She's basically kind of shy and serious, Vicki is, and I think she figured she was doing the equation wrong. She turned to Mr. Blake and said, "Is that okay?"

"It's fine, Vicki," he said. *He* looked embarrassed too, but I guess he figured he couldn't say anything. But instead of making her finish it, he said, "Can someone else come up and explain to us how Vicki got the result she did?"

Vicki went back to her seat, which is way in the back, and all the boys turned to watch her. The next time I saw her, around lunchtime, she was all buttoned up. Maybe one of the other girls told her.

I fucked up with Vicki two years ago, when she first came to our school. I think she had sort of a crush on me. It's hard to tell. It may have been that she was new in school and our last names begin with almost the same letter, so we were seated together right from the start. She wasn't flirtatious so much, but she used to stop me in the hall and ask me things. I never knew how to handle it. Partly, I just wasn't into girls much back then, but also I didn't know what she had in mind. Now she hardly ever speaks to me. In fact, I think she might have a crush on Otis, because I've noticed her staring at him sometimes in class. He thinks she's okay, but she's not his type. If he could get anyone, he said, it'd be Marcella. The trouble with that is she has these older brothers that look like something out of the Mafia. I think if you ever tried anything with her, you might end up out cold in an alley somewhere. I'm a coward from way back, so I'm content to admire her from afar.

After lunch I was standing around in the hall waiting for the bell to ring, when Vicki came over to me. She did look nice in that lacy dress. "I like your costume," she said.

I shrugged. "I never even read the book. You can tell, I guess."

"Well, it's still a good costume. . . . You know who you look like? Kevin Kline in *The Pirates of Penzance*. Did you see that?"

I felt really pleased because no one else seemed to have noticed the resemblance. "I can't sing," I said. One of my classically dumb remarks. Like I said, I'm not the smoothest talker around girls.

"I feel so uncomfortable," she went on. "I'm wearing this horsehair crinoline my mother lent me, and it itches like crazy! But the thing is, Scarlett was supposed to have this really tiny waist or something! Supposedly guys could put their hands around her waist. Mine's twenty-four! I don't think anyone could do that with me."

Okay, you want a perfect example of what I'm like with girls? The second she said that, I reached down and tried to put my hands around her waist. It was true; they didn't go around. Vicki kind of jumped backward, like I'd been about to rape her. She didn't run away, but she looked really embarrassed. Why do I do things like that? I don't seem to have the art of leading up to things gradually. After that we just stood there awkwardly.

Just then Russ Pharr walked up, flexing his muscles. He winked at Vicki and me. "How's it going?" he said, and walked on. I had the feeling he winked because of the incident with Vicki in math class. What a jerk.

After he'd gone, Vicki made a face. "Gross," she said.

"God, he's so conceited! He must think he has such a great body or something." She said it like *she* didn't think he did. That made me feel better.

Otis won first prize as Rhett Butler. I thought for sure Marcella would win as Scarlett O'Hara, but she didn't. Those judges must be blind. They gave it to this girl Marsha Moss, who isn't even especially pretty. Maybe it's because she has red hair. Maybe Scarlett is supposed to have red hair.

Someday I'm going to see the movie.

FOUR

||||

WHEN *I* GOT HOME *M*OM WAS OUT, SO *I* SMOKED A LITTLE IN the bathroom. I try not to smoke at home *ever*, because Mom has a nose like a bloodhound when it comes to pot, but I've figured out a way to do it at times when it's raining really hard. I blow the smoke out the bathroom window and then close the window when I'm done. I didn't have much, just a little to take the edge off. I'd thought I would change back into regular clothes, but to tell the truth, I kind of liked wearing the sword and hat. I still think I looked good, even if not the way Rhett Butler looked.

When Mom came home and saw me, she looked startled. I explained.

"Jase, that's really a valuable sword. I wish you'd ask me before you borrow it."

"You were asleep."

"Okay, well, next time ask." She started going into the kitchen.

"Did you ever see *Gone With the Wind*, Mom?"

She thought. "This is strange, but I think the only time I saw it was on our honeymoon, in Florence. It was dubbed in Italian. *Via Col Vento*."

"Is it some kind of love story, or what?"

"Sort of, but you might like it, Jase. There are great battle scenes. The history is kind of one-sided, but . . . Hey, is Ty home yet?"

I shook my head, kind of surprised, because Ty never comes home during the week unless Juliet's whole family has pneumonia or something.

"I left word at school for him to be home for dinner. I guess I'll call the mansion." That's Mom's word for the Moscowitz home, which is in the ritziest part of town.

For dinner that night we had what was almost a regular dinner: hamburgers, corn on the cob, and sliced tomatoes. Cooking is not one of my mother's strong points. This wouldn't have gotten her a job at a fancy French restaurant, but it smelled good.

Just as we were about to start, Ty breezed in. "Hi Mom, hi Jase."

"Where were you?" Mom snapped. "I left word at school for you to come straight home."

He looked taken aback. "Juliet had to go to the dentist."

"So?"

"Well, they were going to give her Novocain and she thought she might be feeling funny, so she wanted me to wait for her."

"God, does she have a choke collar for you too?" Mom said. "Do you blow her nose for her?"

Ty looked really pissed. "Look, I'm here, okay? What's the big fuss? You said be home for dinner."

Mom sat silently for a minute. Then she said, "Well, Jase knows this already . . . but your father moved out yesterday, announcing his intention to marry some lady he's been making it with, and I thought you ought to know."

Ty put a big bite of hamburger away. "Okay, I can live with it."

Mom just looked at him. "Christ," she said.

"Christ what?" He looked innocent.

"Your parents are getting divorced, and all you can say is, 'I can live with it.'"

"Well, Mom, I mean, you're not exactly, I mean you're not like Juliet's parents."

Mom slammed her hand down on the table. "I'm going to be sick. The perfect parents: a lobotomized housewife who spends every Saturday shopping with her daughter buying her diaphragms in every shape and color and an ambulance-chaser lawyer who—"

"They love each other, okay?" Ty said.

"Spare me," Mom said.

"Mom, listen, I'm not *blaming* you that Dad walked out. I'm just saying—"

Mom smiled grimly. "Gee, thanks. Thanks a whole lot. . . . Are *you* not blaming me too, Jase?"

I shook my head.

"Here I was afraid you'd all be so traumatized, and it seems about as significant as if the Orioles lost the Series."

Suddenly Ty got this really solemn expression. "No, I'm sorry, Mom . . . It must be rough."

"It is," Mom said. "And whereas I don't want to lay a big duty trip on either of you, I would like a little more . . . I mean, you two are all I have left."

Ty looked very uneasy. "What d'you mean?"

"I mean, I'd like you to start spending more time at home. . . . You can fuck her on weekends."

I tried not to laugh, but Ty looked indignant. "That's *not* why we need to see each other so much. We just enjoy each other's company."

"Well, you'll enjoy it all the more since it'll be less frequent."

"What do you call less frequent?"

"Two school nights a week, maximum."

Ty stared at Mom in horror. "I'm supposed to see her only two nights a week?"

Mom got up to clear. "You'll get sick of each other less quickly that way."

"We're not going to get sick of each other!" he said, hurt. "We're not *like* you and Dad."

I guess I must have been smirking unintentionally, because Ty turned on me and said, "What do *you* know? Just sitting around jerking off in your room? You wouldn't even know what to do with a girl if you got one."

"Oh, shut up," I said. "Bring Juliet over some afternoon and I'll figure out what to do with her."

"She wouldn't go near you in a million years. She says you're dumb and you're too stoned to talk half the time."

Maybe this was dumb, but I lunged at him and knocked him to the ground. I'm a coward, but I know I can beat Ty up if I want. He started getting up to lunge back at me, when Mom grabbed him. "Ty, stop! Right this minute!"

"Ty, stop?" He looked at her. "How about Angel Face here? Who started it?"

When I was little and had blond curls, Mom used to call me Angel Face. Ty knows I hate it when he mentions that. I would have gone at him again, but Mom said, "You too, Jase. What's wrong with both of you? You're supposed to be the men in the family. I mean it. I'm going to need help, real moral support . . . and you're both acting like you're two years old."

"So, if we're so awful, why do you even care if I'm here?" Ty said, sitting back down at the table, glancing at me sideways. I knew he'd do something **to** get back at me later.

"Because sometimes you're sweet, terrific kids."

There was a moment of silence. I don't think Ty is *ever* a sweet, terrific kid, but I kept quiet. Then Mom said, "There's one other thing. Your father and I agreed we wouldn't announce this publicly, as it were, till Thanksgiving, when the girls are home. . . . So if you talk to them or write them, just don't mention it, okay? Pretend everything is normal."

"I don't get it, Mom," I said. "What's the point of that?"

"Well, Erin takes these things hard, and it's hard enough for her, being away at school."

"Why can't we tell Andy, then?"

"It just seems funny having Erin the only one not knowing. . . . Look, it's six weeks. That's not so bad."

It'll be hard, lying to Andy, because she's so straight about everything. She's also pretty perceptive. I have to admit that I don't keep up my end of our correspondence all that much. But she writes me anyway. I guess I'll just write back about other stuff, like today at school.

"So, I'm supposed to stay here tonight?" Ty said, in this weary, sarcastic way.

"Yes, you're supposed to stay here tonight," Mom said crisply. "Or does Juliet need you to run her bath?"

"How about tomorrow? Do I have to stay here *then* too?"

Mom exploded. "What is this 'have to'? You can't spend three nights a week in your own house?"

"I *said* I would," Ty said, "but tomorrow is Juliet's parents' anniversary, and they wanted me to go out to dinner with them."

You could practically see smoke coming out of Mom's ears, probably because of the anniversary thing and also

34

because of wherever they were going, which was sure to be the most expensive restaurant in town. "Okay, go out to dinner. Just come back afterward."

Ty sighed. "How about weekends?"

"Weekends you can stare into each other's eyes twenty-four hours a day. . . . But I'd like you home Sunday night."

Ty trudged off to his room, slammed the door, and put one of his records on full blast. Mom looked at me. "Love," she snarled.

I wonder about that a lot. I mean, obviously I hope at some point I'll fall in love with some girl, but when I think that it'll make me go around acting like that, I kind of wonder. The one reassuring thing is Ty was pretty obnoxious before he was in love with Juliet.

"Don't fall in love with someone for another year, will you, Jase?" Mom said, getting up to clear. "I don't think I can handle two terminal cases at once. . . . Still, I suppose it's reassuring that someone in the family has a decent sex life . . . other than your father, of course."

The thought of my father screwing this other woman is hard for me to handle, I must admit. I know lots of middle-aged men do that, but if you knew my father—well, he's not like those guys his age on TV, all witty and suave and making brilliant suggestions about legal cases. Of course, I don't know what his girlfriend is like, either. At least he didn't fall in love with Juliet Moscowitz's mother. Then Mom would've really zonked out.

I went back to my room. For the millionth time in the last year, I thought: if Ty could get Juliet, I can get someone. But who? Deep down I was kind of hurt that he said she thought I was dumb and stoned all the time. What if all girls think that?

When I was about to go to bed, I went into the bathroom to brush my teeth. Ty was just getting out of the shower. I glanced at him quickly. Okay, I do admit it. I really feel jealous about his sex life. Before Ty started going out with Juliet, Dad used to tell us all these jokes about Jewish girls, like, "What's Jewish foreplay? Three hours of begging." Or "How do you know when a Jewish girl has an orgasm? She drops her nail file." But so what? I wouldn't care if someone was out cold, as long as they'd let me. But the trouble is, I gather they don't let you unless you're really in love with them *or* a terrific liar. I'm a good liar at times, but I don't think I could do that with a girl. Not on moral principles. I just don't think I could convince anybody, if my heart wasn't into it.

Still I'm not going to take up figure skating. I may be desperate, but there are limits.

FIVE

||||

THE NEXT MORNING, REALLY EARLY, SEVEN THIRTY, DAD called. Maybe he called that early because he knows Mom tends to sleep late and they don't have a phone in their bedroom.

"Jase? Hi, is Ty there?"

"Yeah."

"Would you get him? I wanted to talk to both of you a minute."

I went into Ty's room. He was lying in bed with his eyes open.

"Would you knock before you come into my room, jerk?" he said.

"Dad's on the phone. . . . He wants to talk to both of us."

Ty took the living room phone. I took the kitchen one.

"Ty? Uh, I gather Fay told you that—"

"Yeah, she told us," Ty said.

"Well, what I'm calling about is this. I'd really like the two of you to meet Randall. She's very eager to meet you too. I wondered if maybe this weekend, Saturday or

Sunday, you might come over here. We could go to the zoo, maybe. It's right near her house."

The zoo! Does he thing we're in third grade? "Sure, that sounds okay," I said.

"Well, I'd like to, Dad," Ty said, "but the thing is, Mom has set these pretty stringent rules about my seeing Juliet. So, like, weekends are practically the only time I have to see her."

"This wouldn't involve the evening," Dad said. "Just the afternoon. Just a few hours."

Ty sighed. "It's just—there was something we were planning to do."

"Fine. Do it Saturday and come on over Sunday, or vice versa."

"Could I bring Juliet along?"

There was a pause. I could tell Dad was ready to blow up. "Ty, this is a very personal family thing. Randall and I are going to get married. Sure, at some point Juliet can meet her too, but for the first time, I'd really appreciate it if—"

"How do you know Mom'll divorce you?" Ty said.

"Could you let me handle it?"

"Sure, you can handle it."

Dad sighed. "I hope so. . . . So, which day do you prefer?"

I said "Sunday" just as Ty said "Saturday."

"You don't have anything to do Saturday," Ty said to me.

"How do you know?"

"What? Jerking off in your room?"

It's good that he was in the other room because, I swear, I would have lunged at him again and really given it to him.

"Ty? Jase? Look, just pick a day, will you, and call me back tonight?"

38

"Sure, Dad," Ty said, suddenly really polite and ultra friendly. "We're really looking forward to meeting her."

"Yeah," I said. Which was half true.

After we both hung up, I went back into his room. "Listen, will you shut up about that jerking off stuff? You should talk. . . . I just don't go around boasting about my sex life. I don't need to."

He laughed. "Your sex life! . . . The day you have a sex life, I'll become the first Jewish astronaut."

I looked at him with cool scorn. "Like I said, I feel no need to talk about it."

All the way to school I felt great. Those were good lines. I don't know if I convinced him. But still. God, he is such a hypocrite. After giving Dad all that trouble about setting the thing up, suddenly he's so "eager" to meet Randall. I wonder what she'll be like. You figure she's got to be younger than Mom and fairly sexy. Otherwise, why bother? But I imagine her sexy in a more subdued way. Not in a Marcella way. Maybe she'll look like Leslie Stahl, that newscaster on TV, blond, with glasses, but very self-possessed. I wouldn't mind having a stepmother that looked like Leslie Stahl.

There were no major events at school. The only surprising thing was when Ms. Korbel asked me to stay after class. I hadn't flunked the Bio quiz, so I wasn't sure what was up. I motioned to Otis that I'd meet him for lunch, since that was our next period.

Ms. Korbel had gone back to her usual way of dressing, after her brief moment as Olivia Newton-John. It's too bad. I mean, I know she couldn't dress like that every day, but she could dress a little bit more like that. It wouldn't hurt.

"Jase, I wondered if you were ever free weekend nights?"

"Uh, sure . . . pretty much." What whirled through my mind was this movie I once saw with Otis, called *Homework*. It was about this teacher—she was a million times sexier than Ms. Korbel—who for some reason got a mad crush on one of her students and decided to "initiate" him. She really did a job. By the end of the movie they'd done about everything you can do and still get an R rating.

"I don't know if I ever mentioned that I live with my father?"

I shook my head.

"Well, he's eighty years old. He had two families, really, and I'm the youngest child of the second one. Both his wives died, my mother and the other woman. So, to make a long story short, he lives with me. . . . And he's a darling person, really, very gentle and sweet, but in the past year he had a mild stroke. He's not senile, he just sometimes forgets things. I have a housekeeper who stays with him during the day, but at night, if I go out, I hate to leave him alone. . . . I wondered if by any chance you'd be willing to come and, well, babysit for him? He goes to bed early, nine or so, so you'd have plenty of time to do homework or watch TV."

I never heard of anything like that. Babysitting for an eighty-year-old grandfather? But I said, "Sure."

"I'd pay regular rates, two-fifty an hour. . . . Would—I know this is a little last-minute—but would tonight be possible?"

"Yeah, I could do that."

"I'll be back early, ten-thirty at the latest."

I didn't think Mom would mind, since I'd be earning money and it'd be for a teacher. Ms. Korbel gave me the address and smiled. "Thanks *so* much, Jase, I truly appreciate it."

40

I felt a little disappointed. Sometimes my fantasies about things are so real, I tend to forget how unlikely they are. I told Otis about it. We were sitting outside eating our sandwiches. They let you leave the school grounds, as long as you're back on time. "Maybe it's just a lure," he suggested. "She'll get you there, Grandpa'll be off in bed, and—whammo! She'll jump you."

"Sure." I sighed.

He looked at me sideways for a second, drained his can of Coke, and said, "Okay, are you ready for this one? Marcella asked me out!"

"Oh, come on."

He laughed. "I swear. I'm sitting at home and Mom comes in. 'There's this girl with a very funny accent on the phone, Otis.' I wonder. Can it be? No, forget it. I go to the phone. She says, real soft, 'Otis? I hope I'm not disturbing you.'" Otis can imitate Marcella's Italian accent real good. "'Not at all.' Well, it seems there's some Italian street festival in the city Friday and she wonders if maybe I'd like to go. She's going with one of her brothers, and her parents."

"You better watch it, man. Those brothers are the kind that kill people. I mean it."

"True . . . But it's a street fair. I figure we don't have to stay in a pack every second. Anyhow, it's a first step. . . . Oh, wait, this is the best part. She says, 'We'll have to go in my parents' car, and it's not too big. We may be a little squashed. Is that all right?' I wanted to say. 'Marcy, honey, I'll squash up with you *any* day.'"

"Maybe she'll sit on your lap." God, I was getting depressed. This was all I needed. First Ty, then my father, now Otis. Even Ms. Korbel probably has some hot thing going. I bet I'll be the last fifteen-year-old virgin east of the

Mississippi. Dad once took me aside and gave me the classic "don't take advantage of girls" talk, but when I asked him how old *he'd* been when he first did it, he admitted he was fourteen. He said it was a coincidence, that he had a cousin who really liked him and they were on the beach one day and kind of got carried away. So it wasn't like from then on he was at it day and night. He said it wasn't till college that he met a girl he really cared for, that Cerelia Blade, who ended up dumping him for someone else.

Otis had just been sitting there, staring off into space. "You know what I really like about Marcella?" he said.

"No, tell me," I said, trying not to sound too sarcastic.

"Well, okay, her figure, and her voice—I really dig that Italian accent—and her eyes, those big soft eyes. . . . But it's her smell. You know what she smells like? Homemade pasta. My sister got this machine to make pasta and that's what it smells like. Or maybe it's olive oil. My mouth practically starts watering when I go near her."

"Well, don't drool into her lap while her brother's around."

"Don't worry, man. I can handle it."

Mom was cool about the babysitting job. I gave her the phone number. Actually, it's not far from our house so I decided to take my bike. She said she wanted me home at the latest by eleven.

When I rang the bell, Ms. Korbel answered it right away. She looked a little more dressed up than she does at school, but not that much. Her father was standing right behind her. He was a little guy with thin white hair and glasses. He had his pajamas on. "Daddy, this is the boy I've been telling you about—Jason Lieberman. My father—Vernon Korbel."

Old Vernon looked delighted to see me. He reached out and shook my hand. Then he turned to Ms. Korbel. "He seems like a fine young man, Betsy." Then, turning to me, he said, "I don't let Betsy go out with anyone who isn't going to treat her right."

"Uh," I started, but Ms. Korbel said, "Daddy, I'm not going out with Jason. Remember? I'm going to a concert. Jason is going to stay here and keep you company."

She took us both into the living room. It was a small house, neat, but not especially fancy. "Daddy likes to watch 'Whirly Girls,' which is on from eight to nine," she said. "You don't have to watch it with him. And then sometimes he likes a little snack. But he's usually pretty tired by then." She took me inside and showed me his bedroom. "Just kind of help him, and, if he wanders out, lead him back. He may not, but sometimes, if he doesn't fall right to sleep, he does that."

"I get it," I said.

Ms. Korbel kissed her father good-bye and left. I wonder who she was going to the concert with. She said she'd be back by ten-thirty. Vernon had settled down in a big armchair. I turned on "Whirly Girls" for him. I had a little homework, but I didn't feel much like doing it so I watched the show with him. Mostly I watch sports on TV or an occasional horror movie, if a good one's on that I haven't seen yet. Boy, was this a dumb show! I wondered why an eighty-year-old guy would want to watch it. It seemed like the kind of show nine-year-old girls would watch. It was all about two girls in junior high who were giggling all the time and worrying about when boys would start liking them. They were both pretty cute, and it really bugged me. In real life those girls would have their choice of anyone they wanted. But the show pretended it was a big deal, trying to

43

attract boys. But Vernon really liked the show. He laughed louder than the laugh track at the dumbest jokes. During one of the commercials he asked me, "Which one do you like best?"

I wasn't crazy about either one, but I said, "The dark-haired one, I guess."

He shook his head disapprovingly. "You're young," he said. "You'll learn. That one's a schemer. Stay away from those. Pamela—she's a real darling."

I shrugged. It was the kind of show you could watch and think about a dozen other things and still follow the plot. When it was over, I turned off the set and asked him if he wanted a snack.

"Well, let's see what surprises the refrigerator has for us," he said, and padded in. I followed him. He spent a long time looking at all the stuff and finally decided to have a cup of tea and some cookies. "Will you join me?" he asked.

I said I'd have a Coke. Then I put the water on to boil for his tea. They had a big copper teapot. Suddenly, when I was bringing the tea in, he looked up with a really worried expression. "Where's Betsy?" he said, glancing all around the room.

"She went to a concert," I said.

"By herself?"

I didn't really know, but I said, "No, she was meeting a friend, I think."

He shook his head. He still looked really worried. "I love Betsy," he said, dumping a whole lot of sugar in his cup. "I love her to excess in fact. I'd give my life for her in one second. . . . But, you know what her big problem is?"

For some reason I thought he was going to say that she

had such lousy students at school, but he said, "She's too naive about men."

"Yeah?" I said.

"Look at that guy last week, that bald guy," he said. "Now it's true, I've had lots of experience. Those men walk in the door, I take one quick look at them, and I know. I can read their minds! I know *exactly* what they're thinking about. . . . Not Betsy. 'Daddy,' she says, 'he's an engineer. He loves dogs. He gardens.' Bullshit. They feed her a line. They make things up. . . . Look, I did the same thing. That's how I know. You size up what they want to hear and you tell them. But I worry about her day and night."

I didn't exactly know what to say. "I think she's smart," I said. "She's a good teacher."

"Of course she's smart!" he said indignantly. "You won't find a girl smarter than my Betsy." He squinted at me. "I bet you have a girlfriend," he said, grinning. "Some nice little girlfriend like the ones on that show."

"Not exactly."

"Why not?"

"I don't know, I just don't. . . ." Since he seemed interested, I said, "I act funny around girls."

He looked worried again. "Boy, I'll give you a piece of advice that'll stand you in good stead the rest of your life." He paused dramatically. "Learn to dance! Are you a good dancer?"

I shook my head.

"That's the key," he assured me. "Look at me. I'm not the handsomest man that ever walked the face of the earth, not the greatest lover, but I could dance, and I got the two sweetest, prettiest wives any man ever had. . . . I'll tell you where to start. Learn to waltz first—no woman can resist a good waltz. Then the tango."

"Okay." I wasn't sure what the tango was, actually. I think they do it in South America, Brazil, places like that.

"I'm too tired now, but next time you come over, I'll give you a few pointers. You take charge, you lead them, but gently. Don't overdo it. Women hate it when you overdo it." He winked at me. "So is it a deal?"

"Sure." I followed him into his bedroom. I thought he might feel offended that I had to help him into bed, but he didn't seem to. I pulled the covers up around him. "I'll be right inside," I said.

"You tell Muriel I was a good boy," he said.

"Sure," I said, wondering who Muriel was.

I took a stab at my homework and did some of it, but it's hard to concentrate in someone else's house. Anyhow, it was past ten and Ms. Korbel had said she'd be back at ten-thirty. She did come back then. She was with this guy. He was tall and heavy and completely bald, though he didn't look that old. Maybe he was the one her father was worried about.

"How did it go?" she asked me.

"Fine. Who's Muriel? He asked after her."

"Oh, that was his first wife. He gets them mixed up. Fanny was my mother, but sometimes he calls *me* Fanny." She turned around. "Gunther, this is Jason."

"Hi," I said.

Gunther grabbed my hand and shook it like he wanted to take it home with him.

"Would you like Gunther to drive you home?" Ms. Korbel asked.

"No, that's okay, I have my bike. I don't live far from here."

She paid me. I put the money in my pocket. It won't be bad having a little extra cash. Biking home, I wondered about Ms. Korbel and that Gunther. I wondered if her father was right. Was he going to jump her the second I left? Maybe she wanted him to. But how come she picked a bald guy? She's not bad-looking. This guy didn't have one hair on his head! Otis once said some women find that sexy. I can't figure that. I guess some of them find *anything* sexy. And I wonder if he knows about one of her breasts not being real. What do guys do, after they know, I mean, if it's some rubber thing? I guess you could squeeze both of them— they'd probably feel about the same. But how about once she takes her bra off? Maybe you get used to it.

I wish I didn't obsess about this kind of thing so much. Hell, I don't even know how to handle a regular situation with a regular girl where everything is where it's supposed to be. Still, I think Vernon's wrong. I think Ms. Korbel can handle herself.

SIX

||||

WE ENDED UP VISITING DAD AND RANDALL SATURDAY. TY
said Sunday Juliet's family was going to do something else
to celebrate their anniversary—some movie or something.
But one slightly awkward thing happened. In the middle of
the morning—we were supposed to get there around noon—
Andy called. I answered it and we talked for a while. I knew
I couldn't say anything about Mom and Dad, so I just talked
about general things. I told her about babysitting for Ms.
Korbel's father and Senior Day at school.

After a while I forgot about it, till she said, "Hey, is Dad
around? I wanted to ask him something."

"Uh, no," I said.

There was a pause.

"Is anything wrong?" Andy pursued. "Is he okay?"

"He's fine," I said.

Then Mom got on the other extension. "So, how's life?"
she said really cheerfully.

"I'm working my ass off, but otherwise terrific," Andy
said.

"How's your social life?" Mom asked. She was really

doing a perky interested-mother number. I had the feeling that would get Andy more suspicious than anything else.

This time there was a slight pause before Andy said, "Well, I met someone."

"Who is he?" Mom asked.

"A guy."

"Whew," Mom said. "Want to tell us a little more or—"

"Listen, why don't I wait till I see you guys over Thanksgiving?" Andy said.

"Is he a student?" Mom persisted. Andy's cautiousness was obviously making her suspicious. Also, it's not like Andy to not tell you everything.

"No, I met him last summer on that summer intern job. He works in the district attorney's office."

"He's a lawyer, then?" Mom said.

"Right."

"Well, we'll look forward to hearing the whole story over Thanksgiving," Mom said.

"Give Dad my love, okay?" Andy said.

Mom didn't say anything. I said, "Okay."

When I hung up, I walked into the kitchen. Mom said, "Something's funny."

I shrugged.

"I bet he's a drug dealer, or he writes kiddie porn, or—"

"Mom, come on. She said he works at the district attorney's office."

"So? I bet he's into S&M, or he's Polish and they communicate with sign language, or he's from Mainland China and he wants her to move back there with him, or he—"

"Mom, listen, we've got to go."

"Oh, right." She stared at me hard. "Jase, listen, I want

a full, and I mean full, report. Look in closets, under beds. Not just, 'Yeah, she's okay.'"

I laughed. "Don't worry."

I met Ty at the bus stop. Randall lives in the Bronx, near the Bronx Zoo, and Dad said we should take a cab to her apartment when we got off at the George Washington Bridge. On the way Ty didn't say much. He just stared moodily out the window, probably reliving his latest bang with Juliet. Now even Andy has a boyfriend. God, if one more person I know pairs off, even with an elephant, I don't think I can take it.

"Andy called," I told Ty, just to try and get some kind of conversation going.

"Yeah? How is she?"

"She's got some guy evidently. She didn't say much about him."

Ty wrinkled his nose. "She ought to lose some weight. Otherwise she's only going to end up with losers."

Jesus, he can get me mad! "Wally wasn't a loser," I said. That was the guy Andy went with in college.

"Sure he was. I never saw a guy in such lousy shape physically. His chest was *concave*, practically. And he told me once that without his glasses he couldn't even see. He was almost legally blind!"

"So? He wore glasses. What's the big deal?"

"Anyway, all I'm saying is guys can get away with stuff like that to some extent, but girls have to be—you know. Or who's going to want them? Like Juliet. You know when we met she weighed a hundred and twenty? Which isn't fat, but it was too much for her size. She didn't look good, especially in that skating costume. Her rear end hung down. . . . But once she started getting interested in me, she got motivated and lost twenty pounds." He smiled smugly at me. "Now she's perfect. That's what the gym teacher at school told her. She said, 'You've got a perfect body.'"

That's what you get when you try and talk to my brother. Can you imagine how hard up and sick a girl would have to be to lose twenty pounds just to get his interest? I swore I wouldn't say a word to him till we got there, but about a minute later I found myself saying, "I wonder what she'll look like."

"Who?" Every time I raised a new topic, he kind of tore himself away from looking out the window, like he was doing me a big favor by giving me his attention.

"You know—Randall."

"She's probably a nice middle-aged lady."

"Really? How come he'd want someone like that?"

"Well, what'd you expect? He's dating Raquel Welch?"

"So why change from Mom? *She's* a nice middle-aged lady."

"Oh, she's off the wall," Ty said dismissively. "Look, he got somebody. I just hope she's not a real drag. Juliet's friend Kathy has this stepmother and she says it's a real pain going over there, she does such a number, trying to act interested in their private lives, all that crap."

It's funny. Till this moment I never thought that if Dad marries Randall, I'll have a stepmother. I don't like the sound of that.

We rang the bell. Dad and Randall answered it together. She was standing in back of him, smiling a little uncertainly. I don't know. I guess she was somewhere in between Leslie Stahl and what Ty had said he thought she'd be like. I'm not good about guessing women's ages unless they're all wrinkled and hunched over, because if they dye their hair, how can you tell? To me she didn't look a *lot* younger

51

than Mom. She had short dark hair, an okay figure, rimless glasses. She reminded me a little of this woman I used to take cello lessons from when I was in third grade.

"Hi, I'm Randall," she said, shaking my hand and then Ty's.

Dad seemed kind of embarrassed. I felt weird too. It was, like, what was he doing here with this strange lady, whether she was nice or not? She called him "Mort"—that's his name—but once, when she went into the kitchen to get us something to drink, she called out, "Darling, do you know where the corkscrew is?" Darling! That really spooked me, hearing someone call my father darling. And I think maybe he called her darling once too.

What was funny was, you got the feeling she really liked him. I don't mean to say my father is such an ogre that I can't imagine anyone liking him. Like I said, he's really smart and he's always been pretty good with me. Ty used to say he was an absentee father because he was never around much when we were little. Maybe that was because he loved his work or maybe the tension around the house got to him. It was like when he and my mother were in a room together, it was *always* tense. Either they'd just had a fight and weren't speaking, so it was "Could you ask your father what his plans are?" or "Do you know if your mother will be here Saturday?" Or there'd be real knockdown, dragout fights, where they'd both be yelling and slamming doors. I don't mean they socked each other, but it wasn't just like disagreeing about whether to vote Republican or Democrat. So what was odd here was there was none of that. It was all so weirdly calm.

After we sat around for a while, Randall said, "Maybe we could go to the zoo now." She reached out and touched my father's hand. "What do you think?"

"Sure, I'm game," my father said. He looked at us. You could tell he was nervous, probably from wanting us to like her. "How about it, boys?"

Ty cleared his throat. "Dad, the thing is, I promised Juliet I wouldn't be back too late."

"You just got here," Dad said, obviously trying to restrain himself.

"Yeah, well, an hour or so, sure, I can manage that."

Dad looked at me and smiled. "How about *you*, Jase? Any elaborate plans we should know about?"

"Not especially," I said.

Randall got her coat. Going down in the elevator, she said to Ty, "I had a friend named Juliet in high school. It used to drive her crazy, because every time she liked a boy, everyone would call him Romeo. 'Wherefore art thou,' all that."

"We don't go to the same school," Ty said stiffly, "so I don't have to worry about that."

Juliet goes to the fanciest private school in our district, needless to say.

"Of course, in our day social life hardly existed," Randall went on. "Did it for you, sweetie?" she asked, turning to my father.

"An occasional crush," Dad said. "That's about all."

"I once told my niece, Delia, how old I was when I lost my virginity, and she almost fainted. She couldn't believe *anyone* could've been that old!" She laughed.

I wondered how old she was. I wondered if Dad told her about his cousin and that time at the beach. Randall wasn't so bad-looking, but I gather things were different then. Mom once told us she was so ashamed of having "gone all the way" with some guy before she got married that she even thought of having some operation before her wedding that made you a virgin again. That sounds kind of grisly. Anyway, Dad said he didn't care one way or the other. Mom says what men say and what they feel is another story, but I don't personally see Dad as the type that would care especially. *I* certainly wouldn't. I mean, I don't know if I'd want to marry someone who'd made it with millions of guys, unless I'd also made it with millions of girls, which, at the rate I'm going, doesn't seem all that likely. But I wouldn't mind if she had a general idea about what to do and all that.

The Bronx Zoo is huge. We'd been there a couple of times as kids, but I didn't remember it much. Or maybe they changed it around. It was a nice day, cool, but the sun was out so it wasn't bad walking around. I like it when the animals look like they don't mind being there so much. I mean, obviously no one knows what they're really thinking or feeling, but in that zoo in Central Park, and in some others I've been to, the animals look the way I feel on the days I go to school unstoned: miserable, like they want to scream "Let me out!"

We watched the elephants and the tigers and then moved on to some monkeys that were outside. I was glad, because the smell in the monkey house can really get to you. They ought to bottle it so people could spray it on criminals who try to attack them. After that Ty went to call Juliet, and Randall said she had to go to the ladies' room. That left Dad and me, standing outside.

"So, what do you think?" he said, as soon as Randall was gone.

It was funny, his being that eager for my opinion. The fact is, I thought she was okay, but what if I hadn't? I really would've been in a bind. "Yeah, she seems nice," I said, and he looked pleased. "She's different from how I pictured her, though."

"Oh? How did you picture her?"

I didn't want to say "prettier" or "more like Leslie Stahl." All I could think was to say, "More different from Mom, I mean."

"She's *completely* different from Fay," Dad said.

"She doesn't seem that much younger is what I meant," I said, trying not to say anything that would get him mad.

"She's forty. . . . Oh, I'm not going to do a number with some twenty-two-year-old." Dad grinned at me. "What do you take me for, Jase?"

I grinned back. "I don't know, Dad."

He became serious. "No, the way we met was indicative. Randy did an article for *Human Rights*. It was on disarmament. That's her specialty—she's a freelance journalist who used to work for a newspaper, but the last decade or so she's mainly done surveys and articles. She handed it in, and it was excellent, much more tightly organized than half the stuff I see, but we just needed another slant. I hadn't made that clear when we'd discussed it. I thought she'd scream her head off because it had obviously taken a lot of work, it was a long piece. But all she did was ask a few questions, and two weeks later, she handed in a perfect piece, just what I wanted. No hysterics . . . That's what she's like. I can't describe how wonderful it is to be with her. I feel like I've spent thirty years listening to a drill outside the window and suddenly it's stopped. It's—incredible."

Well, I know what he means about Mom. She isn't exactly the most soothing person on earth. But still, though I was glad for him, I felt funny hearing about it. I know my parents are probably the least well-suited couple that ever got married, but in some peculiar way I still wish they'd hung in there.

We walked around a little more. Randall said, "I feel I'm so lucky living near the zoo. Some days I feel so pent up, working at home, and I walk over here and watch the animals for a while, and it's like taking a Valium. I come home and I feel terrific. Like, *they're* not obsessing about deadlines and word structure, so why should I?"

Ty kept looking at his watch and saying, "It's three," or "It seems to be past three-thirty," till finally Dad laughed and said, "Okay, why don't we drop you two off at the bus station."

"I hope you can stay for dinner some time," Randall said, more to me.

"Sure," I said.

"Or we could take them to that Mexican place," Dad suggested. "Jase likes Mexican food, or used to. Do you still?"

I nodded.

On the way home I started feeling not that great. Ty was going straight to Juliet's, but I'd have to face Mom and all her questions. "What'd you think of her?" I asked.

He shrugged. "Okay . . . nothing to write home about. They seem to get along okay."

"I thought she'd be sexier," I admitted.

"Maybe she's great in bed. . . . You can't always tell by looks."

How does he know? The only person he's done it with is Juliet, as far as I *know*. I don't know. I guess I'd rather not think of that, since I'll never know anyway.

When I got home Mom wasn't even there, so I biked over to Otis's. He'd been to that street fair with Marcella the night before. Usually he calls me Saturday, but maybe I left too early.

56

"Yeah, it was good," he said, but much more calmly than I'd expected. We were in his room. Otis's house is an apartment, actually. It's pretty small. Just the living room, his mother's bedroom, and his room. They had a bigger place, but once his two older sisters moved out, they figured they didn't need all that space.

"What're her parents like?"

"Okay. They didn't hassle me. They sat in front, and Marcy and I took the back with Joe. That's her youngest brother, the one in Mr. Deyner's class."

"But did you get any time alone with her? Or did they go everywhere with you?"

He smiled and put down his sneaker. He'd been trying to fix this really ripped-up old sneaker with that gooey stuff you squeeze out of a tube. "We had one real break. Her parents said they had to go see some friends. So they go off and we're standing around with Joe, and all of a sudden he says, kind of embarrassed, that he has to go see someone and would it be okay if we met back where we were in an hour? So I said sure."

"Weird," I said.

"Marcy said she thinks he likes some girl who lives in the Village, but he doesn't want their parents to know. She says she just gets that feeling, but she doesn't actually know. . . . But, like, we were alone in a sense, but there were about nine million people running around screaming. Mostly we just ate tons of stuff. I ate so much I got kind of sick. They had all this great stuff, raw clams, stuff like that, and Marcy kept saying, 'Try this, try that.' I thought she'd think I was anti-Italian or something if I didn't try everything. By the end I was ready to duck into the bushes and heave it all up."

"So, *nothing* happened?" I was disappointed. "You didn't even see her mole?"

He laughed. "Not exactly . . . No, in the car we sat kind of close together, and we held hands once her brother took off. I just get the feeling it's kind of an old-fashioned family, so I didn't want to blow it on the first date."

"As it were."

"As it were, right. . . . Oh, and at the end her father takes me aside. 'Otis,' he says, 'you seem like a very nice young man. You do me a favor, okay?' 'Sure, Pop.' 'My Marcy, she still feels a little lost in school, so many people rushing around. You keep an eye on her, okay? Make sure no one takes advantage of her.'"

"Other than you."

"Right . . . But they didn't seem prejudiced or anything. Usually you can tell, even if they bend over backward not to show it."

That must be really tricky, to have to worry about what the family of the girl you're going out with thinks not just of you as a person, but even of you just as a member of some particular group or religion. I'd hate to have to have extra stuff to worry about, in addition to the basics. Those are complicated enough.

I hung around Otis's a while longer, but I figured I better get back for dinner. When I came back, Mom was unwrapping a pizza. "I couldn't hack cooking tonight," she said. "Is pizza okay?"

I'd have pizza every night if we could. Usually it's Mom who says we need green vegetables and fresh fruit. The pizza was from this good place, not far from where we live.

"So: describe," Mom said. "Unexpurgated edition."

"She's just not," I began. "She's . . . I don't know. Dad said she was forty, she wears glasses. She's not that—"

Mom's mouth was half full of pizza. She took a swig of beer. "Career lady, huh? Zoomed right out of college into some terrific job, probably was engaged once but the guy died. . . . Or maybe she's just made it with a zillion married men, like Josie."

Josie Gercek is one of my mother's best friends. She's never been married, but I'd never known she made it with a zillion married men. She sure doesn't look like that type.

"She writes articles," I said, taking another slice.

"Yeah, she would," Mom said morosely. "Brainy . . . I bet she went to Barnard or Bryn Mawr. . . . You know what makes me sick? *I* did that once."

"Did what?" I shoved the mushrooms to one side and drank some beer out of the can. Mom says beer is okay if I just have one can and it's not a school night.

"When I was right out of college, I had this thing with my boss, some married guy, and I sat there and *wept* at all the stories about his rotten marriage and how trapped he felt and how all he wanted was a little peace and quiet. And right at that moment God was looking down, thinking: Okay lady, some day *you'll* be married and your very own husband will be dishing out the very same bullshit to some innocent young thing and *she'll* be sitting there, 'Oh, Mort, oh darling . . . I'll bet you haven't had a moment's peace in twenty-seven years.' Fuck."

Mom never eats that much. She just had one slice of pizza and left most of the crust. Now she just sat there and stared off into space. "I get the horrible feeling this is real," she said. "Like, it's not just a masochistic fantasy I've cooked up to torment myself. She's a real person, right? She exists!"

I nodded and half-laughed. Sometimes you can't tell if Mom is trying to be funny or not.

She covered the rest of the pizza. "Well, they'll live happily ever after. There's little enough happiness in the world—" Then she broke off and suddenly whirled on me fiercely. "I am going to be *okay*!" she said, as though I'd been saying the opposite. "Don't *look* at me that way, Jase."

"I *know* you're going to be okay, Mom," I said quickly.

"I don't want one droplet of pity from anyone in this family," she muttered, half to herself, going into the kitchen. "Not one blasted drop. Who says I can't get a job and a husband and all the rest of it? I studied Chinese literature. How's that for topical? They can send me to China. Why is everyone assuming I'm going to fail?"

"We're not," I said.

But it was like she hadn't heard me. "Okay, so it's a man's world. So crinkly, gray-haired almost-fifty-year-old men are considered adorable, and crinkly, gray-haired almost-fifty-year-old women are tossed into the moat. That's just a statistic. I'm a person, not a statistic."

"Sure," I said. "I know."

God, I wish it was Thanksgiving and Andy were here! Or that Mom hadn't made that dumb rule that we weren't allowed to say anything till then. I thought of breaking it. I thought of making up some excuse and biking down to the corner where there's a public phone and calling Andy, only making her swear to pretend I hadn't said anything. She wouldn't. You can trust her. I even put my jacket on, but then I took it off again.

Otis's parents were divorced when he was four. He can't even remember when they were married! He's seen his father some, not a whole lot, but the point is, it'd be a lot easier if it happened when you were that age, a whole lot.

SEVEN

SCHOOL IS THE SAME. NOTHING MUCH. I'M STILL BABYSITTING for Vernon. I've gotten sort of fond of him. His mind does wander. Like, I've been going there almost a month, but still sometimes he doesn't remember my name, or he'll tell me stuff he told me the time before. One night he taught me how to waltz. I didn't have the heart to tell him that kids my age don't do a hell of a lot of waltzing. When I came over, he had this record out, "Tales from the Vienna Woods." Ms. Korbel told him he shouldn't get overexcited, and he said he wouldn't.

I could see how he must have been a good dancer. Naturally now he moves pretty slowly, but once he got into it, he was bouncing along. First I was supposed to be the girl, so I'd get the idea of how it was to be led by someone. Then *he* was the girl and I led *him*. I kept being glad no one I knew was around to watch, because it must have been a pretty strange scene. After about twenty minutes he was pretty winded and said we'd better stop, but that he thought I had a lot of natural ability. He said we could start on the tango next time.

When Ms. Korbel got home, she took out this photo

album and showed me a photo of Vernon dancing. It seems he was head of something called The New England Ornithological Association, and every year they had a big party. You had to get dressed up in a tuxedo. You could tell from the photo that Vernon was really getting a bang out of it. He looked taller, and he was beaming at the lady he was dancing with. Ms. Korbel said that was Fanny, his second wife. She was kind of attractive, in a fairly low-cut dress, but not like Marcella; it didn't just hang there. They must have been near my parents' age, but they looked really happy.

"They really loved each other," Ms. Korbel said wistfully. "Sometimes I think that's why it's taken me so long to decide to get married. I want to be as happy as they were, and I know that's unusual these days."

"Yeah, well, my parents are splitting," I said, trying to sound fairly casual.

"Are they?" She looked really concerned. "What a pity. I'm so sorry, Jason. I'm not sure if I ever met your father, but your mother was at a conference once last year and she seemed like such a lovely person. So alive and interesting."

"Well, they . . . never basically got along all that well, so—"

"Is there another— Well, maybe that's too awful to even think, but sometimes one of the two meets someone else and—"

"My father," I said. "He met somebody."

Ms. Korbel looked thoughtful. "It always seems easier for men, somehow. . . . Of course my brother, who's a bachelor, says it isn't but *I* think it is." She paid me money. "I'm sorry, in any case. It's always hard on the kids."

I guess at least I won't have the problem Ms. Korbel

mentioned, not wanting to get married because of being afraid I can't be as happy as my parents!

A couple of days after that Ms. Korbel asked me if I could babysit Friday. It was the end of class, and while she was talking to me, Vicki Katz was gathering her papers together. When Ms. Korbel walked out of the room, she came up to me. "I didn't even know she had a baby," she said. "I didn't think she was married, even."

I explained about Vernon.

Vicki listened with that serious expression she usually has. She has big black eyes that stare right at you while you're talking. She never looks all around the room, the way some girls do, like they're hoping someone better will come along to rescue them or something. "That's nice of her," she said finally.

"Well, it's her father," I said.

"Still . . . We had my father's mother living with us once, and it drove everyone crazy. Of course, she was more forgetful or senile or whatever than he sounds, but in the end they put her in a home. She died six weeks later and I think it was, like, it was such an awful place she figured she'd just as soon die."

"Yeah, well . . ." I cleared my throat. There are two kinds of girls that I'm really terrible with. One is the kind like Marcella, who are so gorgeous that, even if I'm about six feet away from then, my brain just freezes. The other kind is at the other extreme, the really shy, nervous ones who are girl versions of me, who bite their nails or are always hunched over, looking at the ground. They make me as nervous as the first kind, because you can tell *they* don't know what to say or do either. Vicki's kind of in the middle. She's definitely pretty. Like I said, she has these dark eyes and a good, though not sensational, figure. Her hair's black too, and she wears it in some kind of braid. Anyhow, all of a sudden I found myself saying, "You'd really like Vernon. He's a great guy."

"I'd like to meet him someday," Vicki said eagerly.

"Well, uh, how about Friday? . . . That's when I'm going over there. You could, like, come over."

"Would Ms. Korbel mind?"

"No, she wouldn't mind." I don't know for a fact that that's true, but I think it is. Ms. Korbel seems pretty relaxed for a teacher.

Vicki smiled up at me. I guess because she's so small, I feel about six feet four when I'm talking to her. When we're standing up, that is. I suppose Russ Pharr feels like that with everyone. "That would be terrific," she said. "So, I'll see you Friday."

For the rest of the day I kept replaying that scene in my head. What's strange is, that if I had thought of it ahead of time, asking Vicki to come over while I was babysitting Vernon, I never would have asked her at all. Or I would have done it so dumbly that she'd probably have said no. But the fact that it just happened, she just happened to be there when Ms. Korbel asked me, and I found myself saying it before I'd had a chance to think it over or wonder what the chances were that she'd say yes—that was what made it work. With me it's always bad if I have a chance to think things over.

Also, what I like is this isn't a real date. So I don't have to go through any big thing of where should we go or what should I wear. It'll be more in between being at school and an actual date. How bad can it be? I mean, if it's terrible, we can just do our homework or something.

Vicki told me her brother would drop her off on his way to some date he had. I was glad, because that eliminated the hassle of picking her up. I told her to come about eight-thirty. Vernon had decided I was as good at waltzing as I'd ever be. He said he was going to start me on the tango. Luckily just after he said that the bell rang, and it was Vicki.

She looked nice. Pretty much like she looks at school, but better in some way. She had a red sweater on, and jeans, and cowboy boots. I introduced her to Vernon. He really looked pleased. It was like I'd invited her over for *him*! He said, "Jason knows I like dark-haired girls. . . . I knew he'd pick the prettiest one he could find for me."

Vicki turned red. "Thank you."

Then he turned to me. "Before the tango, let's go over the waltz one more time. . . . Find the record, Jason."

I found "Tales from the Vienna Woods."

"Can you dance, my dear?" Vernon asked Vicki.

"Sure," she said uncertainly. "Some dances."

"How's your waltz?"

She shrugged. "I never learned that one."

"Well, young lady, this is your chance. . . . This young man has learned at the hands of the master. He's not a master yet, but he's getting there." He put on the record and showed Vicki the basic steps. Then he said to me, "Okay, boy, take it away."

I felt really pissed. If I'd known this was going to happen, I'd have told Vicki to come at nine-thirty, when Vernon was asleep. But there was no getting out of it. I put my arms around Vicki and tried to remember all Vernon had said. While we danced, he stood there, watching us like a hawk. "Lilting, lilting!" he yelled out, making his hands like a megaphone. "It's light, you're dancing on feathers!" Suddenly he took the record off. To both of us he said, "Have you ever heard a Mozart quartet?"

"No," we both said together.

"A waltz is like Mozart," Vernon said. "Light, delicate, but with a soul. Do you get what I'm saying?"

I nodded, mainly to be polite. Vicki said, "I *think* so."

He put the record on again. After saying to me, "If you'll permit me . . ." he took hold of Vicki and waltzed her all around the living room. You should have seen him. I mean, he's a little guy, not much taller than Vicki, and he doesn't have much pep, but there he was, dancing her around, smiling and, like, you could tell he'd once been really good at it. It must be hard having been good at something and then not being able to do it anymore. I guess that happens a lot when you get older. Like, Dad says he used to be good at tennis and he's still *pretty* good, but he just can't run the way he used to. He gets winded.

After that we all had a snack in the kitchen.

"You go to school with this young fellow?" Vernon asked Vicki, who was drinking hot chocolate.

She nodded.

"I bet he's smart, right? Top of the class?"

Vicki hesitated. "*I* think he's smart," she said diplomatically.

"*He's* a smart boy and *you're* a smart girl," Vernon said with satisfaction. "Two smart kids . . . Don't get into trouble, you know what I mean? Smart kids don't get into trouble."

God, what a thing to say! I felt like stuffing a cupcake in his mouth. But after that, when we put him in bed, he just smiled and said, "Have a wonderful evening."

It's funny. I always feel weird putting Vernon into bed or helping him into bed. Maybe it's that I think I'd mind if someone had to help me do that, at that age. But it doesn't seem to bother him. He's told me other things do, but that doesn't.

When we were inside, sitting on the couch, Vicki said, "He's really nice."

"Yeah, he is."

Then all of a sudden I started getting a slightly sick, strange feeling. I mean, I'd said it was like we were in school and we could just do our homework, but it wasn't. It was just the two of us. And I didn't *want* to do homework. I wanted to start making out with her, but I never know how you start those things going. There was a long silence, Vicki looking off at the wall, me looking at her. Finally I just kissed her. I couldn't figure out how to lead up to it, so I just did it. It wasn't a long kiss, but it was nice. Her lips were soft, and she didn't pull away.

She looked up at me. "Have you had a lot of experience with girls?" she asked, like she was working up the courage to ask that.

I didn't know what to say. I guess I was scared that if I said "no" she'd think I was too peculiar, so I said, "Yeah, pretty much."

"With, like, a lot of people or just one?"

"Basically just one."

"Who was she?"

Shit. This is one of the big troubles with lies, something I've discovered before. You can tell one—fine. But it never stops there. You end up having to tell about a hundred others to cover for that one, and by the time you're done, you realize it would've been a lot easier to tell the truth.

"She was a friend of my sister's."

"You mean, was she older than you?"

"Yeah, about . . . five years or so."

"Oh." Vicki thought about that. Then she looked up at me again. She looked really pretty, her eyes especially. She has very long eyelashes. "So I guess she must have been pretty experienced?"

"Yeah." I swallowed.

"My brother had a girlfriend who was older than him. He said she taught him everything he knows." She laughed. "Of course, I don't know how much he knows. . . . Did she with you?"

I nodded. What else could I do?

"So, did you, like, do everything with her, or what?"

Boy, did I want this conversation to be over! I hesitated. "Almost everything."

"What *didn't* you do?"

"Um . . . well, she wore braces, so oral sex was kind of—"

"Painful?" Vicki suggested.

I nodded. I knew I was bright red, especially my ears. That happens if I lie or am embarrassed.

Then she did a funny thing. I'd forgotten Vicki had braces. They aren't the kind that cover a kid's whole set of teeth so all you see when they smile is metal. Andy and Ty both had that kind. It was more like a thin strip of metal going across the front. Anyway, she reached in and took it out. "It's just a retainer," she said. "I'm supposed to wear it all the time, but I don't have to *always* wear it."

I was really feeling strange. It was the way you feel when you've smoked too much pot too fast on an empty stomach, like the room was getting larger and smaller at the same time. Maybe it was realizing the dumbness of all those lies. Now she'd think I was supposedly this great lover who knew everything. I jumped to my feet. "I'll be back in a sec," I said.

I went to the bathroom. I just stood there, leaning against the wall, trying to give myself some kind of pep talk. Like, who cares about Vicki Katz? She's just some girl. You never even have to see her again. Yes, I do. I have to see her every day at school. Okay, you never have to talk to her again. But the thing is, I like her, and I get the feeling she might like me. So, just go back there and do it. Do what? Whatever! Stop thinking about it.

I took a deep breath and went back to the living room. Vicki was still sitting on the couch. Her retainer was still on the floor. I sat down next to her and tried to smile.

"*I* haven't had that much experience," she said suddenly. "That's why I was asking you. So, like, if I do something wrong—"

"You were fine," I said quickly. "You didn't do anything wrong."

"Well, we didn't do anything that much so far . . . I mean, we don't *have* to if you don't want. I just wanted to sort of, like, warn you."

"Oh, that's okay," I said magnanimously.

There's this expression we learned in English last year: Deus Ex Machina. It was something like when a god suddenly appears and does something unexpected to resolve the plot. Well, that's what happened with me and Vicki.

All of a sudden the lights went out! Not just in the house, but even the street lights outside. It was so pitch black, you couldn't see a thing. Vicki sucked in her breath. "What happened?" she said, sounding scared.

"I guess it must be a blackout," I said.

"Are the doors locked?"

"Sure." I wasn't sure, but I wasn't about to go crawling around looking for the back door.

"Maybe they'll come back on in a minute," Vicki whispered.

"Probably," I whispered back.

Only they didn't. A few minutes later Vicki said, still softly, "Do you think she has some candles?"

"Maybe . . . only I don't know where they'd be."

She sighed. Her body, right next to me, was trembling a little. "I know this is dumb, but I feel horribly scared. I guess it's from all those horror movies. There was this one on TV where this woman is, like, blind, and well, it's the opposite, she turns *off* all the lights so the guy who's trying to kill her can't see either."

"I never saw that one." I reached over and felt for her hand. It was icy cold.

"Thanks," she said, like I was doing it just to make her feel better.

Then I put my arm around her. "This is a pretty safe neighborhood," I said. I haven't the vaguest idea if that's true. For all I know they've had a dozen rapes and murders in the last month. But Vicki sighed and, leaning back, said, "I'm glad."

Then we started kissing. It was a million times easier than before. I guess that's why people make out in the movies, though it's never pitch black there. But it's almost like you're a different person in the dark. And the girl is different too. You don't have to watch her expression and wonder what she's feeling or thinking or how dumb you might look. And you notice things you don't so much with the lights on. Like Vicki had this terrific smell. It wasn't perfume. Maybe it was just shampoo or soap. She let me reach under her sweater and touch her breasts, but she wouldn't take her bra off. Or anyway, it wouldn't come off and she didn't help me. But who cares? It was still terrific. Whatever little guy pulled the wrong switch and caused that blackout, I'd give him a hundred dollars if I had it. Even a thousand.

Then all of a sudden the lights came on again. That was embarrassing in a way, it was so sudden. Like, there I was with my hand under her sweater and both of us semi-entangled, and all of a sudden we could see each other. We both sort of pulled apart. She looked embarrassed too. Then she smiled.

"This must be why the birth rate rises right after blackouts," she said.

I laughed. I like the way she just blurts things out that way, even though before, when she was questioning me about how experienced I was, it made me nervous.

"Was I okay?" she asked. I guess she meant in relation to what she'd said before, about not having done that much.

"You were great," I said, wanting to start kissing again. She had been, I wasn't lying.

"But, like, were you comparing me in your mind to that other girl?"

"No, not at all . . . She wasn't that much, really. It was more that she was—"

"Available?" Vicki suggested.

"Right."

"Was she on the Pill?"

I nodded. I was really sorry we were back on this conversation again, though. There were better things to do than sit around discussing a girl who didn't exist.

Vicki looked thoughtful. "I guess that's what *I'd* do, if it ever came to that . . . I mean, you know, rather than get pregnant like Marcy did last year."

"Marcella?" I was kind of shocked.

Vicki looked embarrassed. "I thought . . . I shouldn't have said that. Will you not tell anyone? I thought everybody in our class knew. The girls all knew. See, her parents are these really strict Catholics, and they wouldn't have wanted her to have an abortion. She had to go with her brother."

I thought about her and Otis. "Was it some guy from school?"

She shook her head. "Some older guy, I think, maybe a friend of her brother's. . . . Listen, Jason, don't tell, promise? Because, like, we're not *best* friends, but I like her and—"

"I won't tell," I said.

Ms. Korbel came home not long after that. She said Gunther would drive both of us home. He let Vicki off first. In bed I kept thinking back over everything, all my lies, the blackout, finding out about Marcy. One weird thing is that by now I almost could imagine that girl in my head, the one I supposedly made it with. I think I was thinking of one of Andy's friends that used to come around a lot a long time ago. In fact, I was nine and they were seventeen. Belle— that was her name. She was sort of chubby, like Andy, with curly blond hair, but she had a very easygoing, relaxed personality. A lot of Andy's friends treated me like some little brat or monster, especially when they had to stay home and babysit for me. But Belle loved board games like Monopoly, and I was good at them; the three of us would play for hours. She and Andy would make buttered popcorn, even though they were supposedly on diets, and they'd both talk as though I weren't there. That is, they'd joke about boys and sex; I heard a lot of interesting stuff. Or Belle would say, "Jase, tell me sincerely because you're a guy . . . should I let my perm grow out?" The fact that she saw me as a guy when I was this little shrimp who weighed around seventy-five pounds made me feel great. Who knows? Maybe she really did like me. Sometimes we'd have pillow fights and she'd tickle me and giggle and lean over me, laughing. For years I had quite a few sex fantasies going where Belle and I were the same age and ended up on a desert island somewhere. Even without the buttered popcorn *or* a Monopoly set, I think we could've had a really good time.

But that was all fantasy. Whereas I think Vicki *really* likes me. Anyhow, during that blackout she sure acted like it. Boy, I wish there was a way to arrange a blackout every time she came over. I think I will ask her to come babysit with me again. I suppose I could just get up and turn out all the lights, but that would seem peculiar. I'll figure it out. Don't worry.

EIGHT

||||

*F*OR *THANKSGIVING THIS WAS THE PLAN* M*OM AND* D*AD HIT ON*.
Erin and Andy were coming in on separate planes Thursday
morning. Dad would pick them up at the airport and bring
them back here, like everything was normal. We'd have our
usual Thanksgiving dinner at around two or three, and
sometime during the day, maybe while we were having
dinner or at the end, Mom and Dad would make a "public
announcement" of the divorce thing. Ty and me were
supposed to act "natural," like this was the first we'd heard
about it.

I'm not crazy about Thanksgiving anyway. It always
seemed like my parents had their worst fights around
holidays, especially Christmas. Either Dad got Mom the
wrong present, or once he just gave her money, saying she
should buy whatever she wanted, and she said that made her
feel like a whore, just finding a check on her desk. Stuff like
that. Maybe all families feel that way a little. Like holidays
should be this great cozy warm time and it isn't. Probably
even in "normal" families it isn't.

I slept late, partly because I like to, partly because I
wanted the day to be as short as possible. I got up around

noon, showered, and then took a walk and got stoned enough to see me through the rest of the day. It was viciously cold out. I was glad to get back inside.

Mom was in the kitchen doing stuff with the turkey. Ty was in there with her, helping out with something. "Wow, it's cold out," I said, putting my hands on the oven to get warm.

"Where'd you go?" Mom asked.

"Just for a walk, to get some air, you know."

"Well, help me set the table, okay, hon?"

I got out the plates. Ty was looking through the oven door at the turkey. "Looks good," he said. Then he turned to Mom. "You know, Juliet's family always has goose for Thanksgiving. Her mother says it's juicier and it doesn't—"

Mom glared at him. "Ty, listen to me. I do not want to hear *one* word, and I mean *one*, about Juliet's family today or I'm going to throw this blasted turkey straight through the McKonekeys' front window."

The McKonekeys are our next-door neighbors and their front window is stained glass. They brought it back from Europe.

"I just thought you might be—" Ty began, but Mom put her hand over his mouth.

"When're we going to meet Vicki?" she said to me. I'd mentioned her a few times because of the babysitting.

I shrugged.

"Vicki Katz?" Ty said. "You're going out with Vicki *Katz*?"

"It's not going out so much, it's just—"

"Boy, is that typical," he said.

"What?" I asked.

"You're just copying me . . . as usual."

"What're you talking about?"

"*I* start going out with a Jewish girl so *you* start going out with a Jewish girl. They're both five feet tall, good at sports—"

God, I felt like killing him! Also, I never knew Vicki was any kind of jock at all. She never talked about it. "What sports is she good at?"

"Basketball! She's on the team!" He acted like not knowing that meant I was a complete moron.

"So, who cares? I didn't even know she was on the fucking team. . . . Copying you! I wouldn't copy you in a million years!"

"That's all you *ever* do," he said. "The way you fixed up your room, the way—"

Mom grabbed him. "Ty, shut up this second! This is the stupidest conversation I've ever heard. . . . Now, will the two of you show some ounce of sensitivity? I'm a wreck, okay? Do you want me to spell it out? W-R-E-C-K."

"You mean, because of Dad?" Ty said.

Mom just looked at him. "No, because Guy de Rothschild just had a bad year in Burgundies . . . of course because of Dad!"

"But you, like, never got along," he said. "So what's the big deal?"

Mom was hunched over the counter with her hand over her eyes. "It's no big deal. I mean, it's just a mere twenty-seven years of my life, and I have so many men falling over themselves to marry me or take me on exotic trips to Port au Prince that I hardly have time to cook one lousy turkey for Thanksgiving."

"You'll find someone," Ty said, not that enthusiastically. "Juliet's mother's sister did."

"Tell me about it," Mom said. "I want to hear all about Juliet's mother's sister."

"Well, she got divorced—"

At that Mom went screaming out of the room. I just looked at Ty. "She *told* you not to talk about them."

"I was trying to cheer her up," he said sullenly. "All I meant was—"

Just then the door opened. It was Dad with Erin and Andy. Andy ran right in and hugged us. She's a very hugging kind of person. She looked the same. Whenever I haven't seen her for a while, I forget that she's not that good-looking. But I like her so much then I forget again. Like, Erin's a lot prettier, especially now that she's gained some weight, but we never have much to say to each other. She was standing shyly and smiled at me.

"Hi, Jase," she said in this almost whispery voice she has.

"Hi, Er."

They went into their rooms and did stuff, called people, so we didn't sit down to eat till late, almost four. The table looked nice—Erin lit the candles that Mom always puts out for special occasions. Dad said we could all have a little wine. Erin said she'd just have water.

It was a strange meal, the first half maybe more so because I sat there waiting for Dad to say something. It all seemed so horribly phony, everyone talking cheerfully about school or whatever they'd been doing. It's always a little like that, but what made it weird was Andy really was in a good mood, and the fact that Mom and Dad were just putting on this total act and Erin and Andy didn't even know about it—well, I hated it, that's all. I couldn't even eat much. I shoved the food around and tried to make it look like I was eating, but I couldn't get much down.

Finally, just after we'd finished the main course, just

before dessert, Dad looked nervously around at all of us and said, "There's something Fay and I have to tell you."

Total silence. Everyone looked at him except Mom, who was staring into space, and Ty, who was looking down at his plate.

Dad really seemed nervous. "For years," he began, "maybe some of this has been apparent, I hope not too much, but for years—"

"Oh, just say it!" Mom suddenly burst out.

Dad looked at her in an agonized way, then back at Erin and Andy, who were sitting side by side. "We're getting divorced," he said quietly.

After a moment Andy said, "I'm sorry . . . I guess I kind of saw it coming, but—"

Then Erin burst into tears. She just sat there with her face covered with her hands, sobbing. Everyone stared at her.

Dad got out of his chair. He walked over to where she sat and put his arms on her shoulders. "Sweetie, don't," he said, almost in a whisper.

"I don't *want* you to!" Erin sobbed. "I can't stand it!"

"We don't want to either," Dad said. "But we just—"

"He's found a lady he likes to fuck better than me," Mom said. "That's all."

Dad looked at her like he wanted to kill her. "That *isn't* all! . . . Why do you do this?"

"Because I like truth," Mom yelled.

"That's not the truth. It's an ugly and stupid distortion."

Like I said, I'd gotten quite stoned, plus two glasses of wine. But I still felt really rotten. I looked at Andy. She looked awful too.

"Please don't quarrel now," Andy said.

Dad took Erin by the hand. "Let's go inside and talk about it," he said.

Mom just sat there, staring after him, her mouth set. Then she turned to the three of us. "Dessert, anyone?"

"What is there?" Ty asked, interested.

For once I was glad for the way Ty never loses his appetite. Mom brought in pie and ice cream and we all had some. We didn't talk about anything much. It was the opposite, like everyone tried to think of things to say that were about anything other than Mom and Dad. For some reason I thought of Vicki. I wondered what she was doing right then, what her family was like, whether her parents got along.

Dad stayed in Erin's room with her a long time. When he came out, we were all, except Mom, in the living room. Ty had turned the game on TV, Andy was reading, and I was lying on the couch, not doing much of anything. "Well, I think I better be going," he said in this "everything's under control" way. "I have the feeling my presence here doesn't exactly . . . You all have my number." He looked at Andy. "Maybe we could have lunch tomorrow? Would you be free?"

"Sure," she said. She smiled. "I'm free, Dad."

He waved at us and left.

After a while Erin came out of her room. She looked red-eyed and funny. She sat down at the end of the couch and started watching the game with Ty. I know she doesn't know anything about football or care, but I guess she wanted something to do. At five-thirty Ty said he had to be going. He told Mom he'd be staying at Juliet's. Then Mom came in, also looking strange, and said she was going to see a double feature and did any of us want to come. Erin said she did, but Andy said, "I've got a lot of work, Mom."

"I do too," I said, though I knew I wasn't going to do

any of it. But I didn't think I could sit through a double feature either.

After Mom and Erin left, it was just Andy and me, alone in the house. That felt better, especially having Mom and Dad gone. She sighed and raised her eyebrows. "Jesus."

"What was weird," I said, "was *we've* known since September. But they made us not tell. He moved out eight weeks ago."

"I knew something was funny," Andy said. "Dad never being there when I called."

"Randy seems okay," I said. "Like a nice person, pretty much."

"I met her."

"When?"

"They had a party once. I saw her talking to Dad. You could tell . . . I mean, not how it would end, but that something—" She frowned. "I guess I'm a little worried about Mom. She seems so on edge. She told me she doesn't sleep more than four hours a night."

"I didn't know that." All I know is Mom's always asleep when I leave for school in the morning, but that's been true for a long time.

"What does she do while you're at school? Is she looking for a job or anything?"

I shrugged. "She didn't say anything about it."

"She ought to get out and do something," Andy went on. "Meet people. It's funny. This friend of mine said for a man the worst thing that can happen ego-wise is losing his job. For a woman it's losing her husband. I don't think that's true so much for my generation, but maybe for hers."

"Yeah, I guess." I never thought about it so much.

Suddenly Andy reached out and touched my arm.

"Listen, Jase, don't let it drag you under, okay? It must be the toughest for you, in a way. I mean, we're not here."

"I'll be okay," I said. "Don't worry."

"Good."

We didn't talk much after that. But even that conversation wasn't as good as ones with Andy usually are. It was like everyone was acting strange, including me. I realized we were probably all strange people, but no one was even acting like themselves.

"I'm glad Erin cried," Andy said, just before taking up her book again. "I wish *I* could."

I know what she means.

NINE

*T*HE REST OF *T*HANKSGIVING VACATION WASN'T QUITE AS BAD AS that first day. Friday I went over to see Otis, and we went bike riding. The sun had come out; it felt good to move around. He knows the family situation. But I didn't feel like talking about it, and we didn't.

Saturday I called Vicki. Just for the hell of it. I didn't really have much to say. "Do you feel like coming over for a little while?" she said suddenly.

Normally I might've, but I wasn't sure I could act in any kind of regular way. On the other hand, I didn't feel like just sitting in the house. "I can't stay too long," I said cautiously, "because my sisters are going back to school tomorrow."

"Oh, sure. . . . Well, listen, it was just an idea."

"No, I'd like to." Vicki lives around ten blocks from me. Close enough to bike. And if it gets sticky, like I feel uncomfortable, I can just say I have to get back. I wanted an excuse like that, and that one was at least partly true.

Vicki's father was in the living room watching a Jets game when I got there. He was a heavyset, gray-haired guy with glasses who waved at me, but didn't get up. "When the football season starts Daddy is just glued to the set," Vicki said. "Mom says she always wants to divorce him in fall and remarry him in spring."

I guess that could've been an opening for saying something about my parents, but I didn't feel like it.

We went up to her room. It was nice, nothing special, neater than mine. A big fish tank in the corner. The trouble was, I didn't feel like doing anything other than making out. By now I've been with Vicki enough so sometimes we can talk pretty easily. She's fairly talkative when she gets going. It isn't a big strain being with her at all. But today I didn't feel up to doing anything, even listening. She started in telling me about her brother's girlfriend, who'd come over for Thanksgiving dinner.

"She thinks she's such a big deal because she's getting a degree at Harvard. I mean, Daddy's terrific and he never went to any Ivy League school. And she's acting like that makes her so superior to us, just because she went to all these fantastic schools. So what? Lots of really smart people can't afford to go to schools like that . . . don't you think?"

"What?" I said.

"About schools," Vicki said. "Don't you think that's true?"

"What's true?" I said. I had sort of heard her and not heard her. Like, I knew what she was talking about, but I wasn't totally following.

There was a silence. Then Vicki turned around, looking really mad. "Are you stoned or what?"

I just shrugged. Vicki knows I smoke a little, but that hadn't been why I hadn't heard her. I just don't give a damn about her brother's stupid girlfriend or where she goes to college.

"Well, then just go home," she said, "because I don't want to sit here trying to make conversation with some spaced-out dope!"

Normally, maybe I'd have gotten mad and said something sarcastic back or just walked out, but I felt so shitty, I couldn't. Sometimes I think I *am* just a spaced-out dope. Vicki stood there, looking at me, obviously expecting me to say something. When I didn't, she said in a less mad voice, "What's wrong, Jase? Is something the matter?"

I shook my head. I kept looking over at her fish tank. It was a big fancy one, the kind I'd wanted Mom and Dad to get me for my tenth birthday. It had filters and a rock castle on the bottom and lots of different fish swimming back and forth. They said it was one, too expensive, and two, took a lot of work to keep up.

"Is everything okay at your home?" Vicki persisted.

"My parents had a fight."

"Oh." She went over to me and put her arms around me. "I'm really sorry," she said.

It's funny. All I said was "My parents had a fight," which is the understatement of the year, and she was all warm and loving again. Girls are hard to figure out. "I like your fish tank," I said.

We went over, with our arms around each other, to look at it.

"What kinds are they?" I asked.

"Well, guppies, of course, and a couple of angel-fish. . . . Those two in the back are kribensis. And there's an eel someplace." She looked thoughtful. "I haven't seen him in a while. Sometimes he's under that rock. He might have died, I guess."

"It's really nice," I said. I liked standing there with her, our arms around each other, the room dimly lit.

"The only thing I hate is when they eat each other," Vicki said. "They just do it! The kribensis, especially. I feed them plenty, but once I came in and there was this one poor little scared fish and they kept biting at his tail, and finally they just plain ate him! Just out of meanness!"

"Get rid of them," I suggested.

"I'm going to. . . . I think I'll take them back to the fish store and tell them. I'd hate to just flush them down the toilet, even if they are mean."

After that we walked over to her bed and lay down. I'd thought I was feeling really horny. In fact, that was the main reason I'd come over, but now I just wasn't in the mood. I liked lying there, with my arms around Vicki, and I kissed her a few times, but that was all I felt like doing. It was so warm in the room, I was afraid I might fall asleep. Just to keep myself awake, I slid my hand under her sweater. Up till now she's always wanted to keep her bra on or, at any rate, not helped me any to take it off, but this time she just sat up, took it off and lay back down again.

Maybe it was just bad timing. It was like she was giving me some sign that she would go further, but, right at that moment, I didn't especially feel like it. I did stroke her breasts and it felt good, but I didn't get manic with excitement the way I would have normally.

"I have inverted nipples," Vicki said suddenly.

"What're they?"

"They— It's just, like, if I have babies, they won't be able to drink out of them. They'll have to have bottles instead."

"Oh." Then, because it seemed like she wanted a compliment, I said, "They *feel* nice."

"My breasts aren't that gigantic, but . . . Were that other girl's?"

"Which one?"

"You know, the one . . . your sister's friend."

"No, she was completely flat-chested," I said.

That cheered Vicki up a lot. "But she was still sexy?" Without waiting for me to answer, she went on, "I think that's true. I think lots of sexy-looking girls aren't really sexy in how they *feel* and lots of girls who don't look especially . . . are."

"Sure," I said. "That's probably true." Most things are as much true as not true. It's easier to agree than to argue.

Then we just lay there and I did fall asleep. I had a funny dream that I was swimming underwater, scuba diving, and these fish were trying to eat each other, or maybe they were after me. I wasn't as scared in the dream as I would have been if it was real. I knew I had to hide from them, and I did in some kind of old shipwreck. I could see this big eye of one of the fish outside, but he never came in.

When I woke up, Vicki was standing over the tank, feeding the fish. She came over and sat down on the bed and kissed me. "You fell alseep," she said, smiling.

"I guess—" I thought of offering some explanation, but she didn't seem to care. Then I looked at my watch. It was almost dinner time. "I better get going."

"I'm glad you came over," she said.

"Me too." I put my sneakers back on. "I like your nipples," I said, and she blushed. I did too. It was probably a dumb thing to say. I just wanted her to know I appreciated her taking her bra off. Next time I'll pay more attention.

At home Erin had gone to bed early because she wasn't feeling well. So it was just Andy, me, and Mom for dinner. We had chicken that Andy helped Mom make; it wasn't bad. Then, while we were having dessert, Mom said to Andy, "So tell us about this guy you've met."

I'd completely forgotten about Andy having a boyfriend, the one Mom was sure was into S&M or from Mainland China. I looked at her, but she looked uncomfortable. She looked quickly from me to Mom. "He's . . . I like him a lot." She cleared her throat. "I mean, basically I'm madly in love with him."

"Sounds wonderful," Mom said. "And he's a lawyer?"

"Right." Andy still had a wary expression.

"So, what's the problem?" Mom asked.

There was a long pause. "Well, it's just . . . he's married."

"Separated?" Mom asked.

"No, married."

Mom laughed bitterly. "Don't tell me. He's been married twenty-seven years and has four kids."

Andy smiled and shook her head. "He's been married seven years and he has two kids. One's three and one's six. . . . Mom, listen, he made a mistake. People do! He married the first girl who ever liked him. They met in fourth grade! He was shy, scared of girls. He didn't know what he was doing. It's not his fault!"

"What are his intentions?" Mom said. "Is he going to leave her?"

"He wants to, but . . . well, she's—she doesn't work and she's—I think it's partially an act, but her hold on him is that she's this totally helpless creature. *I* think she's about as helpless as a piranha, but—"

Mom gulped down the rest of her wine. "Well, good luck, hon. . . . Husbands can be stolen. Ask Randy to give you a few tips."

Andy looked like she was trying to restrain herself. "It's not *like* Randy and Dad! I *knew* you'd think that. It's *not!* Sallie's twenty-nine. Why can't she get a job? Or another husband?"

"Search me," Mom said. "Lord knows the job market for untrained housewives couldn't be better. They're combing the streets for them."

Andy ignored that. "She *says* she loves him . . . but she's just using him as a meal ticket so she doesn't have to get off her duff and go out into the big cruel world and fend for herself."

"I thought the kids were just three and six."

"So? They're in school all day. . . . She says she's scared. What of? Is someone going to bite her? She had this job once and they fired her, but that doesn't mean *everyone's* going to fire her. Does it?"

"It could," Mom said. "She might just be the type. In and out. Fire and hire. Sallie the loser." She sighed. "What are his wonderful qualities? I mean, to make up for all this other stuff. Is he great in bed? Tell us. We need some vicarious, titillating stuff to finish off the weekend."

Andy flushed. "He's a kind, warm, brilliant, lovely person."

Mom poured herself another glass of wine. "Then congratulations, hon . . . because I've never met *any* of those and I always wanted to. It sounds like you've got the last good man left on this planet, and if I were you, I'd just bump little wifey off quietly and send the kids on a one-way trip to Grandma and Grandpa . . . don't you think, Jase?"

"I think—" I began, but Andy just turned white and said, "No wonder Dad left! No wonder he couldn't live with you!"

Mom didn't say anything. Her face just crumpled. She got up and went into the kitchen. I thought Andy would apologize and go in after her, but she stormed off into her room. Maybe I should have stayed at Vicki's. When I went into the kitchen, Mom was standing there, looking out the window. She looked awful. I tried to think of something to say, but I couldn't.

I was really scared she was going to cry again, the way she did when Dad walked out. But she didn't. She was shaking a little, the way you do when you're cold, but she didn't cry. A minute later Andy walked back in. "I'm sorry," she said.

Mom just made a gesture.

Andy looked at me. "I better—my plane's leaving soon. Want to go with me, Jase? I'll pay for the cab."

"Sure," I said.

In the cab Andy said, "He *is* nice . . . and it's *not* his fault."

"Yeah, he sounds . . . good."

I just said "good" because I couldn't think of any other word, but Andy said, "He *is* good, Jase. You've *got* to believe me. He's a good person. In every sense. . . . But it was dumb, telling Mom. I should've lied. I just hate doing that! But I should've."

"Yeah," I agreed.

At the airport we hugged each other good-bye. "Listen, you better write, you jerk," Andy said. *"I'm* the one with all this work. You're just goofing off in that half-assed high school."

I laughed. "I'll write."

I got a cab home. I love driving at night. Maybe I'll be a bus driver when I grow up. Not a city bus, but the kind that goes cross-country. Otis's brother-in-law once let us drive his truck, and it felt great, having a vehicle that big under your command. Flying might be neat too. I've thought of that. Pilots make tons of dough, and there isn't that much traffic up there. As long as the traffic controller isn't bombed out of his mind, I don't think you'd really be in much danger.

TEN

||||

I DIDN'T THINK MUCH MORE ABOUT THE CONVERSATION I'D HAD with Andy about Mom looking for a job, but one day I came home from school and there Mom was, sitting at the kitchen table, more dressed up than usual, circling things in the newspaper. As I walked in, the phone rang.

Mom jumped up. "Let me get it," she said to me, and picked it up. "Yes, this is she. Fine. Yes, I'd like to, I'd like to very much. Four is perfect. Right, no, that's perfect. I'll be there in an hour, or whatever. My watch is in the next room, but I can see by the clock that . . . terrific. That sounds perfect." She hung up. Then she looked at me. "How did I sound?"

"Okay," I said. I hadn't been listening that much.

"I think I said perfect about a hundred times. Didn't I? There are so many other words, but I just— Is it this is she or this is her? I always forget."

"What?" I said. I felt hungry, so I began rummaging around for a snack.

"Don't they teach you grammar at that lousy school?" She sighed. "Oh, Christ, this is the first one where they'll even *see* me. The others won't even see me!"

"The other who?" I began spreading peanut butter on some stale crackers.

"The other job things."

"*Are* you looking for a job?" I knew Andy would think that was good.

"Looking? I'll tell you what I'm doing—you want to know? I have called or written every fucking human being I have ever met in my entire life asking them if they know of anything, *any* job, no matter how menial, no matter how disgusting, anything! And you know what the result has been?"

I shook my head.

"Nothing!" Mom almost screamed. "They won't even call me for an interview! They won't even let me clean toilets or be a checker at a supermarket! I went to some bookstore, and the guy said 'Can you work a cash register?' So I said, 'No, but I can learn.' He just looked like, forget it—I mean, can I blame them? They have nine million applicants for any job, and here am I, hopeless, aging, hobbling in on all fours. Of *course* they'd rather hire a twenty-two-year-old beauty queen with eight MBAs—who wouldn't?"

"Don't any of your friends have any, like, connections?" I asked. That's how one of our teachers said you get jobs. She was giving us advice for summer jobs.

"Jase, don't you *listen*? I just told you. I *have* called friends, I've called acquaintances. I've called every human being I have ever *met*. They all say I'm overqualified because nine thousand years ago I studied Chinese litera- ture. Or one guy said, 'So, why don't you go live there?' 'Where?' I said. 'China. You like Reds so much, go live there.' I said, 'I studied twelfth-century Chinese poetry.'

'So, why don't you go live there?' He had a totally one-track mind! This was for a job as a secretary in a pet shop!"

I was looking at the kitchen clock, which is set in the stove. "Mom, you told them you'd be there at four. You said that'd be perfect."

She grinned. "Jase, would you mind getting down on your knees and giving a short prayer for me while I'm gone?"

"Sure," I told her. "Only get going. You're going to be late."

An hour later Ty came in. "Where's Mom?" he asked.

"Out looking for a job," I said.

"Who's going to hire *her*?" he said. "They aren't even hiring regular people, people who have skills."

"Don't you think she should even look?" I had the feeling he was right, though.

"Sure, if it gives her something to do."

Around five-thirty I set the table and kind of got dinner going. Mom posts this menu on the refrigerator, and the deal is that whoever's there should get things going. It was just hamburgers and frozen beans, so it wasn't too hard. The only thing was, Ty and me were so hungry we started eating before she got there.

She came in with a package of fried chicken from Colonel Sanders. "What're you guys eating?" she said.

"The menu said hamburgers," I explained.

"Oh, Christ, I forgot. Want some fried chicken to wash down your hamburgers?"

"Sure," said Ty, who can eat anything. He put a piece of chicken on top of his hamburger. "Did you get the job?"

"Are you kidding? Who's going to hire *me*?"

"Someone might," Ty said, ripping into his chicken leg.

"Someone might," Mom said, sitting down. "True.

Anyway, it's an existential act. I go, I make an ass of myself, they shove me out the door, the next day I go again."

"How do you know already you didn't get it?" I asked.

Mom poured herself some wine. "Here's how I know. I get there and first the woman gives me this little speech, how the last person who had the job, secretary for some campus newsletter, thought it was going to lead somewhere. I guess for some weird reason she couldn't see spending her life in an airless little room with no windows typing letters. 'She thought it would be a stepping-stone,' the woman says. 'Do *you* regard it that way?' Who me? God forbid. A stepping-stone? Never! Lead to something better? Of course not! So I grovel, I flatten myself in front of her, and she flings this typing test at me, only—here's the catch—to be done on a typewriter with a *carbon ribbon*. She locks me in there, I start manically typing, make a thousand mistakes. She keeps checking in. 'How's it going?' 'Fine, fine.' So at the very end I take out the liquid paper to correct all the goofs, and *splat*! The whole *bottle* sprays out over the sheet, the typewriter, me. . . . The lady comes in, takes one look, smiles a tight, hideous, grim little smile, and says, 'Uh . . . we'll get in touch with you.'"

I'm always doing stuff like that when I'm nervous, so I knew exactly how Mom felt. Even when you don't make mistakes, at the last minute you do one supremely stupid thing. "Still, they might call you," I said, just to say something encouraging.

"Sure, if they ever need someone to wreck their typewriter and jam all the keys with liquid paper, maybe they'll call me. Listen, I'll be lucky if they don't send me a bill."

"Juliet's mother says you need a degree," Ty said.

"Sure you do," Mom said. "You need a degree, self-confidence, good looks, a perky, cheerful manner. . . . And right after dinner I'm going to swallow the contents of a little bottle that says 'Drink Me' and I'll magically attain all those things." She stared off into space, her eyes blank.

"What's for dessert?" Ty got up.

"I don't know. You tell me. Hemlock?"

"Is there any ice cream?" Ty opened the freezer door. "Wow, heavenly hash. Great. Thanks for getting that, Mom." He kissed her.

Mom smiled wanly. "So, tell us about the Ice Show, Ty. When is it?"

ELEVEN

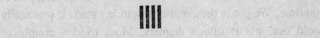

THE BIG EVENT FOR DECEMBER IS THAT TY IS GOING TO BE IN this Ice Show. The school where he takes lessons rents this place once a year to put on a benefit for the handicapped. We've been to it before and Ty was in it, but this year he has a whole act to himself. Juliet has some smaller part. Wouldn't it be great if they both fell flat on their faces? Right in front of maybe eight hundred people! I guess I'm a sadist at heart, but the only reason I'm going is the secret hope that that'll happen. It won't, I know that. But it might.

I'm also going because Mom says I have to. She gave me this lecture about how Ty is really, deep down, very insecure because of being short and not getting on with Dad, and how ice skating is the one thing he's ever been good at. So we have to pretend to be really impressed.

We got a bunch of extra tickets. I would have asked Otis. but he thinks figure skating if for sissies (*he* said that, not me, remember) and his brother-in-law is taking him to a Rangers game that Saturday anyway. So I asked Vicki. She got all excited and said she'd love to.

The night it was taking place, I got slightly more dressed up than usual. I wore a blue sweater Mom got me for

Christmas and jeans and my sheepskin coat. Mom looked pretty good. She had on an orange dress and her hair was brushed out.

"Is my eye makeup crooked?" she asked, as we were about to leave.

It was, but I told her no because I was afraid we'd be late. Mom is frequently late, and I hate that. I like getting places on time. We got in the car and it wouldn't start. It was really cold out, about fifteen degrees. Mom tried a couple of times, but the engine wouldn't catch. "Oh shit," she said.

"We can get a cab," I said. "There's a cab company you can call where they come to your house."

"They're crooks!" Mom said vehemently. "I won't pay ten dollars just to go fifteen miles."

She climbed out of the car. "We'll hitchhike," she said. "It's right off 303. Everybody's going in that direction."

"Mom, listen—"

"We'll only get in with someone who looks nice, okay? If he has little beady eyes and is sweating profusely, we'll say no. . . . We'll wait for a lady, some gray-haired friendly lady."

Man, it was cold! I hadn't brought gloves because I thought we'd just drive there and back. I stuffed my hands in my pockets, and we went out to the road leading to the main highway. Cars pass pretty fast there, but not as fast as on the highway itself. We both put our thumbs up, but no one stopped. I knew we were going to be late. I just hate that with shows, where you have to brush past millions of people to get to your seat. I would have *lent* her ten dollars, for Christ's sake.

"Let's go back and get a cab," I said.

"By the time they come, it'll be too late," Mom said

hoarsely, hopping from foot to foot. She stepped out into the middle of the road, waving her hands over her head.

"Mom, come on, that's dumb," I said. "Get back! They might not see you."

"They'll see me," Mom said. "I'm wearing red." But as I started going out to drag her back, she yelled, "Jase, are you crazy? Do you want to be run over? . . . Oh great, look, someone's stopping."

The person who stopped was a man. He didn't have beady eyes and he wasn't sweating profusely. He had gray hair and said in a friendly way, "Where are you folks heading?"

Mom told him the Sarcar Auditorium.

He leaned over and opened the door. "Well, hop in. I'll take you up to Ridgeville. I'm a little late so I can't go all the way there."

We both got in the front seat. The car was really nice and warm. Even if that guy had a criminal record printed on his front window, I'd have gotten in. Looking over at us, he said, "That was a dangerous thing to do, lady, standing in the middle of the road like that. What if I hadn't seen you?"

"How could you not see me?" Mom said.

"I'm a safe driver. What if I'd been one of these crazy teenagers, some kind of drunk driver. What then?"

"Then, we wouldn't be having this conversation," Mom said. "But you weren't. You were a nice guy. God looked down and said in Her infinite wisdom, 'Give 'em a break.'"

The man chuckled. "You mean *His* infinite wisdom. God is a man."

"She is?" Mom turned to me. "We were brought up to think she was a woman. How do you like that, Jase? God is a man? She's got balls and everything? I thought she was a plump serene old lady in a white toga whose hair stayed curly without a permanent."

"What religion do you belong to?" the man asked.

"I was raised as Presbyterian," Mom said.

"So was I," the man said. "They don't believe in a woman God!"

"Well," Mom said. "I never paid a whole lot of attention in church."

There was a pause.

"Usually I don't believe in picking up hitchhikers," the man said, "but you two sure looked cold and forlorn. I said to myself, those two'll be frozen stiff in ten minutes."

"We were," Mom said. "We appreciate your generosity."

She told him about the Ice Show. He said he was from Minnesota and everybody always expected him to be a good ice skater, but he wasn't. "I hate the cold," he said. "And I'm pretty lazy too. About the only exercise I get is this mechanical bicycle my brother got me last Christmas. While I'm on it, I read."

I knew we were going to be late, even with the guy picking us up. He drove pretty slowly, and it was ten past eight when he let us off. "Jim January," he said, shaking Mom's hand as she got out. "If you ever need a lift again. It's easy to remember. Just like the month. I live out in Palisades. Where're you folks from?"

"Twelve Lemmon Drive," I said.

After he drove off, Mom said, "*Never* do that, Jase. Never."

"What'd I do?"

"You told him where we live."

"So?"

"What if he's an ax murderer?"

"So, why'd we hitchhike with him, if he's an ax murderer?"

"I didn't say he *was* an ax murderer," Mom said. "I just said, don't go giving out our address to every person you meet."

"I don't." We were hurrying along the highway. It seemed colder than it had before. Finally we reached the driveway that led to the auditorium.

Just before we got to the front door, Mom said fiercely, "And don't get any ideas in your head about fixing me up with anyone! I'll fend for myself or I won't fend for myself. Do you have that straight?"

Sometimes my mother is really something. Here we're fifteen minutes late, the temperature is down to zero, and she wants to get into a big conversation about my fixing her up with guys—something that never entered my head. "I got it," I said. "Rest easy."

Needless to say, we were late. The whole auditorium was filled, and as I'd expected, our seats were right in the middle of a row so we had to cross over about twenty people. Vicki was there already. She looked up at me anxiously. "Where were you?" she whispered.

"Our car broke down," I whispered back.

God, you should have seen her. It's lucky she doesn't look that way every day, because the way she looked that night, she would definitely have been in that category of girls who make my brain freeze so I can't remember my own name. She was wearing this scoop-necked white dress made of some soft fuzzy material, and you could see—well, I'd seen most of it already, but she looked great. She had her hair loose with a ribbon on one side.

"You look nice," she whispered, smiling at me.

"You too." I was so stunned I just sat there staring at her,

99

forgetting to take my coat off, forgetting that supposedly we were here to watch my brother be a hotshot on the ice.

Okay, I'll come right out and say it. My brother is a good ice skater. One number he just sort of danced with a girl—I couldn't tell if it was Juliet or not. But at the end, just before the intermission, he had this whole number to himself. He did all kinds of stuff—I don't know the technical names. He jumped in the air and did double turns and landed on one foot. One thing I can tell you. He looked scared. Not all the way through. But when he did that turn and had to land on one foot, you could tell he was afraid he wasn't going to make it. Maybe not everyone in the audience could tell, but I could. But he managed to get through it without falling on his face, and when he was done, the audience gave him a big hand.

Mom looked pleased and happy. "Let's go out," she said. "I need a smoke. . . . Hi, Vicki, I'm this guy's mother."

"Hi," Vicki said.

We went out to the room where they sold drinks and candy. I bought Cokes for me and Vicki and a big box of M&M's. Just as I was coming back, I saw the Moscowitzes bearing down on Mom. Mrs. Moscowitz is definitely one of the best-looking women of that age group I've ever seen. I mean, she has a really great figure and she always shows it off. She was in this very form-fitting black dress that was sexy, even compared to Vicki's, in a different kind of way. She has fluffy blond hair and long dark red nails. He's this kind of chunky guy with a beard. He looks like a businessman type, but he dresses strangely. Like tonight he had on a leather jacket with long fringes and cowboy boots.

"Well, wasn't Ty sensational?" Mrs. Moscowitz said to all of us.

"Yeah, he was great," Vicki said.

"I bet you're as proud as proud can be." She beamed at me.

I just made some gesture which could have been interpreted any way.

To Mom she said, "What an improvement over last year! I couldn't believe it. I know he's been practicing a lot, but still."

Mom said, "Juliet looked nice, too."

Mrs. Moscowitz frowned. "She hasn't been on yet! That was Alison Glass."

"Oh." Mom bit her lip. "We got there a little late so we didn't check our programs. She just looked a little like Juliet. . . ."

"I don't see the resemblance at *all*," Mrs. Moscowitz said. She looked at her husband, who was wolfing down some salted peanuts. "Did you, dear?"

"What?" Mr. Moscowitz said.

"Alison . . . do you think she looks at all in any even *slight* way like Juliet?"

He shrugged. "Which one is she?"

Mrs. Moscowitz turned away impatiently, back to Mom and us. "I was just so devastated to hear about you and Mort," she said. "I've been meaning to call, but I've been so busy."

Mom cleared her throat. "Well, it just . . . happened," she faltered.

"I know!" Mrs. Moscowitz exclaimed. "It does! And to the unlikeliest couples. We know this couple, the Burkes, who've been married as long as we have, and suddenly, bingo, he took off with this woman—I mean, I hate to use this kind of word, but with a floozie. That's what she was. I told Bill, 'I don't care if they were at our wedding and we were at theirs. I simply won't have that woman in my house!' . . . And they were one of the happiest couples you'd ever meet—weren't they, dear?"

"Who?" said Mr. Moscowitz.

"The Burkes!" Mrs. Moscowitz said. "Weren't they the happiest couple we knew?"

"They're divorced," he said.

"Not now! Before!"

"They *seemed* happy," he conceded.

Mrs. Moscowitz grabbed Mom by the arm. "I know just how you're feeling," she said, "but let me tell you. The one who is left gets the last laugh. It *always* happens that way. I've never seen it fail. Here's Harry with that dreadful woman, and Jackie, who was bereft, just devastated, has met the nicest man in the *world*. He adores her! He says his life didn't begin till he met her, and he's been married three times."

Just then the intermission bell sounded. "So don't give up the ship!" Mrs. Moscowitz called, as we started back to our seats.

Mom has this expression she learned to make in boarding school, to scare kids she didn't like. She can roll the pupils of her eyes back so all you see are the whites. I used to love it when she did that when I was little; it really made my flesh creep. Anyway, as soon as the Moscowitzes moved out of sight, she did that.

"Are they friends of yours?" Vicki asked me.

"They're my brother's girlfriend's parents."

"He was awful," she said. "He just stared at my breasts the whole time!"

I don't know exactly why Mr. Moscowitz would do that because, like I said, his wife is kind of stacked. But when

Vicki said that, I looked at hers, and it was true, they looked extremely nice. It just shows he has good taste.

"I *hate* it when middle-aged men gape at girls my age!" Vicki went on. "It's truly gross."

The second half of the show was pretty much like the first, except Ty's big number was over. He did come on again with a girl that must've been Juliet, because they beamed at each other all through the dance and he handed her this rose when it was over. In the middle I started holding hands with Vicki. It wasn't the perfect setting to make out, obviously, with Mom right on the other side of me, but she looked so pretty and I felt really turned on. Then she did this very sexy thing. She began running her finger along the palm of my hand, up and down, just lightly. Maybe if I hadn't been fairly turned on already, it wouldn't have had any effect, but after a while I felt like just dragging her out of the theater and jumping on her. Shit. What dumb timing again! We couldn't even go anyplace afterward. I put my arm around her and let it slide as far down as it could; I don't think either of us paid much attention to the second half of the show.

At one point she took the program and with a pen she had in her purse wrote, "I'm glad no one can see what's in my mind!"

I wrote back, "Same here."

Well, obviously our minds had something going, even if we couldn't do anything about it. I just hoped my erection would go away before we had to leave, or that she wouldn't notice.

When the show was over, I helped Vicki with her coat, kind of half hugging her while I was doing it. Then, about a second later, I saw my father coming up the aisle. Randy was right behind him. They started going past. I wasn't sure he would see me, but suddenly his eyes caught mine. He hesitated and then waved. I waved back. I glanced over at Mom. She was watching him too. "This is all I needed," she muttered.

Dad and Randy moved on up the aisle. Mom just stood there. Vicki didn't understand why we weren't trying to get out of the theater. I didn't want to say anything. I'd told Vicki about my parents getting divorced, but I didn't want to go into the whole thing right then. Finally, after about five minutes, when Randy and Dad had disappeared, we went up the aisle.

Vicki's father was picking her up; he drove us home. Mom sat in the front next to him, and Vicki and I sat in the back. That wasn't too much better than being in the theater, but we did fool around a little in a surreptitious kind of way.

"Would you like to come in for a minute?" Vicki's father asked when we passed their house.

"I'm a little tired," Mom said, "but thanks anyway. Some other time."

Back home I went into the kitchen to get something to eat. God, I felt so pissed at Mom. I know she was spaced out from seeing Dad and Randy, but so what? Why couldn't she just go there for a half an hour? Vicki and I could've gone up to her room and . . .

Mom came into the kitchen too. "She's not even pretty!" she said. "Do you think she is, Jase?"

I thought she meant Vicki. I said, "I think she's beautiful."

"In what way?"

"Well, everything . . . her eyes, her hair, her figure."

Mom glared at me. "Maybe my eyesight is failing. She just looked to me like a tall, fortyish lady with glasses."

Then I realized she meant Randy. "Oh, her," I said.

"Who'd you think I meant? Mrs. Moscowitz?"

"I thought you meant Vicki," I muttered, pouring myself a glass of milk.

"Vicki's sweet," Mom said dismissively.

"Why didn't you want to visit her parents?" I said. "We wouldn't have had to stay long."

"It's almost midnight!"

"So? Tomorrow's Sunday."

Mom looked angry. "Look, what do you want? I got through the evening, okay? I got through what's-her-name and her spaced-out husband and Mort and his sweetie. . . . Am I supposed to start jumping through fiery hoops now? Give me a break!"

I didn't say anything.

"What is Vicki's father—a dentist?"

"Yeah."

"So, I'm supposed to spend the few remaining conscious hours of the day talking about root canal work with some dentist just because you're fucking his daughter."

"I'm *not* fucking his daughter." I just wish I was.

"Well, you will be in around three seconds."

I laughed. "Thanks for the encouragement, Mom. I think it might take a little longer than that."

"Just say boo and that kid'll be wrapped around you in no time flat. She's nuts about you. And then you'll end up living at her house, like Ty is at Juliet's all the time. What do I need a nine-room house for? I have no kids left! They're all so busy screwing around they can't even *live* here!"

Oh, boy. She was really off. "Mom, come on . . . I'm just dating her. It's *not* like Ty and Juliet."

"It will be."

"It *won't* be. Relax."

How ironical can you get? I feel delighted if I can get Vicki to take her bra off, and my mother has us living together and making it every night.

Mom sighed. "Well, okay, maybe I'm a little premature. Maybe I'm a little—I don't know what." She yawned. "God, I am so tired! Sleep well, hon, okay?"

Luckily I had a joint left over. Once I was in my room, I got into bed and smoked. I wasn't up to doing the whole bathroom routine; it was too cold to open the window. Anyhow, I figured by morning the smell would be gone. It was perfect. I turned on some X-rated movies in my head, and while I was getting sleepier and sleepier, Vicki started doing everything I'd been imagining while we were at the ice show.

TWELVE

||||

*M*S. *KORBEL IS GETTING MARRIED. SHE TOLD ME ABOUT IT* the last time I babysat for her. The wedding's going to be in February and she wants me to come. I said sure.

She seems pretty happy. She's marrying that bald guy, Gunther, and she says they'll live right in her house because she's afraid otherwise Vernon would be disoriented. "I hope he's okay at the wedding," she said. "It'll be small, but even so—"

"I think that's so romantic!" Vicki said, when I told her.

It's funny how girls think it's romantic if *anyone* is getting married. Like, Vicki doesn't even know the guy. Maybe Ms. Korbel'll be miserable. I hope not, but you never can tell.

There's just one thing I feel bad about. It's not a major thing, but it's that even though Vicki and I are getting along pretty well, really well, in fact, Otis isn't getting anywhere with Marcella. What pisses me is she gives him this line about how she doesn't want to go that far because she's an old-fashioned girl and all that similar garbage, and here Vicki told me she was pregnant last year! I haven't told Otis that, but whenever I see Marcella, I feel angry at how she's treating him. I wonder if it's because he's black. Yet, why would she go out with him if she was really prejudiced?

"You can't predict with girls," Otis said. We were at his house after school. "Like, Marcy looks so sexy, but she isn't, and Vicki doesn't look like much, but I guess—"

That gave me a guilty pang. Maybe I've been exaggerating the stuff with Vicki. It's certainly not anything like my mother was raving on about. Even after the ice show, though we've made out quite a bit, I'd say we're a long way from doing it. A *very* long way.

"Sometimes I get the feeling Marcy really wants to, though," Otis said, "but I figure it's her religion. Catholic girls are strict. They've got to save themselves for their husbands, or some such."

"Yeah," I said.

Maybe he picked up on my tone, because he said, "Yeah, what?"

"Nothing."

"You sounded kind of sarcastic."

"I bet she's not saving it," I said. "That's all."

"What do you mean?"

"I just bet she's not a virgin . . . In fact, I know she's not."

"How do you know?"

I hesitated. I didn't want to get Vicki into trouble. All I wanted was for Otis to wise up. So I said, "Some guys were talking—"

Otis was looking at me with a really intent expression. "What guys?"

"Just some guys . . . I forgot who."

"How come you never mentioned it?"

"It was just sort of . . . Listen, it was probably a

rumor. You know the way guys sometimes—" I suddenly wished I hadn't brought the whole thing up.

Otis looked thoughtful. "It figures. Like, she's always going on about how boys can't be trusted and they don't respect you if you let them go too far. She claimed it was her brothers who told her that, but maybe . . . I wonder if he was black?"

"Who? The guy that—"

"Yeah. Maybe if he was, she got the idea black guys can't be trusted."

I had thought the opposite, that Marcella might have let a white guy fool around with her but wouldn't with Otis because he was black. "Listen, forget the whole thing, okay?" I said. "I bet it's not even true."

"I'll ask her, that's all."

My heart started thumping. "She'll just lie. What's the point?"

"If she lies, I want to know that about her."

Me and my big mouth! "Well, if you've got to ask her, don't tell her where you found it out."

He gave me a funny look.

"Because, like, the person who mentioned it wasn't really sure."

"What person? You said before it was a bunch of guys."

"I can't mention who it was. . . . They said not to tell."

Suddenly he smiled. "Vicki, right?"

"O, promise me you won't get Vicki into it, okay?"

"Relax, man . . . God, you're in a bigger sweat about this than I am! So she fooled around a little? Guys are always after girls who look like that. Maybe he raped her or something."

The thing about Otis, which makes him a good friend, is

109

he always tries to find an excuse for the way people act. I'm not like that. I don't care that much why people do things. It's what they do that counts. Maybe I'm more judgmental that way. Not extremely, but, like, in this case if I were Otis, I'd be pissed off beyond belief that Marcy's been doing this whole number about being so coy and shy, and with some other guy she just whipped her clothes off and did everything he wanted.

That night, instead of going home from Otis's house, I took the bus into the city. I'd said I would meet Dad and Randy at a Chinese restaurant near her apartment. In some ways it was easier going without Ty, who'd said he was busy, but it was also more awkward in a way. What was I going to say to her? Dad isn't the most communicative guy on earth, but we kind of get along, so I wasn't so worried about him.

They were at the restaurant already when I got there. Randy looked about the same. She's not bad-looking, but she looks more like somebody's mother than like some hot number that you'd sneak out to meet at a bar. That's all I mean.

"I'm sorry Tyler couldn't make it," Randy said, after we'd ordered.

"Yeah, well, he has to practice a lot," I said. "Ice skating stuff."

"I was really impressed at the show," she said. "My ankles go kerplunk the second I get near an ice rink. I'm hopeless. And with skiing I'm afraid of falling off the tow."

Dad smiled at her. "You're a whiz at Ping-Pong, though," he said.

She smiled back. "True."

There was a moment's pause. Then Randy said, "Do you want to—?"

To me Dad said, "Well, it's just . . . Randy and I have set the date. March fifteenth."

"Date for what?" I asked. My mouth was full of cracked ice from the Coke. I swallowed half of it.

"We're getting married," Randy said. She looked excited and pleased.

"Don't you have to get divorced first?" I asked Dad. He laughed. "That's usually done. . . . Well, I've given Fay everything she's asked for. You see before you a man stripped of everything except his toothbrush and his good name. . . . If this lady can't support me, I'm in big trouble."

"And here I thought the point of getting married was so I could lay back on a chaise lounge and eat chocolates," Randy said.

You could tell they were both joking, but they still seemed nervous. Still, I gathered it was the kind of news people feel good about. All I had at hand was a barbequed sparerib, but I raised it in the air and said, "Congratulations, Dad." I wondered if Mom knew.

"It'll be a small wedding," Dad said. "Financial considerations aside . . . just the four of you and a few friends."

I took another sparerib. They were good—perfect, in fact. Not at all greasy.

"Money is going to be a big problem," Dad said, tossing a sparerib onto the pile.

"Yeah, well . . ." It seemed like it was before too. I didn't get what was so different.

"Maybe Fay will get a job," Randy said. "Don't you think that would be a good idea?"

Dad said, "It's a dandy idea, but I don't think there's a ghost of a chance that—"

"She'd be happier," Randy went on. "I mean, wouldn't she? Feeling independent, getting out, meeting people." To me she said, "My father died when I was twelve, and he didn't leave any insurance and my mother had to work. She didn't have training in anything, but she got a library degree and now she says she couldn't go back to the old way for anything."

"She'll never do it," Dad said. "That's all."

"Why not?" Randy said. "I don't understand."

"She'd rather make life difficult for me."

Randy glanced at me and then back at Dad again. "Well, I don't know. Do you really think—"

"I don't just *think*!" Dad said, "I *know*!" He sighed. "Well, okay, maybe I'm being . . ." To me he said, "Maybe you could mention it to her, Jase? What do you think?"

I took a drink of water. "About what? Getting a job?"

"Yeah . . . because it's for the three of you too. . . . If you want to go to decent colleges, everything. And Randy's right. I think it *would* make Fay happier."

"She might meet someone," Randy said.

"Don't count on it," Dad said.

"Sweetie, you're seeing her as . . . whereas someone else—"

I thought of all those awful job interviews Mom has been going on. She's still doing it, but none of them've worked out. "I think she is looking," I said. "Only she hasn't found anything yet." Then I had an idea.

"I don't care that much about going to college," I said. "Maybe I can just get a job or something."

Dad whirled on me. "Listen, you're going to college! Don't talk like that!"

"I could go eventually!" I said, beginning to really like the idea. "Just take a few years off and——"

"And what?" Dad's voice softened. "Jase, people with college degrees, with training, are having a hard time. What kind of job do you think *you* can get as a high school dropout?"

"I didn't mean that I wouldn't finish high school," I said, though I sure wouldn't care if I didn't. "I just meant if college is that expensive, maybe——"

"We shouldn't have gotten off on this," Dad said. "I'm obsessed with money, or the lack of it. . . . But plenty of families have less and manage. I want all of you to have everything you need to get started. Then, once you're all pulling in fifty thousand a year, Randy and I'll show up on your doorstep and you'll support us in our old age." He laughed nervously.

If I'm a pilot, I probably will be pretty rich. I wouldn't mind lending Dad some, if that were the case.

"Sure," I said. "I'll do that."

"Listen, just drop the money thing, okay?" Dad said. "It's like all obsessions. There's more to life than that." To Randy and me he said, "*I* think I'm the luckiest guy on earth. I'm starting over, I have a new life, a woman I'm crazy about, wonderful kids. . . . So we'll eat hamburgers for a decade or two——"

At that moment the waiter brought the bill. Dad handed it to me, I guess for a joke. Then he took it back and paid with his American Express card.

Mom knew I was having dinner with Dad and Randy. I wasn't sure if she knew they'd picked a day to get married, so when I got home, I just said the food had been good and didn't mention anything about that.

"How are they?" she asked. "Still billing and cooing?"

I shrugged. Then, which may have been stupid, I said, "They seem sort of worried about money."

Mom snorted. "Oh, my heart is wrung. Poor things!" She squinted at me. "I get it. They did a number on you about how I'd squeezed every last cent out of poor, hard-working Daddy, didn't they?" She came closer. "Didn't they?"

"Mom," I interrupted her. "Dad says not to worry about money. He says it'll be okay."

"Who's worrying? I haven't got one worry in my head. . . . What's his problem? I thought for sure he'd pick somebody with an income of fifty thou and a neat little trust fund tucked away. Mort's usually shrewder than that. Blinded by love, I guess. . . . Oh, and speaking of hearts, flowers, sex, what-have-you . . . Vicki called."

That reminded me of Otis and what I'd told him. But when I spoke to Vicki, she sounded fine. I was glad because I didn't feel like I could handle any more stuff for one day. One trouble with all this happening now is it's almost like I'm an only child. No one else is here. Usually I'd say great, but right now I'd rather it was a couple of years ago with everyone running around yelling that they couldn't get into the bathroom or use the car.

THIRTEEN

||||

I DON'T SEE VICKI ALL DAY EVERY DAY. WE HAVE SOME CLASSES together—Biology and Math—but the rest are separate. Like, she's taking French and I'm taking Spanish. I thought Spanish would be easier. Maybe it's easier than French, but it's not *that* easy. I still don't know all that much. But when I go to the city I memorize all the Spanish ads on the subway. *"Estoy sentada dose horas al dias. Los ultimo que necesiro son hemerrhoides"* means "I sit twelve hours a day. The last thing I need is hemorrhoids," in case you're interested. I don't know how much help that'll be on the final.

Another reason I don't see Vicki is she's on the girls' basketball team, and they practice a couple of days a week after school. I went to one game. Girls' basketball isn't the most exciting sport in the world, but Vicki wasn't bad, especially given her height. Of course, compared to the other girls she wasn't as short as a guy her size would be on a boy's team. But she's really quick. She darted around and got past this real stringbean of a girl who's half a head taller than me. I felt excited in a weird way, seeing her. She says it's the only sport she's ever been good at.

Monday is a day she has practice, so I didn't wait for her

after school. I started down the steps to where I keep my bike, when I heard her yelling, "Jase, wait! Wait!"

I turned around and waited while she came running after me. Her cheeks were bright red from the cold. This has been the coldest January in the last fifty years! She has a parka that covers all of her—you can't even see her hair. She looks like an Eskimo, almost. "You told about Marcy!" she said angrily, still out of breath.

"What?"

"You promised you wouldn't, and you did!"

My heart sank. "I just—"

"She was crying in the ladies' room, saying now everybody will know, all the boys, everybody, and they'll call her a slut . . . and it wasn't her fault, even! . . . How could you *do* that?"

I felt really cold standing there. I'd forgotten my gloves, as usual, and the wind was blowing right in my face. "Listen, the reason I did it is, she's been giving Otis this whole big line about being this holy virgin and—"

Vicki's eyes were blazing. "Maybe she wanted him to just like her as a person, not to go pawing all over her! Maybe she didn't want every date they had to be him just trying to rip her clothes off. That's all guys *ever* want to do. That's all they ever even *think* about!"

I wondered if she meant me. I think about other things, sometimes. "I'm—I'm sorry," I stammered. "Okay?"

"No, not okay! You betray my word just for Otis . . . why? Because I'm a girl and girls don't count. Just that dumb male bonding stupidity! Well, I think you're cruel and unthinking and hopeless!"

"Vicki, I—"

"Drop dead!" she yelled, and stormed off.

Shit. What's wrong with me? It *was* stupid, but Christ,

she didn't even let me try to explain. I never knew she had such a bad temper. I biked home, feeling cold and rotten. I wish my parents were rich so I could go on a vacation to Hawaii and lie on the beach. I just feel sick of everything: school, girls, my parents. It's all such a dumb mess.

When I got home Otis called. "You were right," he said.

It's unfair, but right at that moment I felt like I hated him too. How inconsistent can you get? "What did you do? Yell at her?"

"No, I just forced her to tell me what really happened." He laughed bitterly. "Rape! Big rape. He was some older guy who snowed her with a line about marrying her."

"Vicki said she was crying in the ladies' room."

"She'll get over it. . . . Listen, there are five dozen guys in the school that'll line up to take my place. Don't start feeling sorry for her."

"I'm not."

"Fuck girls," he said. "It's not worth it."

"Right."

"You're at least getting something."

"No, I'm not," I admitted. "Not that much."

"I thought she just took her bra off and said: dive in."

"Once . . . And it wasn't like that, and nothing happened. . . . Anyhow, she's not even speaking to me anymore."

"You're lucky . . . Marcy's been calling here every ten minutes. I'm going crazy. I can't take the phone off the hook."

"Put those things in your ears, those wax things."

"Yeah, something."

After I hung up, I tried to argue myself into a better mood. It wasn't like Vicki and I were "in love." So, what's the big deal? I guess partly it's that I hate it when people get mad at me, especially when they started off liking me. I've had that happen with teachers, the ones who have me come up to them at the end of the year and say how disappointed they are in my performance, how they expected better. What are you supposed to say? And I also hate it when people don't let you even try to explain. Who am I supposed to be mad at? Vicki? Otis? Marcy? The guy Marcy screwed around with? If it was a single person, you could go out and jump them and get it over with.

I wish she hadn't used that word "hopeless." I mean, obviously, she wasn't standing there with a dictionary, thumbing through, looking for the perfect word to describe me. She was just mad and wanted to get at me. But "hopeless" is so final, like I'm not worth bothering with at all. Then I think—well, if that's her true feeling about me, how about the last two months? She sure *seemed* to like me. Maybe she was just lusting after my body or something, ha, ha.

That's the other thing. Even though Andy says I'm going to be a real hit with girls at some point, that point doesn't seem to have arrived. I haven't had to fight off packs of sex-crazed girls pounding down the door. So I felt good about Vicki seeming to both get along with me okay and also feel attracted to me. I don't think you can lie about the second thing. I mean, like I couldn't pretend to be turned on by some girl if I wasn't, and I don't think Vicki could pretend either. Especially that time during the blackout. Seriously, I think if we'd had a couple more hours, maybe Vicki might've ended up pregnant too. And not just that time. Lots of times, I've felt that if I just pushed a little harder . . . I don't know. Maybe that was just in my head, but something was definitely coming from her.

What I did was something I haven't done in a long time.

First I put the new Led Zep record, which I really like a lot, on my stereo. I turned it up as loud as I could since Mom wasn't home yet. Then I turned my electric blanket up to ten, the highest number on it. Mom and Dad gave me that blanket a couple of years ago because I'm always complaining about being cold at night. A lot of times I forget and don't turn it on at all, just use it as a regular blanket. If you turn it up high and get in, wrapping it all around yourself, it's a strange feeling, like you're in some hot cocoon, almost like when you're sick and have such a high fever that you feel high. I lay there in the dark, a little stoned (I did the old bathroom routine while the blanket was heating up), nice and hot from the blanket, the music so loud it was like it was coming from inside me, and I felt a lot better.

When Mom came home, I was half asleep. The record had gone off. She came over and looked down at me. "Are you okay?" she said. "You feel hot."

"It's just the blanket," I muttered.

Mom looked at the setting and turned it way down. "Jase, don't do that! You can electrocute yourself."

The fact is, you can't electrocute yourself with an electric blanket unless you're using it while taking a shower or something, but Mom read something in the newspaper about that once. Anything electrical, a hair dryer, a toaster even, she thinks you can electrocute yourself.

"I just felt cold," I said, turning over. I felt like just going to sleep.

She went over and turned the stereo off. "You're sick," she said. "You're coming down with something."

Since I just wanted her to leave me alone, I said, "I don't know."

"What can I get you? Tell me. Are you thirsty?"

I really did feel thirsty. Mom went and got me a big glass

of Coke with a lot of crushed ice in it. She's good at crushing ice. She takes a hammer and whams it. I love crushed ice. I sat up in bed and drank the whole thing. Mom watched me anxiously. Andy gets furious about this, but I have to admit I love it when Mom takes care of me when I'm sick. Having a woman wait on you hand and foot is a great feeling, especially if they're doing it because they love you. I wished I could pretend to be sick, just to get out of going to school, but I didn't feel up to that big an act.

I smiled at Mom. "I feel a lot better," I said.

Even though I said that, she said it was important I take it easy. So dinner was creamed chicken on toast, which I ate in front of the TV wrapped in a blanket. Not bad. I still deep down felt sort of rotten, but a lot better.

February was a lousy month. It's not one of my favorite months anyway. By February you figure winter ought to be over, but it still hangs on and you still forget your gloves or your boots. Vicki wouldn't speak to me. Like I said, we don't have every class together, but we are in a few, and that was hard, seeing her go way to the back of the room or start looking deliberately out the window the minute I'd walk in the room. Okay, maybe it wasn't true love or anything Erin reads about in those Candlelight Romance things, but it was better than nothing. A lot better. And, which I think is typical of me, I never really appreciate things till they're over. Or maybe it's while they're happening, you don't think about them. Whatever.

The ironical part is Otis and Marcy are going together again. She practically came over and got down on her hands and knees and begged him to forgive her for not telling the truth. Why don't girls do stuff like that with me? She said it was just she'd been afraid he would think she was a slut and wouldn't respect her anymore. He said no, he didn't think that, and that he thought the guy who did it was a real turd and if he ever came around again, he'd take care of him good. The thing with Otis, like I've said, is if he likes you, he really does take your side. So I think he talked himself into thinking this guy was some kind of monster just because he wanted to see Marcy again.

Also, which I consider a bad sign, he's stopped talking about their sex life so much. I think people talk about it when nothing much is happening. That's true of me anyway. You exaggerate or build it up to your friends, partly to convince yourself something is happening. Whereas if something really is, you clam up. Anyway, for all I know, O and Marcy are actually doing it. I almost get that feeling. But that he won't tell even me because he wants to "protect her reputation" or something. That could be a figment of my imagination. Most things are. But when I see them holding hands and she's looking at him with this gooey-eyed expression, I feel really shitty. Especially with Vicki either totally ignoring me or staring at me like I'm a bad smell that's drifted into the room.

Andy called. I'd been meaning to write her, but I hadn't. So on the phone she asked how things were and if I was okay.

"Yeah, fine," I said.

The thing with Andy is, you just can't hide stuff from her. I don't know why. You can say, "Yeah, fine," and she knows the whole story, everything you haven't said. But instead of saying, "So, tell me what really happened?" she said, "Jase, listen, I have an idea. . . . Why don't you come up for the weekend. I just handed a bunch of papers in and I'm not too loaded down with work. Would you like to?"

"Sure," I said. The trouble was, I didn't have any money, and I knew Mom and Dad wouldn't lend me any.

"I'll send you some dough. I've been saving. I'm turning into this real skinflint. How's the home scene?"

"Hairy."

"Mom hasn't been—God, I hope she's not home—dating, or anything?"

"Are you kidding?"

"Well, she could . . . I admit, it's harder for women her age than for men, but it's not impossible. Well, listen, that'll be great, sweetie. I can't wait to see you. Take care, okay?"

I felt better after that. She's my sister, true, but there are times when just someone liking you is a good thing. I mean, Otis still likes me, but with Marcy around he doesn't have that much time for me. I wonder if Andy's still going with that guy, the one Mom blew up about. Maybe I'll meet him. I don't care what Ty said, I liked Wally, and I bet anyone Andy would like would be a good guy.

At dinner—Ty was there too—I told Mom about the trip and added that Andy would send the money. Mom turned to Ty. "Are *you* going too?"

He shook his head, like she must be crazy to think he'd give up a weekend with Juliet just to see his sister.

"I just don't like being in the house alone," Mom said. "It makes me nervous. Why did we get such a big house? I'm afraid that guy who picked us up on the road that time is going to come by and strangle me or something."

"Mom, I can't be here that weekend," Ty said. "I promised Juliet I'd be with her."

"Let her stay here instead," Mom said.

Ty didn't say anything. He just looked pissed.

"What—our house isn't fancy enough? Listen, I'll bring

her breakfast in bed, I'll buff her nails. . What does her mother do for her?"

"It's not that," Ty said. "It's just she likes being at home. They're a very close-knit family."

Mom rolled back her eyes. Then she said, "Look, I'm just asking you about one weekend, Ty. . . . Is she going to wither up and die if she isn't at home one fucking weekend?"

Ty looked at me. "Why don't you make *him* stay home? Why *me?*"

"Because he usually *is* home! . . . Oh, the hell with it. Maybe being strangled in your sleep is the best way to go."

Ty sighed. "Mom, okay, I'll talk to her. Maybe Saturday night, after the party, we'll come back here."

"It's these little moments that make life worthwhile," Mom said. To me she said, "So, are you going to meet Andy's paramour while you're up there?"

I shrugged.

"I'm going to give you a letter for his wife. Pitch him out, baby, and get it over with! She's twenty-eight. If I'd done that, twenty years ago, I'd probably be a rich, happy something-or-other."

"You wouldn't have had us," I pointed out.

"True . . . can't win 'em all."

She stomped off into the kitchen. Ty looked at me. "Guess Vicki dropped you, huh?"

"She has inverted nipples," I said coolly.

"What?" He looked totally bewildered.

"I didn't feel like messing around with somebody with inverted nipples, that's all."

That seemed like a good exit line. I got up and went to my room.

FOURTEEN

||||

ANDY AND I HAD DINNER IN BOSTON THE NIGHT I ARRIVED. She took me to this big seafood place that she said she and Marcus go to a lot. That's his name, her paramour, as Mom would say. Andy can drink quite a lot. She had a weird-looking drink called a strawberry daiquiri before dinner and she ordered wine for both of us. I haven't really gotten into alcohol that much. What I like with pot is you can control it. With wine or hard liquor one minute you're fine, the next minute you're ready to puke. It goes too fast.

After we ate, she drove me around. "I'm going to take you to Marcus's house," she said.

I thought she meant into his house, but she just drove by this white frame house that looked like a lot of others. "That is Marcus's house," she said. "There's a light on. That probably means he's in his study working and Charlotte is out at one of her League of Women Voters meetings." She turned the car and drove down a few blocks. "On your right is Marcus's son's nursery school." After a few more blocks, "And on your left is Marcus's shrink's office, where we used to meet every Wednesday and Friday and where we once actually had sex in his car before he went to work." She looked at me. "You've got to understand, Jase. Marcus can be really uptight. He's a great lover, but he'd never done it in a car."

I was a little drunk, but not as much as I think Andy was. "What's great about him?" I asked. Andy's the only girl or woman I know that I can ask stuff like that.

"What *is* great about him?" Andy said. "A very good question. I'm glad you asked that. Because I often ask myself, Is it worth all this shit and creeping around, and then we do it, and I say: Yes, by God, it is. . . . Lemme see. Well, it's all ineffable, you understand. Everything in life and sex, all the good stuff is ineffable."

"Sure," I said. "I've found that." When we're together Andy and I start talking like this, kind of horsing around. I don't know why. I don't do it with anyone else.

"Okay, what is it that distinguishes Marcus Rosen from all the many men who have labored long and lovingly over my incredible body? First, he doesn't rush it. He goes slowly, he savors it. Not like he's doing you a favor or he's memorized some horrible little manual on how to please a woman. You just get the feeling he likes it. . . . It's weird, but lots of men don't like women or sex. I don't know. But he does."

I wonder if someday some woman will ever say anything like that about me. Like that I'm ineffable or a great lover. I kind of doubt it. Maybe I started looking morose, because Andy turned to me and said, "So, what's with Vicki?"

"I screwed up." I told her about what happened.

"She still likes you," Andy said.

"How do you know? I don't think she even liked me that much to begin with."

"She did," Andy insisted. "I know that whole number,

walking out of the room when you come in, looking out the window. She's just trying to prove to you she doesn't give a damn. If she *really* didn't give a damn, she wouldn't be trying so hard to prove it."

I felt too drunk to follow that. "I don't know." I sighed.

"If she doesn't like you, she's a jerk," Andy said. "But she likes you. I'm telling you that for a hard cold fact."

"So, what am I supposed to do?"

"I don't know. Send her flowers. Tell her you like her. It's not all that complicated."

The trouble is, it is. Maybe people Andy's age, who've done it lots of times, forget that. It *is* complicated. Or maybe it's just me. Everything I've thought of doing seems dumb or like it won't work.

We drove back to Andy's place. She just has a two-room apartment, a small bedroom and a living room. But there's a foldout couch. That's where I was going to sleep. Just as we walked in, the phone rang.

"Oh, hi," she said, sounding pleased. "Mental telepathy . . . I was just showing Jase your house. . . . Yeah, I figured she might be, but . . . How come? . . . Yeah, I thought . . . Not at all? Come on, he wants to meet you. Just get away for half an hour. Right . . . Okay, we'll see you." After she hung up, she pointed a finger at me. "Jase, I'm going to give you an invaluable piece of advice: never get involved with a married man."

I laughed. "Don't worry."

"Or a married *anyone*. A married dog, a married giraffe. Even if you take one look at them and little sparks fly out of your ears *and* their ears *and* you hear Beethoven's Ninth in the background *and* they laugh themselves sick at your jokes. . . . Just run, do not walk, to the nearest exit."

I like Andy's place. Maybe someday, if I'm a pilot, I'll have a place like this. Not too big, but fixed up the way I want. A super stereo, lots of records. For the first time in a long while I felt pretty good. I'd brought some pot along, but I decided to save it.

I slept well too, which I don't always, even at home, but especially when I'm away from home.

We spent most of the afternoon driving around or walking around. The other good thing about being with Andy, as opposed to being with a girl of any other kind, is I don't feel like I have to talk if I don't feel like it, or act any special way. It's almost like being by myself, except she's there if I do want to say anything. But she never tries to "draw me out" or gets pissed if I seem silent or out of it, which I think I do a lot of the time.

So for me it was a good day, even though we didn't do anything special or talk about anything special. Then, late in the afternoon, she said we were supposed to meet Marcus at this coffee shop in a hotel near where he worked.

We got there first. Then a man came over to our table and sat down opposite us—Andy and me were sitting next to each other. "Hi," he said, smiling at me. "I'm Marcus Rosen."

"I'm Jason," I said.

"I know." He looked at Andy. "Sorry I'm late. The usual complications."

He wasn't that great-looking. I don't mean I expected him to be handsome especially, but he looked really tired and wrung-out for a guy in his thirties, and his hair was turning gray. He had kind of a big nose and shaggy brown hair that Mom would say needed to be cut.

127

"So, I hear you're a terrific ice skater," he said after ordering a drink.

Together Andy and me said, "That's Tyler."

"Oh." He looked puzzled.

"Jase is the smart one," Andy said.

That made me feel terrific. She could've said "Jase is the druggie" or "Jase is the baby of the family" (that's what Mom used to say and it drove me up the wall).

"I'm failing half my subjects," I half joked, "but—"

"He's not, he just doesn't study, and if you went to the high school we did, you'd understand why," Andy intervened quickly. "They can take any subject and make it so dull, you just stop listening."

"Are you going into law, like your crackerjack sister here?" Marcus asked.

I shook my head. "I haven't decided yet . . . I might be a pilot."

"I hope you don't drink. . . . I always have the feeling those guys are bombed out of their minds."

"No, I don't like liquor that much," I said, hoping Andy hadn't mentioned about the drugs.

"Hey, listen, I thought maybe we might go by your office," Andy said. "It's such a great view. I wanted Jase to see it."

Marcus sighed. His drink had come and he drank a long swallow of it. "Not today."

"Why not?" Andy asked.

He had a funny expression. "Well, actually . . . I got fired yesterday."

"What?" Andy practically jumped out of her chair. "How come? You didn't even mention it when I spoke to you yesterday!"

128

"Well, you know the situation there has been pretty—"

"But I thought what's-his-name had spoken to you and said they had another—"

"Look, what can I say? It's done. I have a month to pack up."

Andy pounded the table. "Shit!" She turned to me. "He's the best lawyer *in* the stupid place. It's all those awful office politics."

"It's a lot of things," Marcus said morosely. "The recession . . ."

"I think they ought to shoot all those guys," Andy said hotly. She'd finished her drink and gulped down the maraschino cherry. "Why can't we go there, though? It's Saturday."

"Some of them work Saturday," Marcus said. "See, that's the thing. A lot of those guys don't have families. They work a seven-day week. How can you compete with that when you have a wife and two kids?"

Andy half-smiled. "I don't know," she said. "I don't *have* a wife and two kids."

Marcus looked at me. "How about you, Jason? Do *you* have a wife and two kids?"

I shook my head. "I don't even have a girlfriend. . . . I used to, though."

"Jase has some girl who I think is crazy about him," Andy said. "He just—"

"No, she's not," I said. "She cringes when she sees me."

"That's the proof!" Andy said. To Marcus she said, "Don't you think that's the proof? You don't cringe if you're indifferent to someone."

"True." But he looked abstracted and kind of out of it. "Listen, I really better get back."

"Already?" Andy said. "It's only six."

"I know, but . . . I'm not in such a great mood, and I just think—"

"You'll get another job," she assured him, leaning forward intently.

"Yeah, I guess," he said, as though he didn't believe her. He stood up and put his coat on and shook my hand. "Nice to have met you, Jason."

After he left, Andy moved over to where he'd been sitting. "Well, I'm sorry."

"What about?" I was beginning to feel starving. I could hear my stomach rumble. We hadn't eaten since breakfast.

"You didn't see him at his best. He's really a total and absolute sweetie . . . which is what's so awful. I mean, I *like* him for feeling all that loyalty to dumb, hopeless Sallie. . . ." She sighed. "I don't know."

Her saying "hopeless" made me think of Vicki yelling at me. "I'm hungry," I said.

Andy grinned. "Then you shall be fed," she said.

We went back to her place and ordered a huge pizza with everything on it. Eating, especially something I like, like pizza, almost always makes me feel better. Andy seemed more cheerful too. While we were eating, a girlfriend of hers called and asked if she could come over. Andy asked me if it was okay, and I said sure.

"Vizhier's from Manila," she said. "She's in my class. I like her a lot."

What a weird name. She pronounced it Vish Air.

When Vizhier came over, I practically passed out. Basically most of Andy's friends look like her. That is, they aren't ugly but most of them haven't been knockouts either. They're usually a little chubby or whatever. This Vizhier had long black hair to her waist and small, perfect features. She looked a lot like this spy in a James Bond movie I once saw. He fucked her underwater a couple of times. In the end he had to bump her off because she was trying to get some kind of important information out of him, but after he did, he looked kind of sad, and you knew why.

"Hi, Jason," Vizhier said. She had a little bit of an accent, not that much, just she didn't talk the way people usually do.

"We've been pigging out," Andy said. "Want any?"

Vizhier looked longingly at the two remaining slices of pizza. "Oh, boy—I wish I could. But I'm on that stupid diet, at least until next week."

The three of us played poker for an hour or two. We didn't play for high stakes because no one had much money, but it was fun. I'm good at poker. I cleaned both of them out. Too bad it wasn't strip poker.

"We have to give Jase advice on how to get this girl back," Andy said.

"He doesn't look like he'd have any trouble with girls," Vizhier said, smiling at me in that soft, beckoning way she had.

"I know!" Andy said. "Isn't he adorable? I mean, what girl could resist him?"

I'm used to Andy horsing around like that, but it embarrassed me, her doing it in front of Vizhier. In another way I liked it. "He *is* adorable," Vizhier said seriously, looking at me.

I wonder if she has a boyfriend. I wonder if she'd ever like someone my age. She must be around twenty-three, like Andy.

"I think boys and girls in this country get into all this

with sex too soon," Vizhier said to Andy and me. *"Much* too soon. Twenty is soon enough. Before that you should concentrate on your studies and your family. That's what I did. I didn't even become a woman til I was twenty-one."

"Become a woman?" Andy said. "What do you mean? Get laid for the first time?"

This time Vizhier looked embarrassed. "Yes."

"I love it!" Andy said. "That sounds so great. 'Become a woman.' I don't know, Vi. I think everyone differs. Some people are ready at thirteen, some at sixteen."

"My brother," Vizhier said. "He says he was ready at fourteen." She looked at me.

I grinned. "I'm ready."

"But be nice," she said in that same serious way. "That's the most important thing. To be kind and gentle." After a second she added, "I'm sure you will be."

When she left, I asked Vicki sort of casually, "Does she have a boyfriend?"

Andy laughed. "She's gorgeous, isn't she? Well, half the professors are drooling over her, but she says she has an 'understanding' with someone back in Manila."

"Yeah, I figured." But I felt really disappointed. I was hoping Andy would say she didn't have anyone.

"She's a little old for you, Jase," Andy said, smiling. "Don't you think?"

I shrugged. "I don't know . . . I guess."

"Stick to Vicki," Andy said.

As though I had a choice! After Andy'd gone in and I was lying in bed trying to go to sleep, I felt berserk with horniness. I kept going over the whole evening, with Vizhier brushing her long black hair back and saying, "Be kind and gentle . . . I'm sure you will be." I jerked off a

132

couple of times, each time inventing variations on my usual themes with Vizhier climbing all over me. Maybe I should go to Manila. Maybe girls like that are a dime a dozen there. Maybe she has ten younger sisters and I could work my way through all of them and then pick the one I like the best.

Vicki . . . Vizhier. Well, their names start with the same letter. But that's about the only resemblance, damn it.

FIFTEEN

||||

Ms. KORBEL GOT MARRIED IN A CHURCH ON FEBRUARY 18TH.
When I came out of class the day before the wedding, I saw Vicki looking at me. I thought of all the advice Andy had given me, but I just couldn't do anything. While Andy was saying how sure she was Vicki really liked me, I felt maybe she was right. But once I saw her again in school, I wasn't so sure. Anyhow, how come guys have to be the ones to start things up again? She could come over and say something to me, if she really wants to see me again.

I thought of all that after I came back from Boston because Ms. Korbel told me I could bring Vicki to the wedding if I wanted. I just said I wouldn't, and she didn't press me about it. Probably Vicki would've liked it more than I did. Girls always seem to get all manic with excitement at weddings.

Everybody came back to Ms. Korbel's apartment after the wedding part. There was food on a long table and records playing in the background. Some people danced, but not everybody. Vernon winked at me. "We need a waltz," he said, "Where did Betsy put the Vienna waltzes?"

"I don't know." I looked for her, but she wasn't around.

134

"I can't dance to this kind of thing," he said irritably. "She knows that. I need real music." He turned to me. "Who should I pick? What lovely lady appeals to you?"

I guess he meant who did I think would be good for him, not me. I saw some woman about his age over near the food and said, "One of those?"

He shook his head. "Not my type . . . I like redheads. Do you see any redheads around?"

There was a woman with red hair in a bright blue dress. I couldn't tell how old she was, but she certainly wasn't Vernon's age and she was tall, about half a head taller than him. "There's one over there," I said.

At the sight of her he perked up. "That's the girl. . . . At my age, you don't need to go through a lot of inner debate. You take one look and you know. Here I go!" He marched off, before I could stop him.

I wasn't sure if I was supposed to prevent him from dancing, if that would be too strenuous. I found Ms. Korbel and she said it was okay as long as he didn't overdo. She said I should put the waltz record on.

The lady in the blue dress evidently like to waltz too. She and Vernon whirled around and around, beaming at each other, both looking like they were having a ball. After they'd danced a while, they came back over to me. I wasn't having such a hot time because there didn't seem to be anyone my age. Also, I didn't know anyone except Vernon and Ms. Korbel, and I'm not that great at going over to people I don't know and talking to them.

"This is Jason," Vernon said. "Jason, my next wife, Marguerite Fagan."

Marguerite smiled. "I'd love to marry you, Mr. Korbel, but I have a husband. He just couldn't come today because he's on a business trip."

"Get rid of him!" Vernon said. I couldn't tell if he was joking or not. "What do you want with a husband who's off on business trips all the time? I'm here, I'm available! Get me while I'm hot!"

"You dance beautifully," Marguerite said. To me she said, "He's a wonderful waltzer."

"That's just the first of *many* talents," Vernon said, raising his eyebrows. "I hate to blow my own horn, but at my age, time is precious. You don't meet tall, rapturous redheads every day of the week." He peered at her hair. "It's natural, isn't it?"

She blushed. "With a little help."

"I'm a sucker for redheads," Vernon said. "Jason knows that. It was the bane of my wife's existence. I'd see one and—*boing!* I was a goner."

Marguerite was smiling at me. "What will I do, then, if you meet another redhead after we're married?"

"If I had you, darling," Vernon said, squeezing her, "I wouldn't need anyone else."

I went to get some more food, and when I came back Vernon was dancing with Marguerite again. I just stood there, feeling really out of it. Maybe because we were in the same room I'd been in with Vicki the night of the blackout, I started thinking back on that. I imagined the blackout had never ended, that it was some permanent thing, and Vicki and I were going to live there forever. There was enough food to last, and we got used to it. Only we couldn't see each other at all. It was like being blind, but as if everyone in the world was blind because *nobody* could see anything. The sun had burned out. There was still heat, just no light. But Vicki and I coped pretty well. I had all these ingenious ideas about what to do to while away the time, and she went along with them.

Ms. Korbel passed by. "Dance!" she whispered.

"I am," I said. "I mean, I will." But she had moved on.

I realized I needed to go to the bathroom. The bedroom was empty, just a lot of coats on the bed. After I got out of the bathroom, I didn't especially feel like going back inside. I began drifting around the bedroom, looking at things, wondering when I could go home. Then I saw this money on the bureau. It wasn't real money. It was store money. I knew about that because Mom once took me shopping and she had store money. It's from when you buy something and return it. With the store money you can buy something in the store, but that's all. I counted it. It was $100—ten tens. Without even thinking, I took half of it and put it in my pocket. I put the rest back just the way it had been.

Then, my heart thumping like crazy, I went back into the room where everyone was dancing. I've stolen things in the past. It never was exactly a habit, I just did it occasionally. Always on impulse and usually something I didn't need. Like once—this is a pretty typical example—I was waiting for the bus and I saw this guy sitting outside a bank. He had a transistor radio with him, and all of a sudden he jumped up and went into the bank, leaving the transistor on the bench. I just went over and grabbed it and got on the bus. I didn't need a transistor. I had one already, a better one than that.

I don't know. It's hard to explain if you've never done it. I guess it's the excitement, that you might get caught, and the feeling that you're getting something for nothing. Also, I've never had much cash to fool around with because both my parents are pretty tight with money. They're tight for different reasons. Dad says it's because he grew up poor and realized the value of money. Mom says it's because she was rich till her father went bankrupt, and she realizes if you become dependent on having fancy stuff and suddenly you don't, you can go crazy, so it's better not to become dependent.

What I was thinking of when I took the money was Vicki. She'd told me her birthday was the same week as mine. Hers is March 2nd, mine is the 10th. I thought maybe if I got her something great, that might be the way to patch things over. But I don't have any cash and Mom will scream at me if I ask her. I used to borrow from Ty, but I hate doing that because he gets all sarcastic, like, "How much do you need *this* time?" A couple of times he even charged me interest! And every second he'd be asking me, "When do you think you'll have that ten or fifteen?" Or whatever it was. It was too big a hassle. I figured Ms. Korbel probably got that money as a wedding present, but I could pay her back at some point.

Still, when I went into the room, I felt really self-conscious. Like I was sure everyone looking at me could tell. That's how criminals get caught, by the way. They look or act guilty so even if they haven't left any clues, they give themselves away.

People were starting to go home. I didn't want to be the first to leave because I thought it might look funny. I think taking just half the money was good, because Ms. Korbel might not have counted it. I waited a little while longer and then said I had to go.

At home I counted the money again. It was still fifty. I haven't figured out what to get Vicki, but for fifty I know I can get something good. Just then Mom opened the door. I slipped the money under my pillow and whirled around.

"I didn't know you were home," she said. "How was the wedding?"

"Okay."

"Are you all right? You look a little funny."

I guess mothers have some X-ray powers when it comes to their kids. "Yeah, I'm fine," I said. "I just had a little too much to drink."

"That's stupid!" Mom said. "I thought you gave all that up!"

Mom and Dad are under the impression I haven't touched drugs since last June, when I swore a solemn oath about it. "Everyone was having some," I said, giving her my most innocent look. That's one reason I got that horrible nickname, just in the family, fortunately: Angel Face. Because, if I want, I can look totally angelic, good as gold. I just kind of open my eyes wide and look right at Mom, and I can practically see her melting right in front of me.

"A little can't hurt you, I guess," she said, in a much softer voice. She came over and rumpled my hair. "You've been so quiet lately, Jase. Are you okay?"

"Sure, everything's cool."

"Erin seems to be having some trouble at school," she said. "I wonder if maybe I should go up and visit her. Would you and Ty be all right alone?"

I nodded. She was standing right over my bed and I was scared the pillow might fall off. "We'll be fine."

"I'll think about it," Mom said.

After she left I counted the money again and transferred it to a side pocket in my school knapsack. I want to get the present tomorrow after school because Thursday is Vicki's birthday.

SIXTEEN

||||

I WALKED AROUND OUTSIDE THE STORE FOR A WHILE. I FELT nervous, even though I didn't think there was any reason to be. What I felt afraid of was maybe Ms. Korbel had noticed the money was gone and had called the store and told them to look out for someone trying to spend fifty dollars in store money. Of course, how could they tell it was me, even if she had? But I wondered if maybe I should just spend thirty instead. Then I got a better idea.

I saw a lady about to go into the store, a motherish type. I went over to her and said, "Uh . . . ma'am?"

"Yes?" Sometimes ladies jump away if you ask them the time even, but this lady didn't.

"I was wondering . . . The thing is, my mother gave me fifty dollars in store money to buy myself a jacket here, but they don't seem to have the kind I need. I thought maybe if you're going to buy something in the store, we could, like, trade off. . . . I'll give you the store money and you could give me cash."

"That sounds fine to me," the lady said. "Could I see it?"

I guess she wanted to check and make sure it was real.

She looked at it carefully and then handed me five tens. "I hope you find what you want elsewhere," she said. "You could try Jackson Brothers. I go there for my son. What kind of jacket are you looking for?"

"Um . . . a windbreaker," I stammered.

"Well, try Jackson Brothers. They have a very large selection."

I tried to smile. "Thanks a lot . . . I really appreciate it."

After she'd gone into the store, I sat down and recounted the money. I decided to go to Bloomingdale's, which was down the block a little. I didn't feel like running into the lady again.

I still felt nervous for no special reason. I knew I hadn't cheated the lady. It was a fair trade, but I decided to just buy something nice as fast as I could and then go straight home. On the first floor they had a sale on cashmere sweaters. They were all heaped up in a big pile. The sign said they were marked down to $42.00.

I didn't know Vicki's size exactly, but I decided to get her pink because she once said that was her favorite color. I showed the saleslady a pink one. "I have, like, this sister," I began. My heart was beating really fast, even though there was absolutely nothing to be scared about. "Only I'm not sure what size she wears."

"How old is she?"

"About fifteen."

"And is she very . . . well developed?" The saleslady was pretty well developed herself. I tried not to stare below her neck.

"Fairly much."

"Probably a thirty-four would do, but why don't you take a thirty-six? Girls like them a little loose." She smiled. "And she might grow into it."

I gave her the money and she wrapped it up in some gold paper. I put it back in my knapsack. I was a little scared Mom might find it if I left it in my room, but it's only three days to Vicki's birthday so I didn't think it was too likely.

On the way home I suddenly wondered if I was right thinking Vicki had said pink was her favorite color. Maybe it was Erin who said that. Maybe Vicki said it was a color she hated. I couldn't remember why I thought that. Still, most girls like pink. And cashmere is this really soft, nice wool. The more I thought about it, the more I wondered if I should've just gotten her a book. But with a book you don't know if the person has read it already. I could've gotten her a fish for her aquarium. . . . Then I wondered why I was getting her anything. She was the one who screamed at *me*. What if, when I try to give it to her, she starts screaming again, even worse insults? I decided if she did that, I'd say something equally bad back, like that she was ugly and not even that great at basketball. I'd just make it up at the moment.

In class that day Ms. Korbel started talking about cancer. She asked if anyone knew what the difference was between benign and malignant.

"Malignant is the bad kind," Tim Wolf said. "If you have that, you die. If you have the other kind, you don't."

"Is that what most of you think also?" Ms. Korbel went on. "Raise your hands if you agree."

It sounded basically right to me, so I raised my hand. About half the other kids did too. Ms. Korbel asked Otis, who hadn't raised his hand, to explain why he didn't think it was true.

"Because you can operate," he said. "They did that on my uncle. They cut out all that bad stuff, the malignant stuff, and then he had treatments and now he's okay."

Ms. Korbel said that was true, that malignant cells were dangerous but could sometimes be treated. "I had a malignant breast cancer," she said, "which is why I had to have my left breast removed. That was three years ago and I've been well ever since."

Like I mentioned, I've been trying to figure out which breast of hers was the real one all year. But it was funny. Even knowing, they both looked pretty much alike. Ms. Korbel went on to talk more about that, about how everybody would feel if they had to have some part of their body removed, about how much people felt they were valued according to their bodies and how they looked. Of course I don't have breasts, but it would be weird to have something removed you used a lot, like a hand or a foot, having everyone stare at you. In this grocery store near our house the owner has a fake hand. He can use it pretty well, but it's hard not to notice it, even when you've seen it a million times.

When we got of that class, I went over to Vicki. Sometimes she's with her girlfriends, but today she wasn't. "Are you doing anything after school?" I asked.

She looked right at me, frowning. "Why do you want to know?"

"I just wondered. . . . Are you?"

"Not especially," she said in a friendlier way.

"Then, could you, like, meet me?" I felt like I had peanut butter on the roof of my mouth. My tongue seemed to have trouble moving around.

She hesitated. "Okay." She kept looking at me as though trying to figure it out. I didn't know what else to say, so I just said, "See you later," and walked off.

I thought of saying "Happy Birthday," but I was scared . . . I don't know why.

It was a nice day, cool, a little windy. I went outside to wait for her. I was hoping Otis wouldn't come by and see me; he didn't. When Vicki first came out, she was with this friend of hers, Ruth, but they just walked a little bit and then Ruth walked off in the other direction. Vicki looked around and saw me. She walked over to where I was sitting. I still had the present in my knapsack. I figured if she acted awful, I wouldn't even let her know I'd gotten it.

"Hi," she said. She smiled. "So, how've you been?"

"Okay."

"It's been fifty-two days since we spoke to each other."

"It has?" I was surprised she knew it so exactly.

She nodded. "We had that fight on January ninth and it's March second."

"It's your birthday," I told her.

Vicki looked surprised that I remembered. "Yeah."

"Well, I got you this present." I opened the knapsack, took it out, and handed it to her.

She just stood there, her eyes wider, still looking surprised. "How come you got me a present?"

I shrugged. "I just felt like it."

Vicki looked down. "I feel awful . . . I said all those terrible things to you."

"Well . . ."

"See, I thought you'd be getting Marcy into a lot of trouble because she really likes Otis a lot, but it doesn't seem to have mattered much. That made me feel so dumb."

I decided to help her out. "I still shouldn't have said anything."

"You were loyal to him because he's your friend," she explained. "That shows you're a good person."

It's funny—my mother and Andy do that a lot, take something I've done that isn't good at all and find a good reason why I did it. I hesitated. "It was mainly that you said I was hopeless. The rest I didn't—"

"That was so stupid!" Vicki said fiercely. "I have a really bad temper sometimes!" Impulsively she leaned over and kissed me on the cheek. "I apologize."

I felt a lot better.

"Aren't you going to open the present?" I asked, smiling up at her.

"Why don't you come over to my house and I'll open it there?"

"Okay."

We walked to Vicki's house. I wheeled my bike alongside her. When we got there, I parked it outside. The house was quiet. We went up the stairs and into her room.

"I got rid of the kribensis," Vicki said, turning around. "Remember? The fish that were eating the other ones? First I took them back and got two more kribensis, but it turns out all of them are mean. They just have to be. It's genetic, I guess."

"It probably helps them in the ocean," I suggested.

"That's what Daddy said." Vicki looked mournful. "But I still don't like them. It'd be different if I hadn't been feeding them enough." She sat down on the bed and opened the present. For a minute she just sat there, looking into the box. "Wow," she said finally. "It's gorgeous." She touched it. "Cashmere . . . I never had a cashmere sweater. Aren't they horribly expensive?"

"Well, it was on sale."

She jumped up and kissed me again, this time on the lips. "You're such a generous person," she said. "I'm really stingy." She held the sweater in front of her and looked in the mirror. "Pink is my favorite color. *This* kind of pink. Not that pale yucky kind."

"Why don't you try it on?"

Vicki hesitated. "Okay." With her back to me she unbuttoned her plaid shirt, took it off, and then slipped the sweater over her head. I only saw her breasts (she had a bra on) for a second. Then she turned around. "How do you think it looks?"

"Terrific." I wanted to say that I'd liked the way she looked without it even better, but I wasn't sure how that would go over. I remembered how in our argument she said boys only thought of sex. The trouble was I *was* thinking of it, especially because we were in her bedroom and the pink color was almost like skin, in a way.

I stood up and put my arms around her, stroking the sweater on the sleeve. "It *is* soft," I said.

Vicki turned around. "Do I seem prudish?" she said suddenly. "Compared to that other girl?"

"Which one?"

"The one you did all those things with."

I wished I had the courage to admit that was a total lie, but I didn't. "Well, she was older," I said.

We sat down together on the bed. "I went out with Russ Pharr a few times since we had that fight," she said. "I guess you knew that."

I shook my head.

"It was more basically a physical attraction," Vicki went on. "I mean, I can't talk to him like I can to you."

That made me feel totally lousy. Next thing she was going to say she wanted me to be her friend! "He doesn't have much up here," I said, touching my head.

"No, he does," Vicki said. "He just seems that way because he's shy. . . . But I think he has slightly perverse ideas about girls."

I wondered what she meant. I think I have slightly perverse ideas myself.

"Promise you won't tell anyone this, ever?" Vicki said intensely.

"Sure, I promise," I said, sure I was going to hear something that would ruin the rest of my day if not the year or my life.

"Well, once he came over and he wanted to tie me up! With rope! To a chair . . . I mean, all he did was kiss me, and I would've done that anyway. And then he wanted me to tie *him* up. I don't get the point of that. Do you?"

Actually, I do get the point of it, since if someone was tied up, you could do practically anything with them you wanted. But I just said, "He sounds sort of weird."

"He is," Vicki said. "He's going to a psychiatrist, and, like, he comes from a really strange home. His mother keeps having nervous breakdowns, and his father's got M.S., so you can't blame him. But still . . ."

"Yeah," I said. Naturally, I was getting horribly turned on by all these lurid stories of Vicki tied to chairs, but I realized I might fuck up completely by doing anything except sitting there with this totally phony, concerned expression.

"And basically," she said, "he's not even that . . . I mean, he has a good body. He's good at basketball, but that's about all. And he has this weird sense of humor, not even humor. . . . Like I told him about the kribensis? Not the ones you saw, but the other ones we got to replace them, and while I was in the bathroom, he ate them! He said he did it to teach them a lesson. Don't you think that's weird?"

"Definitely." I put my arm around her and kissed her. "He sounds like someone to stay away from."

"That's what Daddy said," Vicki said. "I told him about Russ swallowing the kribensis, not about the thing with the chair, and he said it sounded like Russ had problems."

"I have a problem," I said.

"What?" She looked really concerned.

"Would you take the sweater off?"

"Sure." She slipped it over her head. "What's the problem?"

"Well, it's just that I feel—"

"Me too."

And without my having to explain anything further, we lay down on her bed and started making out. Vicki let me take her bra off—she had a new one that came off more easily—and I fooled around with her breasts for a long time. She let me touch them and kiss them, while she lay with her arms around me. But she wouldn't let me go below her waist. "It's just we might get carried away," she whispered.

I already was carried away, totally. I would've swallowed a whole tankful of kribensis. "Do you think we ever—"

"Sure," she said. "But I have to get used to the idea first."

I don't know exactly what "idea" she meant. I wonder if Vicki smokes pot. I have the feeling if she was slightly stoned she might be a lot more relaxed. She's semi-relaxed, but you can tell she's nervous too. After that, since I knew we wouldn't go any further, I tried to mentally calm myself down. Vicki got up and put her sweater back on. I watched her fish for a while. Watching fish is calming. You'd think they wouldn't be that happy, in a small tank like that, but it looks like a perfect, beautiful world, with the lights dim and the green plants moving back and forth. Maybe I'll be reborn as a fish and drift around in a tank, waiting for some big hand to sprinkle fish food down for me. Not a bad life.

SEVENTEEN

"**Y**OU HAVEN'T BEEN AROUND IN SUCH A LONG TIME, OTIS," Mom said.

Otis had come by after school. We were in the kitchen, having a snack. "Well, I've been kind of busy," he said.

I smirked. Busy! I wish *I* could be busy like that. Mom looked at me. "Have you worked things out for the weekend?"

She meant when she'd be away visiting Erin. "Sure."

"What plans have you made?"

"Mom, I'll be fine . . . I don't mind staying here by myself. It'll be nice and peaceful."

"I could stay here," Otis offered.

Mom looked delighted. "Would you? That would be so good of you. . . . I know I worry to excess at times, but I'd feel a million times better with two of you here."

Otis smiled at her. "No problem."

I was surprised, since he'd been seeing Marcy every weekend for the past couple of months. I wondered if they'd had a fight again. When we went into my room, I asked him. He looked sheepish. "Well, actually, I was thinking it might be kind of a perfect opportunity."

"For what?"

"A double sleepover . . . with Vicki and Marcy."

I shook my head. "Forget it. Vicki'd never agree in a million years. And how about their parents?"

"They could make something up . . . . Why don't you ask her, anyway? What have you got to lose?"

Technically, that's true. Nothing ventured, nothing gained, as they say. But I was scared Vicki might explode again and say all I had on my mind was sex. I didn't feel like risking that. Otis must've seen me looking uncertain, because he said, "How about if I mention it to Marcy and she can ask Vicki . . . I thought you were back together again."

"We are, sort of. . . . It's just—" I looked at him. "Are you and Marcy actually, like, doing it?"

Otis laughed. "Yeah, we actually are."

Damn. I figured they were.

"What's with Vicki?" Otis asked, leaning back in my desk chair. "She uptight or something?"

"I don't know. She kind of goes both ways. Sometimes she's fine, but sometimes—"

"Listen, I wouldn't have gotten anywhere if Marcy hadn't made it with that other guy. I guess I should be grateful to him in a way. It made it a lot easier."

I thought of Andy's friend Vizhier. That's what I need, someone who's done everything, where it isn't a big struggle. I'm not good at struggles. Frankly, I don't basically see why anyone would want to have sex with me, so if they seem reluctant for whatever reason, I don't push it. I've read books where guys do this really subtle snow job, half-pretending they don't want to do it, but all the time keeping on getting the girl more and more turned on, till they're in the middle of doing it and she's still trying to figure out how far to go. I don't think I could pull off something like that. But I agreed to let Marcy ask Vicki. That didn't sound like it could get me into any serious trouble.

Surprisingly, Vicki said yes. She came up to me at lunchtime—we've been taking lunch outside, away from school, now that the weather's nice—and said she'd figured out what to tell her parents, and anyway, they were probably going away that weekend themselves to visit her aunt and uncle. I felt so happy I leaned over and hugged her.

She smiled at me in an embarrassed way. "The only thing is," she said. "Jase?"

"Yeah?"

"I just . . . I'm not sure I want to . . . I mean, I don't think we should necessarily do anything that we wouldn't do otherwise."

"That's okay," I said, disappointed but not wrecked.

"We can sleep in the same bed and everything, only I'm not sure I want to—"

I put my arm around her. Sleeping in the same bed sounded terrific. "We'll just do whatever you want," I said, afraid I was sounding like one of those smooth guys I've read about.

"It's not that I'm not attracted to you," she went on softly, "or that I don't in some ways feel like . . . But I just don't know. I always figured I'd be sixteen at least when I did it for the first time."

"Aren't you?" I'd thought she'd turned sixteen.

"No, I skipped a grade. I'm just fifteen."

"Still, you're mature for your age," I said encouragingly.

"I know," Vicki agreed. "I am in some ways, but—" Suddenly she looked right into my eyes. "Maybe this is some horrible, sexist, backward thing, but I think for a girl it's like, well, it *is* kind of a big deal. Not that you feel you want to marry the person, but . . . I can't always tell how you feel about me."

That was strange, her saying that. I thought I'd made how I felt pretty clear. "What do you mean?"

"Well, like that whole time after we had the fight, you didn't even *speak* to me! You didn't even *look* at me!"

"I was scared you'd cream me if I did."

"It was like the whole thing rolled off your back, and here *I* was going around obsessing about it twenty-four hours a day, whether I'd done the right thing or not."

"I wasn't the one dating other people," I couldn't resist pointing out.

"That's true." She sighed. "Well, anyway, it should be fun, don't you think? I'm looking forward to it a lot."

"Me too." I kissed her. Her face was half in the sun, and it made her skin look shiny and pink. Sometimes we make out a little during lunch hour, but I've found that's basically not a terrific idea. My concentration is weak enough, and when we do that, I totally blank out for the rest of the afternoon, inventing variations on what's happened in which Vicki suddenly turns into a nymphomaniac who can't get enough sex and is stuck on a desert island with me for ten years or so.

Otis slept over Friday, and Saturday, in the late afternoon, Vicki and Marcy came over together. Vicki's parents think she's at Marcy's. Her brother knows the real story. He sounds like a good guy. At the door he smiled at her and said to me, "Take care of her, okay?"

"Sure," I said, not positive exactly how he meant that.

I'd thought we would just order pizza, but Marcy and Vicki had planned a huge Italian meal, with sausages and peppers and linguini and garlic bread. They had everything in a carton and carried it straight into the kitchen. "We'll call you when it's ready," Marcy said.

She looked fantastic. All she was wearing was jeans and a blue sweater, but she has a figure where that's definitely enough to get your attention immediately. Vicki looked nice too, but not in the same league from a purely physical point of view. Otis and I went into the living room, had a few beers, and watched TV.

"She's a good cook," he said, as though I was worried.

"I'll bet."

I don't know if Vicki's good or not—she's never cooked anything. But somehow she doesn't seem so much the domestic type. I was glad it was Italian food, because that's the one kind of food I can eat at any hour of day or night. They called us in when everything was ready. They'd fixed the table up with real napkins and turned the lights down so it was semi-dark. It made it seem like a restaurant, almost. The only bad thing was it made me think of the last fancy meal I'd had at that table, over Thanksgiving.

Marcy served us. She and Vicki had beer too. I was glad because, like I've said, sometimes Vicki is a little nervous, and I thought alcohol might help in that regard. "This is really great," I said enthusiastically.

"My mother taught me," Marcy said. She doesn't have as much of an accent as she used to, but still a little bit. "It's her specialty."

"I can't even boil an egg," Vicki said. "But I figure that's good, because if you're a good cook, once you get married your husband expects you to do all the cooking."

"That's the way it's supposed to be," Otis said in a teasing way.

But Vicki flared up. "According to who?" she snapped.

"I'm only going to marry someone who'll do half of everything."

"Half of shoveling snow and fixing the furnace?" he said.

"Sure," she said, a little less certainly. "I can shovel snow."

"He's going to be half-pregnant too, huh?" Otis helped himself to more garlic bread.

"Why not? Maybe they'll have figured out a way for guys to get pregnant by then," Vicki said.

"No way," Otis said. "It's biologically impossible."

I hope so. I wouldn't want to marry someone and have to be half-pregnant.

"What would be great," Vicki went on, "is if they could figure out a way for the woman to be pregnant half the time, like the first four months, and the man the other half. Like with birds sitting on eggs."

"Nature got it right the first time," Otis said. "Why fiddle around with it?"

Vicki glared at him. "What's right about it?" she said hotly. "It's right that women have to die in childbirth and take all the responsibility in birth control? And husbands can desert their families and—"

"Hey, man, calm her down, will you?" Otis said to me. He smiled at Vicki. "Let's all relax, how about it?"

I didn't know what to say. I looked at Marcy, who was just eating quietly, and then at Vicki, who was looking down at the tablecloth with an angry expression. Why don't I get girls who just eat quietly? I hoped it wasn't going to wreck the whole evening, especially the later part. "Um, could I have some more?" I said, reaching my plate out to Marcy. "Do you cook other things too?"

I figured Italian cooking was a general topic that wouldn't

154

get anyone excited. "I cook a good roast chicken," Marcy said, smiling at me.

"You know what they do at her house?" Otis said. "They give the chicken some whiskey to calm it down, and then, when they cut its throat, the blood comes spurting out more, and it makes it really tender."

Vicki put down her fork. "You buy live chickens and kill them?" she asked Marcy in horror.

"My mother does it," Marcy said.

"Ugh," Vicki looked at me. "How awful!"

"Someone's got to kill them," Otis said. "How about the pig who gave his life for this." He pointed at the sausage. "They didn't just give him an overdose of sleeping pills."

There was a pause.

"I don't feel so hungry anymore," Vicki said faintly.

"What's for dessert?" I asked. I hoped it wasn't anything that had met a gruesome death.

It turned out to be a kind of Italian pastry that Marcy had bought at a store in New York. We had coffee with it. By the time we finished dinner and cleaning up the kitchen, it was almost eleven. Otis said, "Well, see you guys in the morning." I'd told him he could have Ty's room.

I hadn't figured we'd go to bed that early. I'd thought we'd stay up and watch "The Late Show" or something. "*I* don't feel that sleepy," Vicki said, looking at me.

"Me neither," I said.

Marcy and Otis disappeared into Ty's room. That was kind of awkward. It was pretty clear why they were turning in so early. I began feeling uncomfortable, even though Vicki and I have been alone together lots of times. We found a movie on TV. Vicki snuggled up next to me on the couch, and I began feeling better. About a minute later,

Marcy came in. "Do you have any fresh towels?" she asked.

I jumped up. "Oh, uh, sure," I said.

She was wearing this nightgown that was kind of like a dress you'd wear to a dance. It was made of some kind of filmy white material and came down to her ankles. I could see her nipples through it, even though it was pretty dark in the room. I gave her a bunch of towels from the linen closet. "Sleep well," I said, unable to stop ogling her. Lucky Otis.

I was so turned on I felt like maybe Vicki and I should turn in as well, even though I wasn't sure how it would work out. "Maybe we should go to sleep too," I said hesitantly, looking sideways at Vicki.

She whirled on me. "Listen, I told you, we're not going to. . . . Just because *she* does it, doesn't mean *I* do!"

"I know," I said quickly. "I just felt a little tired." I thought of the pot I had in my room and wondered about bringing some out.

"All you did all through dinner was stare at her breasts," Vicki said accusingly.

"Well, she is kind of—"

"So? It's rude. . . . And if all you want is someone with big boobs, go find someone like that!"

As though it were that easy! "Look, she's stacked and a great cook and she puts out," I said, softly in case Otis and Marcy were listening, "but I love you."

I hadn't planned to say it that way—that's just the way it came out. Vicki softened immediately. "I love you too, Jase. . . . Only why didn't you defend me when Otis started in about how women had to be so old-fashioned and everything? Not *all* guys are like that! My brother isn't."

"I should've," I said, wanting her to stay in a good mood.

"If you were married, would you do half of everything?" she asked intensely. "Cooking and all?"

"Sure." I put my arm around her and kissed her neck. Especially sex. I'll definitely do half of that. We began kissing and making out a little. "Listen, Vick, I have this pot in my room. . . . Do you feel like—"

"Sure, I'd like to," Vicki said.

It's funny. With some things she flies off the handle so easily, and with others, where I expect a big fight, she's fine. We smoked a little. I didn't want to get totally stoned. In fact, I was doing it at least half to get Vicki in a more relaxed mood. I think it worked—somewhat, anyway. She let me take off her bra and then pulled her sweater over her head and tossed it on the floor. She began leaning against me. "I wonder how that expression started," she said. "Put out . . . I mean, you're not actually putting anything out."

"True." I wasn't exactly ready for a long linguistic discussion at that point.

"Do you want me to take all my clothes off?" she said suddenly.

I tried to act calm about the idea. "You could . . . only maybe we should go inside." I doubted Otis and Marcy were about to come out of Ty's room, but still.

EIGHTEEN

||||

WE WENT INTO MY ROOM. I'D CLEANED IT PRETTY MUCH. AT least the bed was made, and I'd put fresh sheets on. "Your bed is so small," Vicki said, eyeing it with concern.

"Yeah, sorry." I sat down and looked up at her pleadingly, like a puppy hoping someone would take it home from the pound.

"You can take your clothes off too," she said. "Only, Jase?"

"What?"

"Promise you won't, like, rape me or anything."

I laughed. "Don't worry."

"And when we go to sleep, I want to wear my nightgown, and I want you to wear pajamas, okay?"

"Okay."

She was still talking, but I was so busy staring at her taking off her clothes that I didn't hear what else she said. ". . . that way," she finished. With nothing on, Vicki's body looked great. I mean, I haven't seen any other girls in the flesh besides my sisters, but it looked round and soft and like she was half glowing. "I know I'm too fat," she said, seeming embarrassed by my staring at her.

"No, you're not," I said. "You're beautiful."

We lay down in bed with our arms around each other. The room seemed to be spinning around and around, like we were on the ceiling and everything else was down below. I don't know if it was being somewhat stoned or just the fact of being there together like that. The light was still on in the corner so we could see each other's expressions. Vicki looked down at my cock. It was pointing straight up at her. "Do you want me to do anything special?" she said.

"Whatever you feel like." I felt nervous, despite the pot.

"Tell me what to do . . . I'm scared I'll do it wrong."

"Just touch it." I took her hand and brought it down. She touched it very lightly, like a dog that might bite her.

"You can do it harder than that," I said.

"How hard? I don't want to hurt you." She looked worried. "I thought it was supposedly the most sensitive part of a guy's body."

"It's not *that* sensitive," I said. I took her hand and showed her how I do it.

"What if it just suddenly goes off?"

"It doesn't happen that fast."

Vicki began stroking me. I wished in a way she didn't feel we had to discuss what was happening in such detail while it was happening. I have hard enough trouble concentrating on one thing at a time. I closed my eyes and let myself touch her all over. A lot of things went racing through my head. Bits and pieces of the usual turn-on fantasies I have while I jerk off. But the fact that it was actually happening made me come a lot faster than usual. When I did, Vickie gave a start. Some of the gunk had gotten on her hand. She looked down at it.

"It's not actually so much," she said thoughtfully. "I

thought it would be a whole lot. . . . Did you like it? Did I do it all right?"

I hugged her. "It was great."

"What were you thinking about?"

Jesus, Vicki and her questions! "Just—various things."

"Did you think about Marcy and pretend I was her and that I had big boobs?"

"No."

"When I masturbate I make up these odd stories," she said. "Sometimes from books or whatever. Only I change them around."

I know supposedly girls masturbate. They told us that in Sex Ed, but I can never imagine it. "Don't you ever imagine real people?"

"No . . . Do you think that's strange?"

I shrugged sheepishly. "Whatever works." I wondered if she wanted me to do it to her too. It seemed like that would be a lot more complicated, finding the right place. Otis has a book on female anatomy which I've studied fairly thoroughly, but things are never where they're supposed to be. It's like in science where they show you what you're supposed to see under the microscope and it never looks anything like that. But before I could suggest it, Vicki said, "I guess I'll put my nightgown on."

In a way I was relieved. Maybe she didn't even want me to do it. Vicki's nightgown was pretty, but nowhere near as sexy as Marcy's. Well, I guess she's not the type so much. Just then we heard a sound coming from Ty's room. It wasn't exactly a groan of passion. In fact, it could have been almost anything, a book falling off a shelf or someone turning in bed, but since we knew they were in there, it was embarrassing.

"She really loves him," Vicki said. "I hope he loves her."

"Sure," I said, though in fact Otis and I've never discussed it in much detail. "He does."

"My brother says sometimes guys that age just try to see how far they can get. They, like, pretend to like the girl, but deep down really they don't. He said he even did that once and now he regrets it a lot." She gazed at me solemnly. She still looked pretty, even with her nightgown back on. "You don't seem like that type. Are you?"

"What?" I said. I was trying to find a decent pair of pajamas. Usually I just sleep in my underwear, so most of them were about two sizes too small.

"Do you think you're that type, that would lie about things to girls just to get them to do what you want?"

"Never." It's funny. I wish I knew what type I was. Like, I steal sometimes but I don't think of myself as a thief, and I lie but I don't think of myself as a liar, and I smoke a lot of pot but I don't think of myself as a druggie. I don't know *what* I think of myself as.

I finally found some old wrinkled cotton pajamas that I hadn't worn in a long time.

"Won't you be cold?" Vicki asked. She was already in bed.

"I'll have you . . . and the electric blanket." I showed her how to turn it on. I put it on a low setting.

"Can't they electrocute you while you're sleeping?" Vicki said.

"Don't worry."

I turned off the light. Like I said, basically my bed is just for one person, so we had to sleep fairly closely entwined, which didn't bother me at all. It was a great way to fall asleep, in fact. But in the middle of the night something embarrassing happened. You'll have to believe me about this, because there weren't any witnesses. I guess maybe my subconscious was all excited at being in the bed with Vicki at such close quarters, though I don't remember having any special dreams or anything. I woke up lying on top of her, trying to make her. I had my hand under her nightgown so it was a fairly incriminating position. Maybe I would have slept through it all. I've never heard of that— someone sleeping through their first sexual experience—but I swear I was totally sound asleep when suddenly Vicki said, "Stop that!"

The first time she said it I hardly even heard her. It was like it was coming from far away, so I just kept on. Then she gave me a shove that landed me right on the floor. Man, that hurt. I landed with a thunk. "Hey, what's wrong?" I said, bewildered. It was pitch black and freezing. I couldn't see her or the bed or anything.

"You said you wouldn't do anything," Vicki said. "And just when I fall asleep, you're climbing all over me!"

"I was asleep," I said, climbing back into bed and feeling myself to make sure I hadn't broken any bones.

"You were not! . . . You were saying my name."

That's a relief anyway, compared to various other names I could've said. "Vicki listen, I swear, I was sound asleep. I don't even know what I was doing."

She told me.

"Well, it must've been my unconscious."

"Sure."

"Look, what can I say? I really was totally asleep. But being in such a small bed, maybe I just . . . Do you want me to sleep on the floor? I have a sleeping bag."

"Well, will you promise not to do it again?"

"It might just happen the way it did before, without my even knowing it." I tried to sound contrite.

She hesitated. "Will you be comfortable in the sleeping bag?"

"Sure, no problem."

The problem was getting up out of the nice warm bed with the electric blanket and Vicki and hunting around in my closet for the sleeping bag. I found it. It had that musty, foresty smell sleeping bags get. I unrolled it on the floor. When I was in it, Vicki reached down and touched my hand. "I'm sorry, Jase," she said. "Sleep well, okay?"

"You too."

The other problem was usually I have an air mattress I blow up, which cushions you from the floor or earth or whatever. But that was in Ty's closet, and I didn't want to go in there and interrupt some lurid scene. So I just snuggled down as far as I could and finally fell asleep.

Once you're asleep, you're asleep. It doesn't seem to matter much where you are. Only when I woke up, Vicki wasn't in bed anymore. I looked at the clock near my bed. Eleven! I hadn't expected to sleep *that* late. I washed up, pulled on some clothes and was about to go out when all of them, Otis, Vicki, and Marcy, came into the room. Otis had a white handkerchief in his hand.

"This is going to be totally painless," he said.

"What?" I stared at all of them, bewildered.

"Just close your eyes man. . . . It's a surprise."

Vicki and Marcy were smiling in a friendly way. They were all dressed. I wondered when they'd gotten up. I let Otis tie the handkerchief around my eyes. Then Vicki took one of my hands and Marcy took the other and they led me through the house. I think all they did was take me through various rooms. I wasn't always sure what room I was in, and once I thought we might be outside, but I think it was just they'd opened a window wide. Then they brought me to a chair and sat me down.

"Hey, come on, can I take this thing off now?" I said.

I heard Marcy and Vicki giggling. "In a second."

I heard footsteps and smelled various delicious things, but I wasn't sure what they were. Then someone undid the handkerchief, and they all yelled, "Happy birthday!"

That's right, it was my birthday: March 10th. I'd really forgotten all about it because of the excitement of the weekend. They'd made a big stack of pancakes, and on the top one—there must have been maybe ten of them—were sixteen candles, all lit. I blew them out and looked down at all the pancakes. "These are all for me?"

"All you want," Otis said. "Don't worry. We'll help you out."

Vicki and Marcy brought out bacon and syrup and fresh coffee, and all of them dug in too. "*I* made the pancakes," Vicki said proudly. "It's my brother's recipe."

"They're fantastic," I said, with my mouth half full.

"*I* made the bacon," Marcy said.

"What'd *you* do?" I asked Otis.

He grinned. "I helped out. So, you're sweet sixteen and never been—"

I turned red, thinking of the night before, but Vicki didn't seem to harbor any ill feelings. She jumped up and kissed me on both cheeks and then on the lips. She tasted of maple syrup. I wondered if they'd thought it was funny finding the sleeping bag on the floor. I wondered if Vicki had said anything.

After breakfast they brought out a present. It was an album I'd wanted for a long time: "Sandinista," by the Clash. They must've chipped in, because it's a three-record set and usually sells for around twenty bucks. "Hey, thanks," I said. I was beginning to feel terrific.

"You said you wanted it," Vicki said.

"It's what I wanted the most," I said.

The rest of the morning, till around two, we just hung around the house, listening to records, reading. Marcy had to do some reading for a paper, and Vicki was trying to write a composition for Biology. Ms. Korbel had asked us to write about how we'd feel if we lost part of our body from an operation or an accident or something.

"That was weird that day," Otis said. He was sitting next to Marcy on the couch, playing chess with this computer set Ty got from Juliet for Christmas. "Her telling us how she had to have one of her boobs cut off."

"But she got married," Marcy said. "So I guess her husband doesn't care."

"Well, you don't love someone for their body," Vicki said hotly. After a second she added, "I mean, not *just* for their body. . . . You can love their mind or their personality or something."

It's hard not to let that enter in, though, as it were. I thought of how Vicki had looked in the dim light of the room with her clothes off. I've seen millions of naked girls in magazines with a lot better figures than Vicki had, but it being real makes a big, big difference.

At three Vicki's brother picked up Vicki and Marcy. He smiled at me. "Everything go okay?" he asked.

I tried not to look embarrassed. He sounds like a good guy from what Vicki has said, but she *is* his sister. I hope she doesn't tell him about what happened in the middle of the night.

After they left Otis and I went around the house, just checking to make sure everything looked pretty much like it had before. As I was rolling my sleeping bag up, Otis smiled. "Guess she wasn't ready, huh?"

I felt too embarrassed to describe exactly what had happened. "She took her clothes off."

"And—"

"And we just horsed around a little." I sighed.

Otis put his hand on my shoulder. "Patience, man."

"Yeah, I know. . . . How was it with Marcy?" I wasn't sure I even wanted to know.

He looked dreamy. "Fantastic . . . I guess maybe I love her or something."

"Won't her parents have a fit if they find out?"

"Because we're making it or because I'm black?"

"Either."

He looked uncomfortable. "I don't know. The first, definitely. The second—well, they don't seem prejudiced, they know we're going out a lot . . . I guess they figure we're young and all. They almost bend over backwards sometimes to make me feel it's all cool. I dunno."

I don't know how Mom and Dad would react if I had a black girlfriend. Mom has so many prejudices that I can't keep track of all of them, and they almost seem to cancel each other out. Like, she was raised a Presbyterian but she makes jokes about the church, and she married Dad, who's Jewish, but gets mad if he tells jokes about Jewish girls.

After Otis left, I took one more look around and decided everything was about back to normal. It was lucky everybody left early because Mom came home about half an hour later. I hadn't expected her till after dinner. She looked tired. She said Erin had been okay. "But that school! I don't know. I think if I have to sit through one more bullshit session with one more tight-assed lady psychologist I'll burst at the seams! All this crap about broken homes and

166

how important it is for the parent to 'make it up' to the kid. Who's going to make it up to the parent? Anyhow, was it *me* who shoved off? Why isn't Mort there listening to all that garbage? He's the one who was so eager to start a new and glorious life, quote unquote. And *I'm* the one who has to pick up the goddamn pieces." She glared at me.

"Well, yeah, I guess it's hard," I said.

She looked calmer. "Were you okay, Jase? Did Otis stay the whole time?"

I nodded, trying to look as I thought I would've if that's all that'd happened.

"Oh, and hon, happy birthday! You know, it wasn't till I was coming home that I even remembered. Isn't that awful? I'll get you something next week."

I showed her the album they'd given me.

Mom doesn't know a whole lot about rock music, but she said, "Three records, what a generous gift."

"Well, they all got it together," I said.

"All who?" Mom said, looking at me keenly.

I swallowed. "All, uh, of the guys at school. It was like a collective present."

"Well, that's certainly very thoughtful of them. . . . Did Mort call to wish you a happy birthday?"

I shook my head. Then I remembered that we'd taken the phone off the hook the night before in case Marcy or Vicki's parents called.

"Isn't that typical?" Mom said. "If you heard him go on at parties, you'd think having kids was such a big important deal in his life, but he can't even remember their birthdays!"

I snuck back into the kitchen and put the phone back on the hook. Within the hour Dad and Andy called, so evidently they hadn't forgotten after all. Andy said she was

167

sending me a book, and Dad said he'd give me my present when he saw me next. The next day I got a handmade card Erin had drawn. It was a lot of purple unicorns galloping in a big flowery field. She's nuts about unicorns. Ty didn't even mention my birthday till Tuesday, when he had to stay home. "What're you, sixteen or something?" he asked.

"No, eighty-three," I said. What a jerk. As though he doesn't know how old I am!

He said his present was that he was going to cancel a debt of twenty dollars that I owed him. According to him, it was twenty-four seventy, counting interest. What a generous brother! Then, just as I was sitting in my room trying to get some work done, he came in and said, "What the fuck's been going on?"

"What?"

"In my room. . . . What'd you do—bring some girl here or something?"

The door to my room was open. I jumped up and closed it. "Hey, keep your voice down, okay?"

He looked really pissed. "Why'd you have to use *my* room? What's wrong with yours?"

I wasn't sure how much to tell him. "We just kind of ended up there," I said. I wish I'd thought of changing the sheets, but maybe he would've noticed that too.

He grinned. "Well, I guess you finally made it, huh?"

I felt funny since I hadn't, but I didn't want to admit that. I just shrugged.

"How was she?"

"Who?"

"Well, wasn't it Vicki? Or do you have some harem I don't know about?"

I didn't want to get Vicki into any kind of trouble, but all

I could think of to say was, "She doesn't want me to tell anyone about it."

Ty nodded understandingly. "Juliet was like that at first. She was scared all her friends would disown her or something. But now most of them have gone under, so it's no big deal. In fact, they all keep changing boyfriends every second. They think of us as some old married couple just because we've gone together almost a year."

This was just about the longest conversation I'd had with Ty in almost ten years. Of course, it was based on an erroneous assumption on his part, but still. "Vicki's just fifteen," I said.

He whistled. "Better not let her parents find out or—" He made a motion of slitting his throat.

"Don't worry."

He gave me a farewell wink and sauntered out of the room.

The best present was the album, though. I lay on my bed in the afternoon, remembering the better parts of the weekend and listening to it. It was definitely the best birthday I've had.

NINETEEN

*"W*HY CAN'T *I GO TO THE WEDDING?" MOM SAID. "JUST* tell me."

It was the morning of the day Dad and Randy were getting married. Erin and Andy had flown in the night before, and all of us were having breakfast. We didn't have to be there till three. Actually, I'd woken up feeling crummy. I had a sore throat and a fever of a hundred and one. Normally, I'd have stayed home, but I figured Dad wasn't going to get married that many times. Also, I didn't feel like I couldn't make it, just slightly weak and out of it.

"Because they don't *want* you there," Andy said in exasperation. "Would you want Dad there if you were getting married?"

"Sure I would," Mom said. "I mean, look, we spent the better part of three decades together, we've raised four kids—"

"That has nothing to do with it," Andy said.

"Why can't I at least call and ask her? Maybe *she'd* like me there, even if he wouldn't." Mom laughed scornfully. "I can give her some tips." She made a half motion toward the phone.

Andy leapt up. "Mom, it's masochistic," she said. "Don't!"

Ty got up to get a glass of milk. "*I* don't see why she shouldn't go," he said. "He's her husband."

"He *was* her husband," Andy said. "He isn't anymore."

"So, why shouldn't she be there?" Ty went on.

"Right," Mom said. "At least Ty understands. . . . What do you think, Jase?"

I thought Andy was right, but I didn't want to get Mom too riled up. "You could ask, I guess," I said.

"Daddy wouldn't like it," Erin said, in her soft voice. "I don't think he would." I think she'll call Dad "Daddy" till she's sixty-five.

"Daddy sure as hell wouldn't like it," Andy said. "Mom, come *on!*"

"I think I have a right to be there," Mom said, but weakly, as though she were wavering.

"So when you get remarried, you can invite Dad and Randy, okay?" Andy said.

Mom gave her a withering look. "I'm *not* getting remarried—ever!"

"Why not?" Erin asked. "Then you could have a nice wedding too."

Mom whirled on her. "Do you think I'm crazy? Do you think I want to go through this shit one more time? Stick by someone, raise their kids, cook, clean, the whole *geschmear* while they're out fucking lady journalists and ex-nuns?"

Mom claims that one of the women Dad used to see was a nun for ten years before she decided to get a degree in Italian poetry and teach. Of course, the fact is Mom had boyfriends too, and she wasn't spending a hell of a lot of time cooking and cleaning that anyone could remember. But

I don't think any of us felt like bringing that up. Andy just said softly, "Not all men are like that."

"They're not? Then where are the good ones? Will you show me? Take me there! Is it some special island in the South Seas where they're all secreted away, while the rest of us have to make do with cheaters and bums and—"

"Daddy's not a cheater and a bum," Erin said.

I was beginning to feel really weird. It seemed unusually hot and stuffy in the room. I got up and opened the window. Mom looked at me carefully. "You're sick," she said.

"No, I'm fine," I said quickly. But before I could stop her, Mom put her hand on my forehead. "A hundred and one," she said.

Mom has this strange talent or ability. She can just put her hand on your forehead and tell exactly how much fever you have. Not down to the tenth, but she usually gets it pretty close. "Mom, I feel fine," I said.

"A hundred and one isn't fine."

"It's just one of those twenty-four-hour things. . . . Anyhow, I won't do anything strenuous at the wedding."

"You can't go," she said firmly. "I won't let you, and that's that."

"Mom," Andy said. "Of course he's going. Dad would be devastated if he didn't."

"What if it's pneumonia? What if it's something *more* than a twenty-four-hour virus?"

I was getting nervous. I knew Andy was right—I had to go—but in fact I did feel rotten. "Listen, I feel terrific," I said, trying to smile convincingly at Mom.

"Well, you *look* terrible," she snapped. She glared at all of us. "Okay, he can go, but if he comes down with something serious, I'm—"

Just then the phone rang. Since Mom was nearest to the

phone, she grabbed it. "Oh, hi, Randy," she said. She had a strange smile. Andy looked at me and raised her eyebrows. "No, they're all almost ready. Oh, really? That's a pity. Well, I'll tell them. . . . And now that I have you on the phone, I want to tell you how happy I am for you and Mort. I have to hand it to you. You've succeeded where I failed. There's no doubt about it. I gather from all reports that you've turned him into a loving, sweet stay-at-home, whereas I never saw the guy for twenty-seven years!. . . Of course. . . . No, the circumstances were different, totally different, but that doesn't take one whit away from your triumph, and I just wanted you to know how I feel. . . . Terrific. 'Bye."

After she hung up, Mom grinned at all of us. "So, how *about* that? Is that rising to the occasion or isn't it?"

"She didn't succeed where you failed, Mom," Ty said.

"It's masochistic," Andy muttered.

"Will you stop saying that?" Mom snapped. "If I scream at her, it's masochistic, if I act sweet and adorable, it's masochistic. What am I supposed to do?"

There was a pause.

Ty said, "Maybe we ought to get dressed, okay?"

"Randy says to meet half an hour later. The rabbi or whoever got stuck somewhere on the expressway. His boiler blew or whatever boilers do."

Probably I would have felt a little strange about Dad's wedding even if Mom hadn't acted like that and even if I didn't feel like keeling over and sleeping for thirty hours. I went to my room and got out my suit, the only one I have. I figured I ought to wear a tie also. When we gathered at the door to go, Ty was also in a suit, Andy in a bright red dress with a ruffle down the front, and Erin in a white lacy dress with white gloves.

"Gloves!" Andy exclaimed.

"I like gloves," Erin said.

Ty had his camera. He posed us all in front of the house. We lined up, half in the sun. Later, when the pictures were developed, you could see Mom peeking out one of the windows.

Andy drove. I sat next to her and Ty and Erin sat in the back. She looked over at me anxiously. "Are you really going to be okay?" she asked.

"Sure."

"Don't drink too much," she advised. "Champagne and Coricidin is a fatal mixture."

"Do you think there'll be champagne?" Ty asked.

"I don't know. There usually is."

We were all silent. There is something strange about driving to your father's wedding. I don't know how I feel about it. All I can say is it's a strange feeling.

"I hope Mom'll be okay," I said, half to myself.

"She'll be okay," Andy said, in a not very convincing voice. "Only, God, I wish she wouldn't act like that."

"She loves Daddy," came Erin's soft voice from the back.

"Loves him?" Andy snorted. "They've been at each other's throats ever since the day they met. That's love?"

"I think she loves him," Erin said. After a second she said, "But maybe Randy loves him more."

Andy's hands were clenched on the wheel. "I just wish they'd done this twenty years ago."

"Then we never would have been born," I said.

"Okay, fifteen years ago, how's that?"

Randy and Dad were married in a synagogue. It wasn't a very long ceremony. The rabbi said some things, very general things, about love and marriage and starting over.

Then they kissed each other. And Erin went over and kissed Dad about a minute later, and then we all did. He looked tearful and kept saying, "I'm a very lucky man."

Randy hugged all of us and said how happy she was that we were there and how proud she was to have all of us in her family. That had an odd sound. I don't really think of us as being in her family, even though she and Dad are married. There were some relatives, too—Randy's father and Grandma, Dad's mother, who had flown up from Florida. She and Mom never got along, so I don't know her too well. Andy said she could take her and some other woman to Randy's apartment for the party afterward.

"Mort looks so happy," Grandma said while we were in the car. "I'm glad I lived to see it. I've never *seen* him look so happy."

"He did look happy," Erin echoed.

"He's finally found a woman he deserves who deserves him," Grandma went on, "and I thank the Lord I lived to see it. . . . What a darling girl! And so smart."

"Mom's smart," I said. Somehow she bugged me, going on like that.

"She's smart, but what did she do with it? All these years and she's never worked. She's only been a drain on him and driven him crazy with all her yelling. Is that what you call smart?"

"She has conflicts about working," Andy said. I was surprised she came to Mom's defense.

"So, who *doesn't* have conflicts?" Grandma said. "I had conflicts, but when Mort and Jamie were through college, I said: it's time. And I went out and got a job. Nothing great, but one thing led to another, and now look at me! The business is worth two million, and we started with nothing." My grandmother has a business that makes rubber bath toys for babies. She designs them, and my grandfather used to help her with the business part.

"You did well, Granny," Andy said. "But not everyone has that kind of drive or energy."

"True," Grandma said. "You said it. That's the difference. Without drive and energy, you're sunk. Even with it, it's a hard struggle."

There was food and drink at Randy's apartment, but it wasn't a big party like the one when Ms. Korbel got married. There wasn't any music or dancing. Everyone just stood around talking. Despite what Andy said, I had two glasses of champagne. As long as I was going to feel weird, I figured I might as well feel good as well. Various relatives came over to me and said different things. To tell the truth, I didn't focus too well. I stood there and half-heard what was going on, but it was like my mind was drifting off in space somewhere.

Dad did look happy. Andy was talking to him and some other man, and I saw Erin sitting on the couch next to the rabbi, who was lecturing her about something. I didn't see Ty. I was really beginning to feel woozy and thought I might lie down in the bedroom.

When I walked in, Ty said, "Close the door." I did. He was lying on the bed with the phone off the hook, the receiver right next to his ear. I sank down next to him—it was a big double bed.

"What're you doing?" I said. My words sounded a little slurred or slow.

"Ssh . . . Juliet's playing me 'Stairway to Heaven.' "

"What do you mean? How come?"

"It's our anniversary," he said dreamily, his eyes half-closed. "Of when we first met, and that's the song they were playing at the party."

176

"Oh," I closed my eyes. I could slightly hear the music coming through the phone. I started dozing off when the door opened. It was Dad.

"What are you two doing?" he said sharply.

I opened my eyes. He looked blurry. Ty explained about his and Juliet's anniversary. Dad marched over and put the phone back on the hook. "What absolute nonsense!" he said. "Don't you see how this looks? Randy is terribly hurt. Why do you have to listen to this idiotic song right in the middle of the party?"

Ty looked furious. "It's not an idiotic song!" he said. "What'd you just hang up for? Juliet'll be all upset."

"Ty, grow up," Dad said.

"Why don't *you*?" Ty said. "I love Juliet just as much as you love Randy. You think you're the only person in the world ever to love anybody."

"You're a kid," Dad said dismissively. "It's puppy love. There's no comparison."

"I'm calling her back," Ty said, reaching for the phone.

"You're not!" Dad grabbed the phone. "You're going back in there and act sensibly to my guests." He stared at me. "What's with you, Jase? You look awful!"

"I feel funny," I murmured.

"Oh, God," Dad said. "Did you have too much to drink?"

I shook my head. "Just twelve—I mean, two glasses."

"Twelve glasses?" He looked horrified.

My tongue felt all twisted around. "Two glasses," I said.

Randy appeared behind Dad. "Darling, what's wrong?"

Dad sighed. "I don't know . . . these two are just . . . . Will you both pull yourselves together and get back in there?"

"The rabbi is leaving," Randy said.

177

I tried to get up, but the room started spinning around. I sank back down again. Randy came over and sat down next to me. She put her hand on my forehead. "Goodness, you're so hot!" she said. "Are you feeling okay?"

I tried to say something, but it came out funny.

"I think you might have a fever," she said.

"He does," said Ty. "He has a hundred and one."

Dad and Randy came closer. Their faces looked like big moons floating just over the bed. Dad looked really worried. "Oh, God," he said. "Why did this have to happen today?"

"What should we do?" Randy said anxiously.

"Let's let him lie here. Get him some aspirin. I think he probably just needs to rest more than anything."

I felt like I was some kind of corpse with everyone talking about me as though I wasn't there. Actually, I felt as though I wasn't there. The voices came and went. I remembered Randy brought me some orange juice and made me swallow some pills. Then I must have fallen asleep. I slept heavily, with a lot of crazy mixed-up dreams—Vicki and me together in some kind of traffic jam where someone had been killed. We were supposed to help the person, whoever it was. Then Vicki got caught under a car, and I had to try and get her out. None of it made much sense. It was like ten different movies all running at the same time.

When I woke up, it was so quiet I thought everyone had left. At first I thought I was in Mom and Dad's bedroom at home, because sometimes when I'm sick they let me sleep there during the day. But then I remembered about the wedding. I sat up. I felt better, still slightly out of it, but not as hot. I tried putting my hand to my forehead, but my hand was the same temperature as my forehead, so I couldn't tell.

I went into the living room. I guess the party was over. Andy and Dad were playing chess at the table, and Erin was sitting cross-legged on the couch, drawing. Randy was going around the room, cleaning up. They all looked at me.

"How are you feeling?" Randy asked, coming over to me. "We were so worried! You were tossing around so much and talking in your sleep."

At least I didn't walk in my sleep, the way I used to. "I feel a lot better," I said. I went over and sat down next to Andy. She had Dad in a corner. I used to be pretty good at chess a few years ago—Otis and I played together a lot. But then he suddenly got much better than me, and it wasn't fun anymore.

Dad looked at me. "What happened?" he said in mock horror. "Five minutes ago I was winning. Help me out, Jase."

I couldn't think of anything for him to do. "Better give up," I suggested.

Andy smiled slyly. "I've been playing with Marcus. He taught me that move."

I noticed a lot of wedding photos on the table, taken with a Polaroid camera. It's funny—I was in a lot of them but I don't remember them being taken. In most of them my eyes were half-closed, and I was leaning to one side like I was about to keel over. Ty was standing up very straight with a big phony smile on his face.

"Where's Ty?" I said, looking around.

"Juliet's parents picked him up," Randy said. "She was with them. She does look like a very sweet girl."

Dad made a face.

"What didn't you like about her?" Andy asked.

"I just had the feeling she has him hypnotized," Dad said. "If she said roll over, he'd do it instantly."

"I thought she was sweet." Randy stretched. "God, I'm zonked. Promise me you won't let me get married for another six months at least."

Dad smiled at her and reached out for her hand. "I promise."

She sat on the edge of the chair he was sitting in and put her hand on his neck, caressing him. I saw Andy watching them, and her eyes met mine for a second. Randy looked over at Erin. "What're you drawing?" she asked.

"It's for you and Daddy," Erin said. "It's a wedding present."

She brought it over to show us. It was a little like the birthday card she'd made for me, but it had a couple in a big field with more unicorns dancing all around them. Everyone in the picture had the same big goofy smile: Dad, Randy, and all the unicorns. On top it said in big wavy letters: Have a Happy Marriage.

Dad kissed her. "Thanks, darling. That's lovely. I think you've gotten a lot better in the last year, the way you handle color, everything."

The phone rang and Randy answered it. "Oh, hi, Fay. . . . Yes, no, everything's just fine. . . . Jason? Well, he's feeling a lot better. He had a long nap. . . . Ty went home with Juliet's parents. . . . Oh, I see. I didn't know." She put her hand over the receiver. "She said she was expecting them all back for dinner and it's all ready and where are they." Then she took her hand away again. "They'll set off right away. We didn't know, we just thought. . . . And Jason was sleeping. No, I realize that. It was inconsiderate. I'm really sorry. . . . Sure, you can speak to him." She put her hand over the receiver again. "She wants to speak to you, Mort."

Dad cringed, but then got up and took the phone. "Look,

I'm sorry. . . . What can I say? I know! But the ceremony was at three, they've *had* plenty to eat. It doesn't make sense. I don't think they're even hungry. . . . No, we're not going to keep them here all night. Andy and I were just playing chess, but the game's almost over. . . . Well, thanks, I hope we will be. And I hope you. . . . No, I didn't mean it that way. Of course not! Fay? Fay?" He stood there with the phone in his hand. "Christ. She hung up." He sighed. "She's deeply, deeply hurt that we didn't invite her to the wedding. I mean, God Almighty!"

Randy looked perplexed. "She sounded fine this morning."

"Maybe we better go home," I said. I didn't feel that hot anymore.

"There's a five-course meal awaiting you, evidently," Dad said grimly. "Better tickle your throats on the way out."

I knew I wouldn't be able to eat anything, so that didn't bother me.

Andy drove fast so we'd get home as quickly as possible. When we walked in, there was the dining room all fixed up like for Thanksgiving, with candles and cloth napkins. There was a roast chicken at one end and several platters of vegetables, a basket of rolls.

Mom glared at us. "It's nine o'clock!" she said.

"Mom, we ate about three hours ago," Andy said. "We're not hungry."

"They served dinner?" Mom asked. "I thought it was just a party."

"Well, I'm certainly not that hungry," Andy said, surveying the table.

"I still feel a little funny," I admitted.

"You mean, Mort actually paid for food? I thought he

was so stingy he'd just give everyone ginger ale and peanuts."

"There was food," Andy said.

"I hope you didn't drink anything," Mom said to me. "Did you?"

I shook my head.

"I don't know why I even let you go," Mom said. "What kind of a mother am I? . . . Are you really feeling better, Jase?"

"Definitely," I said. "I just feel a little weak."

"At least they let you lie down," Mom said. "At least they didn't make you stand up and take part in the 'festivities' for six straight hours. . . . Was Dorothy there?"

Dorothy is Grandma. "Yeah, she was," I said.

"Oh, I bet she was happy as a clam," Mom snorted. "You know, that woman hated me from the second she laid eyes on me. I swear. I didn't even open my *mouth* before she decided Mort was 'too good for me.' That if I didn't spend every second *slaving* over him, tending to his every *thought,* I was a disaster as a wife. . . . And look at *her*! Off running her own business, God knows what. . . . Is her hair still purple?"

Grandma's hair is kind of bluish-gray. "It's gray," I said.

"She must've switched hairdressers," Mom said. She looked at the table. "So, what am I going to do—eat all this myself?"

"*I'll* have something," Erin said.

"Will the two of you join us, for company?" Mom said to Andy and me. "You don't have to eat anything. I'm not going to ram it down your throats."

We all sat down at the table. Mom gave Erin a whole lot

182

of food, but just picked up a chicken leg and began gnawing on it. "So, the rabbi got there?" she asked.

"He got there," Andy said. She picked up a piece of celery and bit into it.

"Rabbis must've changed," Mom said. "When we got married, back in the stone age, the rabbi said he wouldn't marry a mixed couple. Was he ever right! Mixed is the understatement of the year. So we had to go to this little Unitarian guy who recited from Kahlil Gibran or some such gibberish. You know what Mort wanted him to read? Ecclesiastes! 'There is a time to be born and a time to die.' At a wedding! Talk about morbid!"

I went to get myself a glass of milk. I felt really thirsty.

"Jase, are you *really* okay?" Mom said. "Tell me honestly."

"I'm better," I said guardedly. "I'll go to bed right after this." The milk felt cool and good going down. My throat was still sore.

"So, come on!" Mom went on. "Tell me about it! Was everybody happy? Was it a good wedding?"

"They were happy," Erin said quietly, buttering a roll.

"She sounds so nervous on the phone," Mom said. "Is that her real personality? Like she's afraid I'm going to scream at her. Why should I? Oh . . . listen, I've changed my mind. I'm getting married. I'm going to marry Jim January."

"Who's he?" Andy asked, frowning.

"He's this potential ax-murderer type who picked Jase and me up a couple of months ago. He's been calling me. He's a widower, he reads Dickens, he used to be an alcoholic, but he's been on the wagon for three years. He builds boats, he's taken a course in Chinese cooking. What more do I want? *I* want to be a perfect couple too!"

"He sounds nice," Erin said.

Mom stared straight ahead for a moment. "He's a fool," she said contemptuously. She stood up to clear. "And I'm going to bed because I'm sick of this day and I want it to be over. Clear up, if you feel like it. If not—leave it for tomorrow."

I was feeling dizzy again, so I went in to bed. Just as I was almost asleep, Andy peeked in. "Do you want anything, Jase?" she asked. "Some juice?"

"No, that's okay."

She came over and kissed me on the forehead. Then she just sat there a minute, staring off into space. "I don't know," she said.

"Yeah." In some ways I was glad I was sick. Everything about the day seemed a little far off, like it hadn't happened. Only it did.

By the way, Andy was right. Champagne and Coricidin are a lousy mixture. Don't ever try it.

TWENTY

||||

I DON'T KNOW IF IT HAD ANYTHING TO DO WITH DAD'S GETTING married, but the next weekend Mom went out on a date. The guy's name was Cole Havel, and she met him on one of those job interview things. He was the person right before her. Neither of them got the job.

"I think someday I may end up in *The National Enquirer*," Mom said. "Eighty-year-old lady goes on one millionth job interview."

I don't get why no one will hire Mom. I mean, I've never had a job except a summer job at a dry cleaner's, but you'd think *someone* would hire her, just give her a chance. I think she's smart.

Cole Havel is nine years younger than Mom, and used to be a contractor. That has something to do with buildings, I guess. He's divorced too, and his wife took their kid, a fourteen-year-old girl, and ran off to Nova Scotia with his best friend. Still, as Mom says, you've got to start somewhere.

The night Cole Havel came to pick Mom up, she was still showering and getting ready. Erin was in the living room with me. She has spring vacation and is going back Sunday night. She's been here since Dad's wedding. "Hi," she said softly, as Cole Havel sat down. "We're going to watch *The Glass Menagerie*. Is that okay?"

"Sure," he said. He looked wistfully at Erin. "You look just like the girl in that play. I bet you have a collection of glass animals just like her, don't you?"

"No," Erin said. "But I like unicorns."

He kept staring at her. "You look just like my daughter, Patsy. Exactly! I can't get over it. Are you fourteen?"

People always think Erin's younger than she is. "I'm almost seventeen," she said. "Is that the daughter that your wife ran off with to Nova Scotia?"

Cole Havel looked embarrassed. "Yeah, it's a terrible thing. She just took her! But I'm going to get her back, no matter what." To me he said, "You're lucky to have such a wonderful sister. I hope you appreciate it."

"Sure," I said. There was something a little weird about the guy. I wished Mom would come out.

"Our parents are divorced," Erin said, almost in a whisper.

"I know that," he said. "I wouldn't date a woman who . . . I wouldn't foul another man's nest. That happened to me."

"She's a very sensitive person," Erin said intensely. "You have to treat her well. Otherwise don't even bother."

Cole Havel turned red. "I've never treated a woman badly in my life," he said. "I think women are goddesses before whom men should worship. . . . Isn't that right, Jason?"

"Yeah, I guess," I said.

"Mom thinks all men are cheaters and bums," Erin went on. "It really hurt her that our father remarried."

186

"Your mother is a wonderful woman," Cole Havel said loudly, almost like he wanted Mom to hear. "She's smart, sexy, talented. . . . She's more than I deserve."

At that point Mom came out. She looked pretty good in a blue dress. She didn't look like a goddess, exactly, though.

"Mom, your slip is showing," Erin said.

Mom yanked up her slip.

Cole Havel stood up. "You have wonderful children," he said. "Beautiful, smart . . ."

Mom beamed. "Right," she murmured. "They are. . . ."

"Your Erin is the exact image of my Patsy. I bet they'd get along like a house afire."

"I go to boarding school," Erin said.

"That's no place for a girl like you," he said. "You belong at home, in the bosom of your family."

Mom glared at him. "It's none of your business," she snapped.

Cole Havel shrugged. "That's true," he said. "It's none of my business."

As he and Mom left, Erin called out, "Have a good time."

After we heard the car start, I said, knowing they wouldn't hear me, "He was weird."

"One of his eyes was a different color from the other one," Erin said.

I hadn't noticed that.

"I like going to boarding school," she said suddenly. "I don't mind. It's good for me. It makes me more independent. I was too clinging before."

"You were okay," I said. I feel like I never know what to say with Erin.

187

"I want to be independent like Andy," Erin said. "I don't want to be like the girl in *The Glass Menagerie*. I hate that! She ended up just living at home with her mother. She was so shy boys wouldn't date her."

"You're not like that," I said, more to comfort her than because I think it.

"I'm a little like that," she said. "I don't know how to act with boys. I don't know what to say to them."

"It's not that hard," I said, thinking of Vicki. "It's not so much what you say."

She was frowning. "I don't know much about sex either, that's the trouble. You should know one or the other, how to talk or how to . . . you know."

"Mom said she didn't do much till college," I pointed out.

"Right." Erin was staring at me in that funny, hypnotized way she has. Then she got up and turned on the TV.

The show wasn't even over when Mom came home. It was only eleven ten. She was by herself. Erin jumped up and kissed her. "Was it nice?" she asked.

"No, it was shitty," Mom said. She glanced at the TV. "Is that still going on? I feel like I've been out for ten hours."

"We don't have to watch the rest of it," Erin said.

I clicked the TV off and we both went into the kitchen, where Mom poured herself a beer. "Okay, kids, it's celibacy from here on in. I'm entering a convent next week. Oh, no, they'll probably have an interview for that, too!"

"He seemed kind of weird," I said.

"He was sort of handsome," Erin said, "except for his eyes being different colors."

"Yeah, you turned him on too. Half the evening he talked

about teenage girls and how wonderful they were, and what a beast and monster his wife was because, for some incomprehensible reason, she couldn't stand him and finally got the courage to walk out. Then he starts in on how he's never 'had,' quote unquote, an 'older woman,' quote unquote, before, but he feels maybe that's what he needs. Someone mature, ripe, exhausted. Like, I'm supposed to be so flattered that this younger man deigns to look at me twice that I'm going to take my clothes off then and there, right in the Paramus Shopping Mall."

"You're no so old, Mom," Erin said.

She looked old in the light of the kitchen, though, tired and thin, with her hair falling in her eyes. "In spirit I'm eighteen, no, make it eight, but sure, my tits aren't where they were once. Whose are? So I have a flabby butt? So does Mort. So does this joker, I'll bet. Do men not wrinkle? Are they drip and dry?"

"You'll meet someone," I said.

Mom whirled around. "I don't *want* to meet someone!" she snapped. "I've done my part in propagating the species and caressing the egos of weak, lying men. A contractor! This guy, this merry Old King Cole, paints *houses*. Some contractor! Do I say I'm a college professor? No, I tell it like it is. Used housewife, devoid of skills, capable of giving a good blow job if properly turned tuned."

Erin turned red. "Mom!"

"Scratch that," Mom said. "No, serious, kids, I mean he expected me to go to Nova *Scotia* with him, kidnap his kid, and then help him raise her. I'm supposed to break the law and then devote my declining years to tending another woman's screwed-up child."

"You have us," Erin said softly.

Mom reached over and hugged her. She started to cry. "Do I?" she said. "Do I have you?"

I hugged her. "Sure, here we are, right here," I said, pretending to joke.

"I thought maybe it was a mirage," Mom said, in a flat, sad voice. "I don't know what's real anymore."

TWENTY-ONE

||||

Ty GOT INTO THREE COLLEGES; VASSAR, BERKELEY AND STONY Brook. It's funny, I thought he'd apply to places that had ice skating, but he says he's giving it up. He says he wants to be a dentist. God, I pity whoever gets to be his patients. He'll probably drill them without Novocain or something.

He seemed pretty happy about having gotten into such good schools, but said he wasn't sure which one to pick; he thought maybe Vassar. Mom went to Vassar and she said she thought that was a good idea, that it was in the Ivy League and a first-rate school. Then Dad hit the ceiling and said he thought it was too expensive, that Ty had to go to Stony Brook because it's a state school and tuition is a lot lower. Ty said Stony Brook was a dumb place and he wouldn't go there.

"Then, why did you apply there?" Dad said.

We were walking around the zoo again, with Randy and Dad. It was a gorgeous day and I kept thinking of Vicki. Things with her have been good lately, and there're only about two more months of school—two blessings. I haven't done too badly at school, all things considered. I think I'll fail gym because I didn't show up except three times.

Otherwise my two lowest grades were History, where I got a C at midyear, and Music, where I got a C-plus. Ms. Korbel gave me a B-plus on my last paper and wrote in the margin of the last exam that I showed "dramatic improvement" since the beginning of the year.

"Look, I applied to a lot of places," Ty said. "I didn't know then where I wanted to go."

"Vassar is too expensive," Dad said. "That's all there is to it. Unless Fay gets a job, I can't afford it."

Ty looked mad. I know he thinks Dad can afford it, but just doesn't want to pay the money. "I just feel like going to a decent college," he grumbled, "and not some cheapo state place with a lot of losers."

"Ty, Jesus," Dad said impatiently. "Stony Brook is a fine school. What does cheapo mean? Just that the parents of the kids who go there aren't rich. They're just as bright."

Ty made a face. "If I can't go to Vassar, I don't want to go anywhere," he said.

"Because of Juliet?" Dad said. Juliet was going to some college near Vassar.

"That's just part of it," Ty said.

"Three months after you're in college, you won't remember who Juliet *is*," Dad said. "You'll have nine million new girlfriends."

"I will not," Ty said, turning red.

"Oh, I give up," Dad said. He looked at Randy and me. "Why don't the two of you say anything? Talk some sense into him."

I guess, though I hate to say it, I can see Ty's point of view. If Vicki still liked me as much as she does now, I'd want to go to the same college she goes to.

"I went to a state college," Randy said. "It was in

Maine, and true, it wasn't the greatest, but it didn't hold me back especially."

After that the subject was dropped. Personally I don't care that much where Ty goes. It'll just be great having him out of the house. Maybe Mom and Dad'll have a rich aunt who'll die and leave them a million dollars. That would solve everything.

The next time we saw Dad he said he had some really exciting news. He said he was going to relocate to San Francisco. Evidently the magazine he works for is moving out there, and he wants to go. Or maybe it's just that he has to go if he wants to keep his job. But he looked pretty happy about it. "If you go to Berkeley," he said to Ty, "you'd be right nearby. You could live with us, even, if you wanted."

"I want to live on campus," Ty said firmly.

"Okay, live where you want, but Berkeley's a terrific school, we could see you all the time. I think this is the perfect solution."

"Isn't it pretty expensive?" Ty said.

"Money isn't everything," Dad said. "I'll find a way."

That didn't seem too consistent with what he'd said last time, but Ty was really pleased. It turns out Juliet got into Berkeley too.

When we got home and told Mom the news, she hit the ceiling. "Berkeley!" she said. "That's three thousand miles away!"

"Yeah, but Dad'll be out there with Randy," Ty said.

"So?" Mom said. "What good will that do me? I won't even see you!"

Ty looked uncomfortable. "You'll see me," he said.

"How?" Mom yelled. "Who's going to pay plane fares back and forth? . . . Anyway, I don't get it. Vassar is a wonderful school."

"Well, it's Dad's money and he's for Berkeley," Ty said.

"Dad's money! Fuck that! I'm just the mother and I don't count? My opinion doesn't count?"

"I didn't mean that," Ty said quickly.

"You're not going to Berkeley," Mom said, "and that's final."

"Well, why don't you get a job and then I can go to Vassar?" Ty asked.

"Find me one," Mom said. "Okay? Will you find me a job?"

He started to answer, but Mom turned to me. "What do you think, Jase? Berkeley is in California!"

"He knows that, Mom," Ty said.

"It's supposed to be a good school," I said.

"It's in California!" Mom said. "All the kids out there will be straight out of *American Graffiti*, big blond hulks who lip-read and play video games all day, and . . . cheerleaders!"

Ty looked like Dad used to when Mom went off. "Mom, first of all, you're thinking of Southern California, L.A. Berkeley's in San Francisco. Second, it's a stereotype, and third, there are cheerleaders everywhere!"

"There are cheerleaders everywhere," Mom said. "How true. . . . And there are husband-stealers and muggers everywhere. I guess you have to go to the moon to escape all that. Maybe I should volunteer for that: first mad housewife on the moon. Then they can clone me and start a perfect society."

"Is that a way of saying I can go?" Ty asked.

"It's a way of saying you're going to go and I might as well like it or lump it. Right?"

Ty looked sheepish. "I'll come home for vacations," he said. "I'll write a lot too. Or call."

"Sure," Mom said, like she didn't believe him. Suddenly she looked at him suspiciously. "You're not going to live with Mort and Randy, are you?" she asked.

"No!" Ty said. "I mean, I might stay with them for a few weeks till I find a place."

"No," Mom said. "There I absolutely draw the line."

"I don't get it," Ty said. "What's wrong with staying there a couple of weeks?"

"You cannot stay there for one *second*," Mom said, "and that's that."

"Will you give me a reason why?" Ty said.

"Yes," Mom shouted. "I'll give you a million reasons, but the main one is they're going to do some brainwashing number on you, saying how awful I am. Randy will crawl around being a perfect, sweet, wonderful little stepmother, and you'll adore her—"

"Mom, I don't even like her that much," Ty said.

"Now!" Mom said. "But after three weeks you'll be eating out of her goddamn hand. I mean, literally as well as figuratively. Listen, I'll pay for it, but you'll stay at the dorm until you find a place."

"Okay, great, I'll stay at the dorm," Ty said.

When Mom had gone out, he looked at me and rolled his eyes. "Holy moley."

"Well, anyway, you're going there," I said.

"Boy, I pity you," he said.

"What for?"

"Being alone with her for two more years? I'd go to West Point first. I'd register for front line service in some war."

"It won't be so bad," I said.

"Yeah, well, for Mommy's little Angel Face, I guess maybe it won't," he said.

I socked him in the stomach. "Shut up, Ty!"

He was winded and wasn't ready to fight back. "Look, who cares? I'm out of it, and the hell with both of them—and you."

What's weird is, I know how Ty feels, and part of me feels the same way. I do feel uneasy when I think of the next two years, of what Mom might be like if Vicki and I started getting really serious. In principle she's not that uptight about things, but if I ever wanted to sleep over at Vicki's, I have the feeling she might get fairly hysterical. Not that that looks like an imminent possibility. And Vicki's parents would never let me. They're not like Juliet's parents. They're a lot more strict, especially about her. She claims they were easier on her brother.

"It's just this classic sexist thing," she said. We were at Ms. Korbel's, babysitting Vernon. He'd gone in really early, at eight. He fell a couple of weeks ago and now he can hardly get around, even with a cane. Ms. Korbel says he stays in bed a lot and just reads or sleeps. She wheels the TV in there so he can watch it without getting up.

"What is?" I asked.

"The way they give Mark so much more freedom than me. Were your parents like that?"

I tried to think. Andy never did much in high school, and Erin's always been so shy, so I guess it never came up as an issue. Vicki put her arms around me and leaned forward so our noses touched. "It must be hard," she said, "their being divorced. I'd die if that happened with Mom and Daddy! When they fight, I hate it so much I can't stand it."

She felt so warm and good. I sat there, my arms around her, just enjoying the feeling. "I love you," I said.

Dad once gave me a big lecture on how I should never tell a girl I love her unless I really mean it. The trouble with that is that you do mean it at the time. When Vicki is acting nice to me, I feel like I love her. That doesn't mean I want to marry her or anything. But it's not just something I'm saying to get her in a more pleasant mood.

"What're you doing for the summer?" she asked, sitting back a little.

I shrugged. "Just hanging around, I guess." I've never been to camp. I guess I could try and get a job at the dry cleaning place I worked at last summer, but that was really boring, just slipping plastic bags over clothes. Their air conditioner was always breaking down too, and some days it was boiling.

Vicki was still sitting with her head on my shoulder, stroking my hair. "I wish you could come to California with us."

"Where do you go?"

"My aunt and uncle have this camp out there. I help the little kids with swimming. It's such a great camp, Jase! Maybe you could be a counselor too." She frowned. "It *is* kind of late to ask them, that's the only thing."

"Is it near Berkeley?" I asked.

"Yeah, pretty near . . . why?"

I told her about Dad and how he was relocating and would be moving out there in a month, at the end of June. Vicki's face lit up. "That's perfect!" she said. "You could stay with them and come up and visit me on weekends. It's so beautiful, Jase! You'd love it, the country and everything. We could camp out. . . ."

I started imagining it, Vicki and me off together in some beautiful unspoiled place on the coast, big waves crashing on the shore, building fires and cooking things, snuggling into the same sleeping bag. They make sleeping bags for two people—I've seen them advertised. I thought of *For*

Whom the Bell Tolls, which we read this year in school, and what a great time they had in his sleeping bag.

"Yeah, it'd be great," I said.

"Do it, then!" She jumped up, she was so excited. "Oh, it's going to be so good. There's this brook I'll show you where we can skinnydip late at night. I love that. The water's freezing, but if you keep moving it's okay . . . and there are raccoons that eat right out of your hand. . . . Why're you looking funny?"

"I don't know if I can," I said.

"Why not?"

I tried to explain. "Well, it's just, Mom got so hysterical about the possibility of Ty just staying with Dad and Randy for a few weeks. If I spent the summer there, she might go bananas. Also, well, they just got married. Maybe they'd want their privacy."

"Ask them!" Vicki is the kind of person who does things the second they occur to her. I tend more to want to mull them over for a while.

"Okay, well, maybe I will," I said slowly.

"Why just maybe?" She looked hurt. "Don't you want to do it?"

"I do want to do it a lot." That was the truth. "It sounds like it'd be wonderful."

She sat down next to me again. "See, the thing is here, it's like my parents or your mother are always hovering around, and it makes me nervous. Even when the door of my room is locked, I feel kind of . . . Whereas out there, it'd be just us. My aunt and uncle are terrific. They trust me about everything."

I kissed her. "Okay, I'll ask them," I agreed.

We didn't make out too much that evening because Vernon kept ringing his bell. Once he needed help going to the bathroom, and another time he wanted some juice. I know he hates having to ask for help all the time, but what can he do? It's the burden of old age, like he said. I hope I don't live that long, to get like that. Seventy or seventy-five sounds old enough to me.

I decided to ask Dad first. I went to his and Randy's house for dinner. Half their stuff was packed up, and Randy was off somewhere. Dad listened while I told him about Vicki's aunt and uncle's camp. "She's not sure I could get a job there," I said, "but I thought even if I didn't, maybe I could live with you and visit her weekends."

Dad looked almost as pleased as Vicki had. "That'd be super, Jase! I'd love it. We'd *both* love it. Randy so much wants to get to know you. What a marvelous idea."

I felt good. "There wasn't much I was going to do here," I said, "except maybe get that job in the dry cleaning place again."

"No, I think it's important for you to see other parts of America. Fay and I really neglected that with all of you. You've never been west of Pennsylvania."

"Vicki says it's really beautiful country," I said, getting excited.

"It is," Dad assured me. "I spent a summer out there between my freshman and sophomore years in college. I stayed at International House, and had my first—well, my first really serious romance."

"Was that with Cerelia Blade?" I said. That's the kind of name you remember forever. You can wake up in the middle of the night and remember it.

Dad laughed. "No, no, Cerelia came later. . . . What was her name? Annunciata . . . She was Spanish. Wonderful black, black eyes like olives and beautiful dusky skin. You didn't know whether to paint her, jump on her, or what." He looked dreamy. "But we lost track of each other. I don't know why. And then crazy Cerelia came careening into my life."

"*Was* she crazy?" Dad never talked about her much, or about any of his girlfriends. Maybe because I have one now, he thinks he can.

"Totally. She was this incredibly brilliant, vivid girl. I was *petrified* of her! If she'd asked me to jump off a cliff I would've. I can't explain it. Sex with her—it wasn't even like sex. There was something insane about it." He sighed. "I guess I thought that was what life was all about, living close to the bone, experiencing things fully, who knows."

She sounded really strange. "Do you have a picture of her?" I asked.

"I do, actually," Dad said. "The question is whether I can find it."

He did. It was in a big folder, full of photos of all the girlfriends he'd ever had. I guess he never showed them to Mom, or at least I never knew he had it. There were even some of the ones he saw when he and Mom separated. The one who was an ex-nun was the cutest. She was sitting on a rock, wearing short shorts and sneakers and winking. Cerelia Blade looked like trouble. Dad had a whole bunch of close-ups of her, and in most of them she was staring right at the camera. She had a nose that came straight down from her forehead, like statues sometimes do.

"I just fell for her nose," Dad said. "One straight line! Beautiful! And for the whole thing. Let's face it, I fell for the whole damn thing."

Just then Randy walked in, carrying a bag of groceries. Dad slipped the photos back in the folder. Maybe he doesn't show them to her, either. "Oh, hi, darling," he said. "Where've you been?"

She put her head to one side. "Guess. . . . Hi, Jason."

"Hi," I said. I still feel a little awkward around her.

"Listen, marvelous news," Dad said. "Jason's going to spend the summer with us in California." He told her about the plan.

Randy looked pleased too. "That's wonderful," she said. "In fact, well, it's funny this came up, because I've been thinking about this. I didn't mention it, but couldn't Jason actually spend the whole year with us?"

"The whole school year?" Dad asked.

"Yes," Randy said. "The schools are so much better out there, and the weather is beautiful. And I thought it might be good if . . . well, maybe it would be easier for Fay, not having the responsibility and all, in terms of meeting new people. What do you think?"

Dad shook his head. "She'd never agree to it."

"Wouldn't she?" Randy asked. "Are you sure? She might be delighted."

"You don't know her," Dad said, as though I weren't there. "She adores Jase. She'd have a fit if he were away for that long."

"I think just the summer is fine," I said. I think Dad's probably right. Also, I wouldn't want to spend the school year out there, whether the schools are better or not. Otis wouldn't be there, or Vicki. I'd have a whole new class, everything'd be different. It's true not everything here is wonderful, but I know about it, I can handle it."

TWENTY-TWO

||||

*T*Y GRADUATED. *MOM AND* I *WENT TO THE CEREMONY AND* watched him get his diploma. Mom looked okay. I wish she'd learn to put on her eye makeup straight, though. It's always kind of wobbly, and since she uses black, it can look a little strange. But otherwise she seemed in an okay mood, even a good mood. The Moscowitzes came too and invited all of us to dinner at some fancy place. I thought Mom would say no, but she agreed.

It was a place with huge menus. Everything was expensive. Even a salad was over ten dollars! But I know the Moscowitzes are rolling in dough, so I ordered a one-pound prime sirloin with a baked potato. That's my favorite meal. They talked a lot about Berkeley and what a great school it was and how nice that Juliet and Ty would be together.

"You know, it's funny," Mom said. "A second ago I had four kids and the house was always a madhouse, the refrigerator was cleaned out in a second, and now——" She gave me a fond glance. "Jase is the only one I have left. It's just the two of us."

"I know," Mrs. Moscowitz said sympathetically. "I feel

exactly the same way. Juliet's my baby, and now she'll be away too. I'm so glad I started working five years ago, or I'd be a basket case, I can tell you."

When she said "Juliet's my baby" Juliet gave her a dirty look. "I'm not a baby, Mom."

"To me you are," Mrs. Moscowitz insisted, "and you always will be!"

Juliet pretended to suck her thumb. "I want a bottle," she said and Ty laughed, as he does at anything she says.

"Of course, we'll be flying out to the Coast a lot," Mrs. Moscowitz went on, "because Bruce has business out there, so it isn't a total separation forever and ever. . . . But I have to admit, beautiful as the West Coast is, I hope so much Juliet doesn't decide to settle out there."

"I've only been there once," Mom said, "but it always seems like another country to me."

"I know! Totally! They never read, everything is just the body, the body. . . . Women our age are considered ancient!" She laughed. "It's just preposterous."

Mom looked morose. "Aren't we ancient?" she said. "I thought we were."

"Of course not!" Mrs. Moscowitz leaned closer to her. "Bruce never *looks* at a woman under thirty-five. He says they're boring, and I think he's absolutely right."

"I'm not boring," Juliet piped up.

"Of course not," Mrs. Moscowitz assured her. "Girls of your generation are different. . . . Don't you think they're marvelous?" she asked Mom.

"In what way?"

"Well, so fresh, so open, so much more frank than we were about their sexuality. . . . I think the whole thing is just *such* an improvement. When they get married, they'll know what they're getting into."

203

"No, they won't," Mom said. "No one ever knows."

Mrs. Moscowitz reached over and patted her hand. "Fay, you mustn't give in to bitterness," she said. "It's terribly aging. It really does actually age the skin. They've done tests."

While they were talking, I was wolfing down my steak and occasionally taking looks at Juliet. I used to think she was so gorgeous, before I had a girlfriend of my own. But now I don't think she's such a big deal. I think Dad's right. The way Ty hangs all over her is pretty sick. I don't think I'll ever do that with Vicki.

Mr. Moscowitz didn't say much during the meal, either. He always looks kind of stoned or just spaced-out, like his eyeballs are revolving in little concentric circles. He slapped down his American Express card without even looking at the bill. I was sitting next to him. It was $205! I wonder if I'll ever be so rich that $205 just for one meal seems like a mere nothing.

After dinner he drove Ty, Juliet, and Mrs. Moscowitz home, since their house came first, and then took us home. Mom gave him the directions to where we lived.

We all sat in front. Mom was next to him, I was next to the window. I like sitting next to the window. I opened it by a push button and let the summer air blow in my face.

"Too bad your husband couldn't come," Mr. Moscowitz said.

"What?" Mom said, whirling around.

"Busy with his work?" he ventured. "What is he? I forget, some kind of writer?"

"He's an editor of a journal on human rights, and we're divorced," Mom said.

Mr. Moscowitz looked surprised. "Oh . . . what do you know? I guess Ty never mentioned that. Been divorced a long time?"

I could feel Mom tense up. "He's remarried."

We were at a stop light. Mr. Moscowitz reached over and patted Mom's hand. "I guess it gets pretty lonely, huh?"

"What does?" Mom said sharply.

"Being alone, not having a man. . . . That can be tough."

"No, I love it," Mom said, taking her hand away. "I'm thinking of changing my sexual persuasion, actually. Women are so much easier than men."

He grinned at her. "Oh, we're not so bad. Give us a chance. That's all we ask for, just a chance . . . right, Jason?" He winked at me.

"Sure," I said.

When he let us off, he said, "Well, if you need any . . . advice, just someone to talk to, let me know, okay? I hate to see a pretty woman go sour on men just because she's met one bum."

"That's kind of you," Mom said crisply. "I'll try and remember that."

He slipped her his business card. "Don't hesitate to call . . . any time."

When we got in the house Mom said, "Oh, God, I love it! He's going to come over and fuck me as a good deed, so I won't turn gay! It would almost be worth it just to send a video to Monica the next morning, but I doubt I could get through it without throwing up."

I guess I was kind of surprised, Mr. Moscowitz acting like that. Also that he didn't even know Mom and Dad were divorced. I would think Ty would have mentioned it. Just then the phone rang. Mom answered it. "Hello? . . . Oh, hi, Randy. Yeah, he's here. . . . No, what plan? I hadn't heard anything about it. . . . No, not a thing. . . . For the entire *summer?* . . . No, well, of course I can see that, but—I certainly *will* have to think about it! . . . Yes, he's right here." Glaring at me, she gave me the phone.

I spoke to Randy a little. I was supposed to have discussed the summer plan with Mom before this, but I kept putting it off. I guess this is it. "I'll call you tomorrow," I said, hanging up.

Mom was still standing there, glaring at me. "What *is* this?" she said. "What was she talking about? What camp?"

This is a major problem with me. I always put things off. I always wait for the right moment. Then, as a result of waiting too long, I get everyone mad at me. "It's this camp Vicki's aunt and uncle run. It's near Berkeley."

"So, what about it?"

I swallowed, feeling extremely uncomfortable. "No, it's just Vicki had this idea—well, first she thought maybe I could get a job as a counselor out there, only it turns out it's too late for that. . . . But she thought maybe if I stayed out there with Dad and Randy, I could, like, visit her weekends."

"But you never said anything! Were you planning on just hopping on a plane and sending me a postcard when you got there?" Mom's voice was shaking.

I looked down. "No, I meant to talk about it, only I forgot."

"What do those two want? Do they want to come and take my house away too? All my clothes? Is there no limit?"

"Mom, it isn't Dad and Randy. . . . It's just—I don't know where else I could stay."

"Well, you're not going," Mom snapped, "and that's that."

"Why not?"

"Jase, for heavens sake! You're supposed to be the sensitive one! Use your head a second, will you? What am *I* going to be doing all summer while you're out there cavorting around with Vicki?"

"You have friends, don't you?"

"But I want someone here when I come home at night." Mom's voice started trembling again. "I don't want to be here all by myself."

I felt shitty. "Okay, well, I won't go then."

She grabbed hold of me. "Do you understand, Jase? Do you? It's just . . . I can't. . . ."

"Sure, I understand," I said, though I didn't really.

Mom was silent a long time. "What kind of camp is it?" she said, in a more pulled-together way.

"Just a regular camp," I said, "for boys and girls. Vicki teaches swimming."

"It's probably a beautiful setting," Mom said flatly.

"She says it is."

Mom turned to look at me. "Do you really want to go a whole lot?" she asked in a softer voice.

I cleared my throat. "Well, it did sound kind of . . . And the only job I could get here would be with the Strassers."

"Yeah, that was the pits, wasn't it? . . . Does Vicki want you to go?"

"She was the one who had the idea."

Mom smiled. "She's totally crazy about you, isn't she?"

"Yeah, she likes me, kind of," I admitted.

"And she must be a sweetie if you like her. . . . Is she?"

I felt uncomfortable talking about Vicki with Mom. "Yeah."

"Are you, as they say, 'doing it'?" Mom said wryly.

"Not yet." I didn't mean to put it that way, but Mom smiled.

"Wait till you get out there under the California moon. . . . Okay, well, I trust you, Jase. You'll come back, won't you?"

"Of course I'll come back," I said, not knowing why she would even ask.

"Because if you didn't—"

"Mom, I'll come back!"

She hugged me. "I want you to have a wonderful summer," she whispered.

Lying in bed, I tried feeling excited, the way I had when Vicki started talking about the camp, but I couldn't. I wish Mom had something to do, some job or hobby or something. Even some boyfriend. Just something to take her mind off stuff and make her happier. But I was glad she'd said I could go. I knew that sometime, in a couple of days, I'd start feeling good about it again, but right now it seemed far away, like it wasn't going to happen.

Vicki went bananas when I told her I was going. "Oh, that's so terrific," she said. "I was so scared you couldn't. When will you fly out?"

"July fifth." Dad had made the reservation for me.

"I'll be going the twenty-eighth." She gave me the name of her aunt and uncle and the phone number and address of the camp. "Do you think your father will let you use his car?"

I don't even know if Dad is taking his car out there. But I guess he'll have some sort of car. "I'll get there," I promised. "Don't worry."

Dad was leaving a week before I was going to leave. I called him to say good-bye, because I didn't have a chance to see him again. Anyway, I'd be seeing him in a week, so it didn't seem that important. "Dad, uh, are you going to get a new car?" I asked.

"Probably . . . why?"

"What kind?"

"I'm not sure . . . possibly a Toyota. Why do you want to know?"

I hesitated. "Well, I just thought if I visit Vicki, I might need to, like, borrow it."

"Jase, listen, you haven't had much experience driving. It's a very winding, steep road along the coast."

"I'd be careful, Dad, I promise."

"Okay, well, we'll talk about it when we see you. I can't tell you how happy I am about this, about your staying with us."

"Me too."

After I hung up I felt a little guilty. Dad's happy because I'm staying with him, whereas I'm happy because I'll be seeing Vicki a lot and having fun with her. I've started getting excited again. I have around six different plots in my head of our camping out on the beach, building a fire, possibly my scaring a bear away that comes out of the woods just by saying, "Scram." To tell the truth I'm not sure if they have bears out there. And I'd be just as glad if they don't. But in the fantasy Vicki is so overwhelmed by my bravery that she plunges headfirst into the sleeping bag. I hope it's really warm too. Because I also have fantasies of us skinny-dipping, like she said.

I think it's going to be a great summer, maybe the best of my entire life.

TWENTY-THREE

||||

THE DAY I WAS SET TO LEAVE, MOM HOVERED OVER ME, checking to make sure I'd packed the right stuff. She seemed really nervous and kept asking me the same things over and over. Even if I told her I'd packed something, she'd make me show her. Then, five minutes later, she'd be back in asking about the same thing again. I wish she'd smoke pot. It might help her a lot. That was one thing I packed very carefully—a bunch of joints I'd bought at the end of school. I wrapped them in tinfoil and put them in with my toothbrush and stuff.

"Maybe I should take in boarders," Mom said. She was sitting on my bed, watching me finish packing.

"Who?"

"I mean, I'd get extra money. Why not? Would you mind?"

"No, I wouldn't mind." In fact, I would mind if they messed around in my room, but I didn't want to get into any hassles so close to when I was leaving.

"But the thing is, who wants a lot of crazy strangers living in the house?" Mom said. "Who needs that?"

"True." I tossed in a sweater. It had a hole in the sleeve, but Vicki said it can get chilly at night by the water.

"Jase, give me that," Mom said.

"I need a sweater," I said.

"I know, but that has a hole in it. Look, it's huge."

"It's the only one I have that fits."

"Okay, well, I'll sew it, it'll only take a sec."

I sighed. "Mom, I don't want to be late."

"You won't be! Relax! God, what a horrible trait to have picked up from your father. 'We're going to be late, we're going to be late.' Are we ever late? No!" She rushed inside to get her sewing box and came back with it.

While I packed, she sewed the rip. "Oh, damn, I'm making a mess of this," she said. "It looks awful." She held it up. The sleeve was all jerked to one side. It looked like a sweater for someone with a withered arm.

"It's fine, Mom." I said, taking it from her.

"Make Mort buy you a new one," she said. "Why should you go around in rags?"

"I will." Dad claims that with Erin still in this special school and Ty at Berkeley without a scholarship, he can barely afford to pay the rent, but I didn't want to get into that. I looked at Mom. She's always bee skinny, but maybe she lost weight recently. She really looked like a rail. You could see the veins on her arms, and her cheeks were all sunken. She looked old, much older than usual.

"Did you pack your bathing suit?" she asked suddenly.

She'd asked me that five minutes ago and I'd shown her the two suits I was taking. I didn't want to talk about the skinny-dipping. Anyhow, some of the time maybe I'll swim with a suit on. I dug down and showed them to her again. This time she looked them over carefully. "Christ, this is ripped too! Your whole wardrobe is a mess. . . .Have you been growing, or what?"

"I suppose." When I was little, I used to get a lot of Ty's hand-me-down clothes, which I hated, but maybe that got Mom in the habit of not buying clothes for me. Except for a few weird outfits I'm fond of, like my red T-shirt with the black suspenders or my pink-striped sweatshirt, I don't much care what I wear. At the very end I put in my felt hat with the feather, or rather Andy's hat—I think of it as mine now.

"What do you need that for?" Mom wanted to know.

For some reason I turned red. "Vicki likes it."

I started to close the suitcase, when Mom suddenly said, "Do you have your toothbrush, brush, comb, all that?"

I nodded.

"Show me."

I started panicking a little because the joints were in the cosmetic bag. I just held up the bag and then stuffed it back under. Mom must have some extrasensory perception, because she said, "I'm so glad you gave up all that stuff with drugs, Jase. Really. I used to worry myself sick over that."

"Well . . . It's not really that bad," I said.

"It is! . . . Listen, I was reading this thing the other day. Those kids who smoked it all through the sixties—now they can't have kids, their brains are just mush, they lie around in a stupor all day. It's criminal—because half those kids started out as sweet, bright kids like you. And now—"

"It's a matter of how much you do," I said. It pisses me when Mom and Dad talk about something they know absolutely nothing about. Like, if there are articles about the dangers of birth control pills for women, Mom says, "Why are they printing all these scare articles?" But if they do the same thing for drugs, she falls for it hook, line, and sinker.

"Will you promise me you won't do anything out there?" Mom said, "because I've heard they're all on cocaine in California. It's everywhere."

"I promise, Mom." As though I could afford cocaine. Anyway, I've tried it and it doesn't do that much for me. I looked at my watch.

Mom leaped up. "I know! I know! We're going to be late. . . . Only we won't be. Don't worry."

We got in the car. It had gas, which was a minor miracle. Mom is renowned for forgetting to fill the gas tank at times like this. Once we were in the car, she drove like a demon. We definitely exceeded the speed limit, but luckily no police cars noticed us. That is, until we made the turn-off to the airport. Just as we did, some little guy on a motorcycle came zooming up and motioned for us to pull over.

Mom grabbed his sleeve. "Look, I'm sorry. I know we were above the limit, but my son has to catch a plane in twenty minutes. His grandmother is very ill, and if he isn't on the plane, she may pass away without seeing him. She's his favorite grandchild. I mean, he's her favorite grandchild."

"Lady," the officer began.

"Officer, please. I have tremendous respect for the law. Just mail me the ticket. Here's my address." Mom wrote it down and then handed it to him. Then we zoomed off to the parking lot. Her face was streaked with sweat. "I gave him the Moscowitzes' address," she said, smiling grimly.

"He has your license," I said. "Mom, I don't—"

"But if you miss the plane, you'll hate me!" she cried.

"No I won't." We were hurrying along to the terminal

213

building. I was carrying my suitcase. Mom had my camera and my tennis racket. It was blazing hot.

We made it to the right gate with ten minutes to spare till boarding time. Both of us were out of breath. Mom put her arms on my shoulders. "Oh, Jase," she said suddenly, starting to cry. I don't mean just cry. She started to sob, her whole body shaking so hard I got scared.

"What's wrong?" I said.

"I'm so scared!" she gasped.

"About what?" I felt so shaky I thought I was going to fall down.

"Everything!"

"Tell me about what."

She started a sentence, stopped, then began again. "You won't come back!" she cried.

"Of course I'll come back."

"They'll keep you out there, they'll say I'm an unfit mother. You won't want to ever see me again!"

"Mom, come on . . . I'm coming back. Don't be dumb. I don't care what they say."

She had her mouth pressed against me so hard I could hardly hear her. "Don't go," she whispered. "Stay here with me. Please."

They were announcing that it was time to board the plane. I felt paralyzed. "I—I have to go," I stammered.

"I just feel so scared," she said again, wiping away her tears. "Am I being silly? Am I wrong?"

"Yeah, it's . . . listen, how about if I just stay for a month? I'll come back in August?"

Her face was red and blotchy. "Will you really? We could go away. We could go to Maine or someplace. You've never been to Maine. We could go to—"

They kept announcing that it was time to board. "Right,"

214

I said, trying to pull away from her. "I'd like to see Maine. I really would."

She gave me one final intense hug and kiss and then broke away and staggered up the aisle.

When I turned around for a moment she was still standing there, tears rolling down her face, looking like a ghost out of hell. The stewardess took my pass and told me where my seat was. It was a window seat, which I like, usually, but I felt too strange and terrible to care. For a second I wondered if I should get off the plane and stay back with Mom. Then I thought how probably, once I left, she'd go home and maybe take a shower and a nap and go out to a movie with a friend, and by nighttime she'd be feeling okay again. I told myself that over and over, but it didn't help a whole lot.

The second the plane was in the air, I went to the bathroom, took out one of the joints I'd put in my pocket while I was packing, and smoked the whole thing. Some guy kept banging on the door, saying he had to go, but I just yelled, "Shut up!" I stood there, inhaling it until it was almost invisible. I don't like to do that, smoke a joint straight down like that, but there was no other way, and I knew I couldn't get through that plane flight otherwise.

When I got back to my seat they were passing out earphones for a movie. It was some Western. I said yes, but when I tried listening to the dialogue, it was so dumb I just turned it off. Once Andy and I took a plane ride together and we made up dialogue to a whole movie. We each took parts and had to watch the movie and say things that had some vague connection to what was happening. It struck us as the funniest thing anyone ever made up. A guy next to us, who had earphones on, kept staring at us, because it wasn't a funny movie and we kept cracking up.

It's hard to do that when you're by yourself—impossible,

in fact. Sometimes on planes I get a kick out of the meals they serve, opening all the packets of salt and salad dressing and everything, but this time it was so putrid, I couldn't eat anything but the roll. I just covered the tray with a napkin and tried looking out the window.

By then I was stoned, but not in a good way. I knew it was a mistake doing so much so fast, but I was more afraid if I didn't take anything, I'd be running up and down the aisles, screaming or something. This way I felt dizzy, like someone had conked me on the head with a large rock. I tried another tactic Otis had once told me about, namely imagining that I had a hot date with one of the stewardesses as soon as the plane landed, that each time she leaned over and said something simple, like, "Can I take your tray?" she was really saying something filthy in a special code known just to the two of us. The trouble was the stewardess who took care of my side of the plane wasn't my type that much. She had very neat blonde hair, and she spent all her time leaning over the guy next to me, a businessman who manufactured ladies' nightgowns. He said he was going to send her some free, and they did a lot of bantering back and forth about what type she was and what she'd look good in. But at the end, when he finally asked her what her address was or her phone number, she started talking to someone else. I guess she figured I was too much of a kid even to be worth leading on like that. The guy looked at me and shrugged. "Need a nightgown?" he asked, and laughed.

I slept the second half of the trip. Or at least I think I did. I kept seeing Mom standing there, crying, even in the middle of a dream that was about something else. I'd half wake up and think, "It's just a dream" and then realize that part of it was, but the part of her standing there was real. Suddenly I wished I'd stayed home. I didn't feel that much like going to California, living with Dad and Randy, even seeing Vicki. I just didn't. I started thinking of the Strassers, who ran the dry cleaning store, and how they weren't so bad after all, and how Otis and I could've had some fun since Marcy's going away for the summer. We could've borrowed his brother-in-law's truck and gone to the beach. He was going to teach me to wrestle. . . .

When I got off the plane, the hot air hit me like someone socking me in the face. Actually, it wasn't any hotter than New York, but the plane had been air-conditioned. I still felt strange, but when I saw Dad, I waved and he came running right over.

He asked about my trip, and we went to get my luggage, just the suitcase. I'd brought my tennis racket and camera on the plane. "We're having a heat spell," he said. "It's rare out here. Usually the weather's perfect. How's it been in New York?"

"What?" I said. It wasn't that I hadn't heard him. It was more that I was having trouble concentrating.

Dad looked at me hard. "You're stoned, aren't you?"

"No," I said nervously.

"You are. . . . You had something on the plane. Christ. What's *wrong* with Fay? Doesn't she watch you anymore?"

"Dad, cool it, will you? I just got a little nervous, being on the plane. . . . I've hardly touched the stuff since last June."

"Bullshit."

It was a great way to start the vacation. "You drink," I said. "What's the difference?"

"I don't get drunk," Dad snapped. "I have a glass or two of wine at dinner. That's completely different. That's

217

civilized. . . . How're you going to get in shape? I thought we'd be playing tennis every day!"

"We will." Christ, this was all I needed.

We were walking toward his car. "I thought we'd play this afternoon," Dad said. "The courts are beautiful. I even made a reservation. But if you're incapable of even—"

"I'll play, okay?" I said. "Just shut up a second."

We drove in silence to the house Dad and Randy had rented. It was a nice place, near the campus. They had a garden in back and three bedrooms. I had the one on the top floor. It was only early afternoon in San Francisco. They let me take a nap. The room was cool, and I fell asleep in a second and slept like a log till Dad woke me at four for tennis.

I got into shorts and a T-shirt and was putting on my sneakers when Dad came in. "Don't you even have a tennis shirt?" he asked.

I shrugged.

"I'll lend you one of mine. I don't want you going out there looking like that."

"Are we going to some country club, or what?"

He came back with one of those jerky alligator shirts that was around two sizes too big for me. He looked at me and shook his head. "Doesn't Fay buy you any clothes?" he said. "You look like a ragamuffin." Just then the shoelace in my sneaker broke. That happens not infrequently. I knotted it up and looped it around. Dad sighed. "Okay, let's see how it goes."

On the way to the courts he said, "We can just rally, if you want. . . . Have you played much lately?"

I shook my head.

"I haven't either, but I've taken a few lessons since I got out here. I want to try and do something about my backhand."

My father has a lousy backhand. Most of the time he tries to run around it and hit it like a forehand. That puts him out of position for the next shot, unless he's playing with someone who hits the ball right at him. Basically he's a junk shot player. His only shot is a drop shot. It bloops right over the net and sinks there. When you miss it, he smiles sheepishly but just goes right ahead and does it again the next time.

We rallied for a while. I was feeling a lot better. I had a headache, but I was back to normal, or at least as normal as I ever go. I had that feeling I sometimes get after being high, where everything seems very sharp and clean, like you just put on a new pair of glasses. "Let's try a set," Dad said. "Okay?"

"Sure, great," I said.

What can I say? I slaughtered him. He did all his usual stuff, but since I knew he was going to drop it, I started running the second I hit it so I'd be there, right at the net. I'd just drop it back so it hardly even went over the net. The few times he got there, I lobbed it over his head or smashed it past him. I mean, face it, my father's forty-nine and I'm sixteen, so it wasn't such a dramatic triumph, but I really enjoyed it. I must be some kind of sadist. At the end of the hour the next two players came on. Dad was so out of breath he could hardly speak. When we got in the car, he laughed and said, "I can see I'm going to need more than lessons. . . . You've gotten a hell of a lot better, Jase. Is that just from not playing?"

I shrugged. I watch tennis on TV, but I think it's more psychology in this particular case.

"I'm delighted," Dad said. "I always knew you could get your game together if you bothered. If you'd stay off drugs, you could really—"

Then I did something dumb. The car was stopping for a

light. I just opened the door and jumped out. I didn't know where the hell I was, but I didn't feel like listening to that shit anymore. I started running. I heard Dad yell, "Hey Jase! Come back! Stop it!"

I didn't pay any attention. I just kept running. To tell the truth, I didn't have much energy left after the game, but I didn't feel like listening to a sermon either, especially one I've heard a dozen or a thousand times before. Once I'd turned a corner which was going the wrong way for Dad to follow, I slowed down a little. I was so exhausted, I thought I might pass out, but I just leaned against a tree, on someone's front lawn, with my eyes closed. A second later Dad came by from the other direction. He leapt out of the car and took my arm. "Get in the car," he said.

"Fuck off," I said. "I'm going back to New York."

His voice softened. "Jase, come on. . . . I'm sorry for what I said. If I didn't care for your welfare, I wouldn't— Look, let's start all over, okay? I won't say another word, I'll trust you. It's your life."

"Right," I said flatly, getting back into the car. I didn't have the energy to agree or disagree. "It's my life."

I closed my eyes on the way back to Dad and Randy's house. When I opened them, there was Randy running toward us, flapping her hands in the air, her mouth open. "What's wrong?" Dad said, in an alarmed way. "What happened?"

"It's Fay," she said. She looked anxiously at me and then back at Dad. "She's—she's dead." Then she looked back at me. "Your mother," she added, like I might not remember who that was.

"Oh, my God," Dad said.

I don't remember what I said. I don't think I said anything. I just got out of the car and went upstairs to my room.

TWENTY-FOUR

||||

THIS IS HOW IT HAPPENED. ON THE WAY HOME FROM THE airport Mom's car smashed into a cement embankment. She wasn't wearing her seat belt, and anyhow, the car just crumpled up in about one second. A policeman was standing nearby giving someone a ticket. He claimed the car just flew into the embankment—there was no other car she was trying to swerve to avoid. "We would've given her a breathalizer test," he said, "only it was too late for that."

So, I don't know. How do you put that together? Did she want to cash it all in, or was she just upset and speeding and the car got out of control? Like they used to say in those books I hated at school, "She took the secret with her to her grave." What bothers me is that I had the feeling from the minute I got on the plane she didn't believe I was coming back. Even though I told her! Even though I promised! I said I'd stay for a month and then we'd go to Maine. Why didn't she believe me? I have nine million faults, but I don't say things and then not do them.

But I hate myself for getting on that stupid plane. Why? To have a fun-filled summer with Dad and Randy? I keep replaying that scene in my mind, only this time I don't get on the plane. We just drive back to the house together, I get my old job at the dry cleaner's, I hang out with Otis.

Last year at school they had us read this book about a guy who was told by a doctor that his wife only had a few months to live. I forget exactly how he put it, but he said he had the feeling while they were telling him that both he and the doctor shrank and became tiny little figures that he was looking at from the wrong end of a telescope. I sometimes have that feeling in the movies. I'm sitting there, watching, absorbed in what's happening, and suddenly I think, I'm watching a movie. I keep seeing the screen, which is something you never do when you're really involved. That's the way I felt all summer. Everything that happened seemed not to be happening or to be happening from far away. I don't even remember all of it.

We all flew back to Rockland for the funeral. The idea was, Dad was going to put the house on the market, and we'd go through our stuff and take whatever we wanted back to California. At the funeral itself everyone was basically sort of silent and awkward. During the lowering of the casket into the grave I did something that may sound weird. I pretended I was someone in a TV show acting in a funeral scene. I pretended we were all part of some soap-opera family, and that I had been told by the director to stay "in character." That was all I concentrated on, staying in character. I even imagined the director congratulating me afterward "That was fine, Jason, fine work."

Back at the house Erin completely broke down. She was crying and clinging to Dad, saying, "I don't want you to be divorced. I want you to stay in this house. I don't want to leave this house."

Dad kept stroking her shoulder and saying, "We can't stay in *this* house, darling. We're going to all move out to

222

California. We'll have a lovely house out there, nicer than this one."

"Why did you leave?" she cried. "You should have stayed in this house!"

"I couldn't," Dad said. "I couldn't live with Fay anymore. I tried to do what I thought was best for everyone."

"You should have stayed in *this house!*" Erin kept saying. "I don't want to leave. I want to stay."

"We're still all together," Dad said. His voice was shaking, and he really looked shot. "We're still a family."

"No, we're not," Erin cried. "We're nothing! We don't even *exist* anymore!"

Dad tried to smile. He pointed to Ty, Andy, and me. "Look, we all exist," he said. "We're all right here."

"No, we're not," Erin said. "It's not real anymore. It doesn't count."

"Oh, my God," Dad said, covering his eyes. "I don't know what to do."

Maybe this sounds sadistic, but part of me was almost glad of the way Erin was acting, even though I knew she was slightly crazy and out of control. Andy came forward and put her arms around Erin. "Let's go into your room," she said. "We can start getting your stuff packed."

"But I'll have to go back to that school," Erin said, looking scared. "They'll send me back."

"You're not going back," Dad said, obviously trying to get a grip on himself. "You're coming out to live with us in California."

"Am I really?" Erin said.

"Yes, of course you are," Dad said. He'd already told her that about ten times. "You'll live right in the same house with us."

"Forever?" Erin demanded. "Through college, everything?"

Dad was having trouble talking. "Through everything—" he started. Then he sat down and covered his face with his hands.

Andy took Erin into her room. Ty and I stood there looking at each other. Ty had a kind of funny expression. He shrugged. "Jesus," he said.

"Yeah, well . . . Are you going to start packing?"

"I packed most of my stuff for college, but there's some extra things."

I went into my room. Someone had put about six empty cardboard cartons on the floor. I started putting just about everything in my room in the cartons. I didn't much feel like looking at each thing and deciding what I wanted to keep. It seemed easier just to pack everything. While I was sitting there I kept getting these flashes of things, like when you sometimes get those sharp pains in your side when you've been running too fast: like Mom holding Dad's clothes up at the end of her foil while he was trying to pack, or her opening the champagne, or the time we went to the Ice Show. One thing I was really glad about was Dad said we could all stay at a Holiday Inn nearby. I didn't feel like staying in the house, even for one night.

When I was finished, I went into Mom's bedroom. I took her collection of swords. I looked for Dad and found him in the kitchen, staring blankly out the window. Randy was making some coffee. She'd been really quiet all day. "I want to keep these," I said. "Okay?"

"Fine," Dad said quickly. "Anything you want. Tell Ty that too. . . . How's Erin?"

"How should *I* know? She's in her room." Maybe it wasn't nice to be nasty to Dad, but I couldn't help it. I wish he had died instead. That's not a good thought to have, but it's true.

Andy and Erin were on the floor, packing Erin's things. Erin had stopped crying, but she still looked awful. Andy looked up at me. "Erin and I may go out and see if we can get wallpaper just like this for her room in California," she said. "That way it'll be just the same as it was here."

"Will it be *exactly* the same?" Erin said urgently. "Exactly?"

"Exactly the same," Andy said gently. "Why don't we go now, honey? I can drive."

We all went into the kitchen, and Andy explained to Dad where they were going.

"I'm sure they have nice wallpaper stores out in San Francisco," Randy said. It was the first time she'd spoken all day.

"It has to be exactly the same," Erin said. She was back to speaking in her quiet, whispery voice. "Everything has to be exactly the same."

I guess maybe everyone was thinking the same thing: that it couldn't be exactly the same because Mom wouldn't be here. But Dad just smiled and said, "Well, you two get some lovely wallpaper."

"Maybe we'll stop for a bite on the way back," Andy said.

"Take as long as you like," Dad said.

The rest of that day is a bit fuzzy in my mind, but we did stay at the Holiday Inn. By evening Erin had calmed down a lot. In fact, she said she was going to bed right after supper. Ty went off to call Juliet.

"Want to take a drive?" Andy asked me.

"Sure," I said. I just couldn't stand being around Dad. It was like all the little things about him that normally I could

225

take were driving me crazy. I wish they'd send *me* to boarding school.

"I think Erin'll be okay," Andy said, as we got into the car. "I hope so, anyway. Poor Randy'll have her hands full."

"I don't want to live there," I said suddenly. I hadn't expected to say that, to have it come out so bluntly.

"Well, you've got to," Andy said.

"Why? Why can't I live with you in Boston?"

Andy touched my shoulder. "Would you want to?"

"Yeah. . . . I could finish up high school there. The schools there're probably just as good."

She smiled, but in a sad way. "I'd love to have you. But I wonder if Dad—"

"Oh, fuck Dad!" I said.

Andy put her arms around me. "It's not that simple," she said.

We sat there with our arms around each other for a long time. I was scared for a minute I might go to pieces like Erin, but I didn't. I just started breathing in a funny way, the way I used to when I was really little and I'd get asthma attacks. "Poor baby," Andy murmured, running her hand over my hair.

The next morning at breakfast we presented our plan to Dad. Or rather Andy did. I mainly sat and listened.

"I could get a larger apartment," Andy said. "And it might be easier for you, Dad, with Erin to take care of."

"Absolutely not," Dad said. "It's an absurd idea. You're just twenty-three years old, Andy. You're not a mother. It's a huge responsibility, looking after a teenage boy."

Andy looked angry. "Are you saying I'm not mature enough? Not—"

"It's not a matter of that," Dad said. "You have your work. You're working around the clock as it is."

"And you're not?" she said.

Dad looked awkward. He glanced at me and then away. "I'm planning on taking as much time off as I can. If they'll let me, I'll only work half the day at first. Jason and I have a lot of catching up to do."

What a lot of bullshit. I took a deep breath. "I'd rather live with Andy," I said, looking right at my father.

"Well, I'm sure she feels flattered at that," Dad said, "but it's simply not a viable option."

God, I hate it when Dad uses phrases like "viable option."

"Our goal, really," he went on, "is to re-create a normal family atmosphere. And I think, with Randy's help, I can try and do that."

"*Re*-create?" Andy said sardonically.

"Children need both parents," he said, getting up. When Erin broke down, he'd seemed almost human. Now he seemed back in his "everything's under control" thing.

After he went up to his room, Andy drank the rest of her coffee. "Well, that's that, I guess," she said.

"It was a good try." Suddenly I had an idea. "Maybe I could sneak off some night and—"

She put her hand on my wrist. "No, Jase, don't. Maybe he's right. I couldn't really be a mother to you, I'd just be pretending."

"That's all Randy'll be doing," I said. "Anyhow, that's not the point. I'd just rather live with you than with them."

"How about for college?" she said. "You've only got two more years of high school. There're lots of colleges in the Boston area."

I began imagining that: me, Andy, Vicki, Otis, Marcella,

all of us living in some big house, taking turns cooking, like one of those communes you read about. "I won't get into Harvard, that's for sure," I said.

"Who knows," Andy said, buttering a roll. "You could try studying now and then."

I grinned. "Thanks."

"Listen, Jase, you're smart. And one day maybe you'll decide to use it instead of misusing it, like Mom."

I didn't say anything. When Dad says things like that, I want to kill him. But coming from Andy I can take it. I know she really cares about me. The waitress came by and asked if we were finished. I ordered some cereal. Then I took a joint out and smoked it a little. "And that's another thing," Andy said. "Cut down on the drugs, okay?"

I looked at her, deadpan. "Only in times of crucial importance," I said.

TWENTY-FIVE

||||

I WROTE VICKI A POSTCARD JUST BEFORE WE CAME EAST ABOUT what'd happened. When I came back, there was a letter from her waiting for me.

> *Dear Jason,*
>   *I was really sorry to hear about your mother. I know how badly you must be feeling. She always seemed like a really nice person to me.*
>   *Do you still feel like visiting me sometimes? I'd understand if you don't, but I'd love to see you, especially if you won't be coming back in the fall. Let me know, okay?*
>
>   *Love, Vicki*
>
> *P.S. I love you and miss you.*

She'd written the phone number of the camp on the envelope. At first I wasn't sure I did feel all that much like going to see her, but after a few days back in San Francisco with Dad and Randy and Erin around all the time, I decided it might not be a bad idea. I asked Dad if it was okay if I borrowed the car. The camp was a two-hour drive up the coast. At first he hemmed and hawed, but when it turned out there was no direct bus connection, he said okay, as long as I drove carefully.

I did. It was a beautiful drive, actually. Not all of the road went straight along the coast, but a lot of it did. There were great views. I brought my camera and took a few shots, but I wanted to save some to take of Vicki once I got there.

Once I saw her, I felt okay. She looked cute in denim shorts and a T-shirt. She kissed me and took me off to introduce me to her aunt and uncle. Evidently they'd agreed to let her take the day off, as long as she was back by noon the next day. "I thought we might camp out," she said. "I borrowed a sleeping bag for you."

I haven't done a whole lot of camping, but this looked like good equipment, a big air mattress. We drove off and got to the campsite around four in the afternoon. It was deserted enough, so Vicki said we could go skinny-dipping if we wanted. It's strange. I'd had so many fantasies about this, being out here all alone with Vicki, but now that the moment was at hand, I didn't feel even mildly horny. I'd noticed that already in the last couple of weeks, that my sex drive seemed to have almost vanished. I spent a whole hour looking through *Playboy,* and even that had absolutely no effect. I just thought: big deal, big boobs, so what.

But Vicki was peeling off her clothes and scampering into the water. "Ooh, it's really freezing," she said. She really had a good tan. It looked like she was wearing a bathing suit, made out of white skin.

I took my clothes off and ran headfirst into the water. I've found that's the only way it works. If you do it slowly and the water's really cold, you never go in. We splashed around a little, and it was fun, but I didn't get wildly excited as I would have even thinking about it a couple of months ago.

"Do I look in good shape?" Vicki said, as she was drying

off in this big orange towel she'd brought. "I've been playing baseball a lot and tennis."

"You look great." I could appreciate the effect visually, even if not any other way.

"You look so pale," she said softly. "I guess you haven't had much of a vacation so far."

"Not much," I said.

I was scared she might want to talk about Mom, just from the way she was looking at me in a concerned way, but luckily she didn't say anything else.

We grilled some thin steaks over a fire and heated up a can of beans. Vicki had packed fresh tomatoes and carrot sticks. All of that, just getting the fire going and cooking and cleaning up got us through most of the evening.

Once it started getting dark, I blew up the air mattress, and Vicki spread the sleeping bag over it. "It's for two people," she said. "Is that okay?"

I laughed. "Sure."

"My aunt and uncle know we've been going together all year," she said. "And they trust me."

Actually, that's a little of a distortion since we only started going together in the winter and then had that fight. We've really only been going together a few months. But I know what she means. It seems longer. I crawled into the sleeping bag next to Vicki. We both had pajamas on because it was kind of chilly now that the sun was down. She rested her head on my chest and began kissing me lightly on the neck. At first I thought I'd just kind of go along with it or that maybe the mood would gradually hit me, but the opposite happened. I suddenly got this horrible claustrophobic feeling, like we were *locked* into the sleeping bag and couldn't get out. And I just didn't feel like being all entangled with another person. I sat up, feeling dizzy.

"What's wrong?" Vicki asked. "Are you okay?"

"I don't know," I said.

"Is it the thing with your mother?"

"I don't know."

Vicki just sat there. "We don't have to do anything," she said. "We can just—whatever." But she sounded disappointed.

"Do you have another sleeping bag?" I asked.

"No." She looked angry. "This one is for two people. Isn't it big enough?"

I took a deep breath. "Look, Vick, it has nothing to do with you. It's just I don't feel like sleeping all kind of wrapped up with someone. I won't get any sleep. And it's a long drive back."

"I'm not going to be *attacking* you," she said stiffly. "I'll just lie there and go to sleep."

I tried touching her shoulder. "I know that. . . . It's me, okay? I just have to sleep by myself. Look, how about—I'll sleep in the car."

Vicki looked like she wanted to kill me. "You mean you came all the way up here just to sleep by yourself in the car? What's the *point* in that?"

"I need to sleep by myself." God, I felt rotten. I shouldn't have come. Except I had no idea I'd feel this way. I was hoping maybe being with Vicki would put me in a good mood, the way I used to feel when I was with her in the spring.

Vicki was sitting there, staring out at the black ocean. "There's an extra blanket," she said. "How about if you use that, on top of the air mattress? Or I can use it and you can sleep in the sleeping bag."

"The blanket's fine," I said, relieved we'd found a solution.

We got the blanket out of the car. It was one of those really heavy Hudson Bay blankets. "This is swell," I said. I knew I sounded a little manic, but I wanted to make up for everything. "This is really a terrific blanket. Where'd you get it?"

"It's my aunt and uncle's," Vicki said.

"They seem like terrific people," I babbled on, spreading out the blanket next to the sleeping bag. "Your aunt and uncle."

"Yeah, they're nice," Vicki said. She hesitated. "My aunt said if I was sure I really loved you, whatever happened would be okay." She gave a half-laugh, half-snort. "Only I guess nothing's going to happen!"

I tried to laugh too. "You can't tell," I said. "I may pounce on you in the middle of the night." I remembered that sleepover we'd had when Vicki had hurled me on the floor. I had a black and blue mark for a month after that!

Vicki got into her sleeping bag and I wrapped up in the blanket. It was comfortable with the air mattress under us. We both lay on our backs, looking up at the stars. "Do you know which is which?" she asked.

"Not really. . . . I think that's the Big Dipper." I never listened that much in Astronomy. Anyhow, to me those things never looked like bears or gods or whatever. They just looked like a bunch of stars.

Vicki reached over and took my hand. Her hand felt warm and good. "Maybe we're too young," she said.

"I guess," I said.

"Sixteen to eighteen is probably the best age," she went on.

"I *am* sixteen," I reminded her.

"Maybe for boys it's different." She sounded sad, though.

233

I squeezed her hand. "It's . . . I'm glad I came out here."

She kissed me. "I am too. . . . Sleep well, Jase."

"You too."

About one second later she was asleep. There are people like that, who can sleep anywhere, under any circumstances. Not me. The minute Vicki fell asleep, I got another funny kind of feeling. Like maybe there were bears or snakes or God knows what waiting around to attack us. I remembered all these gory stories I'd heard about bears dragging people in sleeping bags off into the woods. For some reason I remembered a story of a woman calling out, "I'm dead" as the bear dragged her off. Jesus.

I sat up. My heart was thumping. Listen, everything's going to be okay, I told myself. Just relax. There aren't any bears around here. They're probably all sleeping anyway. I looked down at Vicki, so peacefully asleep, her hand stretched out as though she was still holding mine. I lay down again and took hold of her hand. I had the feeling that if I kept hold of it, nothing bad would happen. And finally, after a long time, I fell asleep.

I visited Vicki a few more times after that. Not much more happened, in terms of sex, but it was like, after that first time, Vicki didn't even expect it and didn't seem disappointed. Maybe she was just getting all set because she thought I wanted it. We had some good times, but most of the time I was pretty silent and strange. I couldn't even think of things to say, even though during the week, when I didn't see her, I'd have long conversations with her in my head.

The last time I visited her, on the way back to her aunt and uncle's camp, I totaled Dad's car. I don't know what happened, and neither does Vicki. It was just all of a sudden we were off the road and into a tree, a really big one that'd probably been there a thousand years. Maybe I got distracted because she was feeding me cherries. Anyway, the car teetered over the edge of a ravine and then didn't fall over. Anticlimax. We got out, a little shaky, and eventually some guys came in a truck and towed the car back. We didn't get hurt at all, that was one of the strange things. At least we were wearing seat belts. The policeman said that made a difference. I have to admit when I looked down at the ravine, I got a little queasy. A close call.

Dad was pretty good about it, in fact kind of amazing for him. He acted like the loss of the car was a mere nothing, said he wasn't sure that had been the right kind of car now that all of us would be out in California. "We'll go pick a new one together," he said.

"Okay," I said, relieved he was acting so cool.

"The main thing is, you're safe. . . . And so is Vicki."

On the way to buy the new car, though, Dad started in on this thing about how I should see a shrink. "It's not that you have any problems any more severe than any boy your age," he said, "but sometimes it's useful to talk to someone outside the family, someone who—"

"Forget it," I said.

"Anyone you like," he went on smoothly. "A man, a woman, a Freudian, a Jungian."

"I'm not going, Dad, save your breath." I hate those guys. I think they're all jerks. I saw one of them at school a few years back, and he was a real Neanderthal. Express your anger. Let it out. Don't let it out. Face it, whatever you do, whether you let it out or don't let it out, it's there. The world is a mess and there's not a whole lot you can do about it.

"Jason, listen, you've been through a very traumatic experience. You *need* to talk to someone about it."

"I'll talk to Andy."

"She's not an objective person. She's involved in the whole thing."

So, he meant Mom. I thought he'd meant the car crash. I turned on him, feeling the anger bubbling from deep inside me. "Listen, if you make me go, I'm leaving home."

"I'm not going to *make* you go. I just thought—"

"Then quit talking about it, okay?"

"You don't think the incident with the car is something worth dwelling on?"

"I won't drive any more, okay? I'll get my pilot's license. There're no trees up there."

Dad sighed. "I think you're making a big mistake. I've found an excellent doctor for Erin. She could recommend someone."

"Terrific. I hope she gets a lot out of it." Comparing me to Erin is crazy! She spent an entire month trying to set up her room out here so it would look exactly like the one back at Rockland. And then, when it was all set up, she started crying and wouldn't stop for three days.

Vicki's aunt and uncle were understanding about the crash too. Actually, at that point the summer was over and she was about to go home, but they didn't scream at me or say I was an irresponsible person. I went to the airport to say good-bye to Vicki when she flew home. She was sort of subdued, and most of the time we just sat there, holding hands and kissing a little bit.

"I'm going to miss you so much!" she said.

"Yeah, me too." I kept stroking her fingers one by one, up and down, knowing that all year long I'd probably think back on all those chances I'd had in the double sleeping bag and wanting to kill myself for not taking advantage of them.

"I'm not going to date anyone all year," she said, her eyes filled with tears. "No matter who."

"Not even Russ Pharr?" I said, kidding.

Vicki looked at me, horrified. "Of course not!"

"Listen, Vicki, you can date people if you want. Seriously. I won't mind."

She frowned. "Does that mean you want me to?"

"No! I just meant . . . do whatever you want."

She leaned her head on my shoulder. "Next summer maybe you can be a counselor at the camp too. Would you like to?"

"Sure," I said. "That sounds good."

We had a long, clinging, hugging kiss good-bye, and then she got on the plane. I stood there till it took off. Vicki didn't have a window seat, so I didn't see her, but I like watching planes take off, that sudden *whoosh* as they rise in the air.

TWENTY-SIX

I'M GOING TO A PRIVATE SCHOOL OUT HERE.

Erin goes to it too. Supposedly it's one of the best schools on the West Coast, which I guess means it costs a lot of money. Maybe Dad feels he can afford it now that he sold the house back in Rockland and doesn't have to support Mom. I guess it is a good school. The classes are small, and there's a lot of "personal attention." If you don't like a subject or fail a quiz, they do a big number about trying to "understand" why. Surprisingly, I'm doing a lot better. I don't know. It doesn't seem like I'm working any harder, but I just end up with better grades. As far as college goes, this might not be so bad.

Mostly it pisses me. I miss my old school, where no one paid any attention and half the teachers would've shot us if they could've. I miss Otis. We write, but neither of us is much good at writing and anyway, it's not the same. Lots of times it isn't even that you want someone to talk to. You just want someone to be with, someone who can understand a lot of stuff without your explaining anything.

He and Marcy are still going together. Maybe they'll even get married someday. He says his mother and her father give them big lectures on how much trouble they'll have "out in the world" with their kids being half-black, half-white. Otis says, "So what?" Not that he necessarily wants to get married at eighteen, but he doesn't seem interested in seeing anyone else. He says it's practically like being married. They just automatically see each other, without having to call up and make dates. I can see how that would be a relief.

Probably there are nice kids in my class and probably, like Dad says, I haven't really tried to find a friend. A lot of them are pretty weird, but I'm not that unweird myself. That isn't what bothers me. I just don't have the energy to go setting up a whole thing again, getting to know someone, inviting them over. I'd like it just to happen, without any of that.

Vicki writes me a lot, even if I don't answer, and tells me everything that's going on at school. I guess I'm glad she keeps on doing it. I wish I could get myself to write back more.

She's been babysitting for Vernon. She says he's kind of stiff ever since his fall, and she has to help him, even moving around the house. On weekends she comes over and takes him to a movie. He's not up to dancing anymore, but they still listen to "Tales from the Vienna Woods," and sometimes she dances all by herself, pretending she has a partner, and he watches her. She says he gets mixed up sometimes about who she is. He calls her Betsy or Fanny or Muriel. But he remembers me. She didn't tell him about what happened, just that I moved to California. He asked if I was keeping my waltzing up, and she told him yes.

Andy broke up with Marcus. He decided to give his marriage one more try. She seemed kind of upset about it at first, but now she says it's for the best, that she's going to use her energy to concentrate on her work. She says celibacy isn't so bad. That might be true if you've already tried other things. But since I've been celibate all my life, I can't appreciate it quite as much.

Erin's the same. Kind of quiet and withdrawn. Still drawing lots of unicorns. She never talks about Mom. It's like it never happened.

Oh, and Juliet dumped Ty. She did it around the first month they were at college, found a new guy and told him to get lost. Boy, did he take it hard! I guess he really liked her, despite his going around saying that she was just an asshole and their sex life hadn't been that great. He's dated a few girls, but nobody special. He's never brought home the same one twice. His opinion now is, quote, love is a crock, unquote, and that you might as well fuck as many girls as you can find, that your wife will be grateful to you later on because you'll know so much about women. Ty lives on campus, but he comes home once a week or so to inform us of his activities.

Once, after Ty left, Randy said, "He seems so cynical." She was clearing the table, but then she went into the next room, leaving Dad and me alone.

I'd been about to go off and tackle some math homework, but Dad said, "I'm glad you're not like that, Jase."

As usual I had only been half listening to what Ty was saying. "Like what?"

"Well," Dad said. "I think it *is* painful when a first love relationship breaks up. It has to be. But to react against that by just trying to score with anyone you can lay your hands on—that's plain dumb."

I just looked at him. I don't think that's exactly my problem. "Yeah, I guess," I said.

"You were very fond of Vicki, weren't you?" Dad pursued.

I made a gesture that meant yes, but didn't spell it out.

"And she was clearly very fond of you, but well—" He grinned sheepishly. "There are other fish in the sea is basically what I'm trying to say, if that isn't a contradiction of sorts."

"What are you worried about? My sex life?" I glared at him. "Relax. I'll do it when I'm ready. I could get a girl tomorrow if I wanted." I'm not sure how true that is, but I really felt pissed.

"Of course you could," Dad said quickly. "Jase, listen to me. I'm saying the opposite. Maybe I'm not putting it well. I'm saying take it at your own pace, go slow, if that's what feels right. I feel like my sex life started at forty-five, in any real sense of the word."

Meaning, I guess, that with Mom it was lousy. "Tough," I said.

He didn't react to that. "It has to all come together," he went on earnestly. "Not just bodies colliding in the night, but affection, warmth, communion. It's a very complex thing."

"Dad, give me a break, okay? I like girls, it'll work out. I think Ty is an asshole about that and everything else. I wouldn't have done it with Juliet Moscowitz if you'd paid me." God, what a liar I am. I'd have done it with her in one second.

"You'll do better than Juliet," Dad assured me. "And, look, really, what I meant to say was I think your priorities are great. You're really trying at school, you're pulling yourself together. I couldn't be more delighted."

I waited for him to add, "If you'd only lay off drugs, you'd be a perfect kid," but he didn't. Which means either he thinks I have or he didn't feel like getting into that. Then I said something so monumentally dumb I just can't explain it. "I miss Mom."

Dad turned green. He still can't handle even a reference to her. "Well," he said. "Of course . . . but you have Randy." He looked at me appealingly, as though pleading with me to agree.

"Randy has nothing to do with Mom," I said, hating him again.

Dad was silent. "Some things just happen," he said softly. "I truly don't feel I was to blame. I can't say I'm sorry for anything I did. I just wish it had turned out otherwise."

I stared at him. Okay, sure, he didn't kill her, and it's not going to help going through the rest of my life blaming him. But I still feel like it's a wall between us that will be there as long as I live.

For Thanksgiving, Andy flew out to be with us. Randy fixed a big turkey and all the usual stuff. When we sat down, I kept thinking of last year and Dad telling us about their getting divorced and Erin crying and all of us watching the football game on TV. Maybe all of us were thinking about that; it was an unusually silent meal. Someone would bring up a topic and someone else would say something, and then there'd be a long pause, like no one could think of what else to say. I didn't eat a whole lot. I've never been crazy about turkey anyway, to tell the truth.

After the meal Dad and Randy went out to some party. That left the four of us with nothing special to do, so we started a game of Monopoly in the living room. I hadn't played for a long time, maybe since when I last visited Andy in Boston that time Vizhier came over, but the old competitive spirit came back and I started doing really well. All of a sudden, just as Andy was paying me—she was the banker—she said, "Last week was Mom's birthday. Did you remember? She would've been forty-seven."

"Yeah," Ty said. He hates for Andy to talk about Mom.

"It's funny," Andy went on. "I still think about her a lot. I even dream about her, which I never did when she was alive."

"Me too," Erin said softly.

Everyone looked at her.

"I dream she's out here living with us," Erin said. "And that she and Daddy never got divorced."

"Well, they never got along that well," Ty said, flipping his playing piece and catching it.

"Do you ever dream about her, Jase?" Andy asked.

"No," I said. It's true. I don't. Sometimes when I'm about to fall asleep I think about her, but she stays out of my dreams. Or rather, I just don't have dreams anymore. I fall asleep and that's that.

"You know, one thing," Andy said. She sounded kind of breathless, like she does when she's upset. "I read this article once about how if you have a parent that kills themself, particularly one of the same sex, it makes you . . . more drawn to doing it yourself. Like Hemingway."

"Did he kill himself?" I asked. I never knew that.

"Yeah, with a shotgun. And his father did too. . . . But what I'm saying is, I'm not going to. Because I think it's a stupid, stupid thing to do!"

"Me too," Ty said. "I'm never doing anything like that."

That left Erin and me. Andy was staring at me. "Say something, Jase."

"What should I say?"

"Promise you'll never do anything like that."

I felt angry. "How can I promise something like that? I don't know how I'll feel when I'm fifty, for Christ's sake."

All of a sudden Andy lunged at me. She knocked me right over and sat on me, pinning my hands back over my head. "Promise," she said, "or I won't move."

Jesus, she really hurt me. My arms were twisted all the way back. "I promise," I said. "Get off me, will you?"

"If you ever do anything like that, I'm never speaking to you again," she said, getting off me.

I laughed. "Jesus, Andy, you practically twisted my fucking arm off," I said, feeling it to make sure it was okay.

Suddenly Andy changed her tone of voice. She came over and stroked my arm gently. "God, I'm strong, aren't I? Wow! Wonder Woman. Men are going to tremble when I come near."

Suddenly Erin said. "Mom didn't kill herself. She died in a car accident."

There was a pause.

"She killed herself," Andy said quietly.

"She didn't!" Erin said. "How do you know? You weren't there!"

"That's true," Andy said. "I wasn't. But I still think that's what happened. And I don't think she'd want us to lie about it, even to ourselves. Remember how she always said she liked the truth?"

"You don't know what the truth is," Erin said.

"No," Andy agreed. "Just what I think it is. That's all anyone ever knows."

I think Andy's probably right, but I also feel, like Erin, that you might as well not tie it all down if you don't know for sure. Even if you were there, and watched what happened, you wouldn't know. Even if you were in Mom's mind. Maybe even she didn't know.

I counted the Monopoly money Andy'd given me—two hundred. I had the feeling if we kept on, I would cream all of them. "Roll the dice, Ty, will you?" I asked.

Andy kissed me and went back to her place. "I'm going to win this game," she said.

I just smiled at her, because I knew I was.